D0327017

Mr. Ryder's Trophy

This story is a fable. The references to real people (living or dead) and historical events are intended solely to lend the fable its proper historical context.

Sleeping Bear Press
310 North Main Street
P.O. Box 20
Chelsea, MI 48118
www.sleepingbearpress.com

Printed and bound in Canada.

10 9 8 7 6 5 4 3 2 1

Library of Congress Cataloging-in-Publication Data
Durham, Shirley Dusinberre.
Mr. Ryder's trophy / Shirley Dusinberre Durham.
p. cm.
ISBN 1-58536-111-9
1. Ryder Cup-Fiction. 2. Golf-Tournaments-Fiction. I. Title.

PS3604.U74 M7 2002
813'.6--dc21
2002007345

Mr. Ryder's Trophy

Written and Illustrated by

Shirley Dusinberre Durham

Sleeping Bear Press

I dedicate this book to all grandchildren, especially mine, and to Samuel Ryder's great-grandchildren, Sam and Tom Ryder-Smith.

Acknowledgments

THE UNORTHODOX NARRATIVE FORM used in *Mr. Ryder's Trophy* is a blend of fact and fancy. The history behind the story, however, is anchored in research, and for this I have many people to thank.

In England, Mary Moore (Mrs. Hector Moore), Sam Ryder's granddaughter and closest living descendant, was a generous source of information and encouragement, as was John Ryder-Smith, who married Sam's other granddaughter Rosalind. John and Rosalind had two sons—Sam's only direct male descendants. Most of the Ryder family anecdotes in my book were selected from the unpublished writings of Sam's oldest daughter Marjorie Claisen, Mary Moore's mother. Rosalind's mother was Sam's youngest daughter Joan Scarfe, a person who contributed much to the Ryder Cup, and who never threw anything away. When Joan died in 1985, Rosalind inherited her mother's household. Then Rosalind herself died shortly after, leaving John with two young sons and a mountain of Ryder memorabilia. He raised his sons well and soon he will get to the memorabilia where he will find the very document that proves my point. I know he will.

The story of Samuel Ryder became the story of Abe Mitchell as well, when in 1996 George H. Underwood of Forest Row, East Sussex, handed me his life's work, and said, "Here." Included in the pile of papers was a history of the Cantelupe Golf Club, a small biography of his uncle Abe Mitchell, tales of Ashdown Forest, and Henry Arnell's centenary history of Royal Ashdown Forest Golf Club. Inevitably, as I learned more about Abe Mitchell, the center of my purpose shifted. George Underwood was also a reader of my manuscript, and he called it "buoyant"!

Brian Currant in England {knight, Prince} went to libraries, ordered books, called the Crown Jewellers, found news stories by always reliable Alan Booth, and, not least, bought our tickets to the 1995 Ryder Cup when we couldn't get them here at the source in Rochester. Brian arranged teas with Ryder expert Bill Murgatroyd, luncheons at Verulam. He "found" George Underwood and John Ryder-Smith. Brian's wife Julia, hostess sublime, dog trainer supreme, helped by being herself, and learning to play golf right in plain sight. Julia's mother Joan Welch explained knapping flints and the protocol of tea, while Hugh Welch allowed his face to be used as the Vicar, which he is.

Edward Asprey of London's Crown Jewellers Asprey & Garrard, with the help of Susan Martin of the PGA of America and Mike Gray of the PGA of Great Britain, obtained the Ryder Cup statistics from the Mappin and Webb hallmark: 9ct gold, made in Sheffield in 1926. Mr. Asprey estimates that in today's market, the trophy, 17 inches tall, would sell for as much as £25,000.

Dr. Margaret Collins was all the things that Dorothy is in the book. And finally in England, I thank the many members and officers of Verulam Golf Club, who have trusted my purpose since the beginning and treated me accordingly.

I could not have done without my celestial navigator, my husband, my source for nearly everything. When I asked George to describe the ins and outs of joining an English golf club, he wrote it out and it can be read in Chapter Three. Our son Bill explained our entropic destiny and several stochastic Theories of Everything, all in "science speak," from his laboratory in California, while our Jim provided "calm talk" to my crashing computer from his corporate headquarters, also in California. Our Adele, an editor for *Cornell Alumni Magazine*, penciled cryptic marks on the manuscript such as "LOL" for "laughing out loud." When she wrote "Thank you, Mom" at the end of the last chapter, I knew I couldn't lose.

Gene Sarazen started a new chapter when he wrote me a letter in February 1997 saying: "The year I won the PGA at Oakmont, Hagen passed up the [1922] PGA just to play this special match with Abe Mitchell at Buffalo." Mr. Sarazen modestly didn't mention that he won the PGA again the following year [1923] when Hagen did play.

Rand Jerris, USGA Library, Golf House, was there for me. He was. Every time I called he was there, and he had all of the answers—except one: who, when, and where was Emmet French, who is strangely missing from Peter Alliss's *Who's Who of Golf*, the best source book of its kind anywhere, according to Rand. I searched for Emmet and found Bill Kittleman who found Pete Trenham, a golf history nut like me. Joe and Jean Lee showed me the value of looking further.

Denis, the pro in my story, is Denny Ferstler and, though handsome, he *is* a good teacher.

Leon St. Pierre of Longmeadow, Massachusetts, shared his vast history of greenkeeping, with a humorous eye to the serious threat from Green Committee chairmen. Dave Oatis of the USGA Green Section also responded when I sought advice.

Thanks, too, to my *readers* and *listeners*. Trisha Lee allowed me to read the manuscript to her while we drove to golf tournaments, and she laughed aloud in all the right places. Dorothy Vagts said she was so helplessly enticed into the story that she was devastated when it ended—and she's not a golfer. George Thomason read it in one sitting in my art studio and he didn't miss a word—and he *is* a golfer. I chose the Howes to read the first version of the manuscript because Sharon and Gordon wouldn't ever say a nasty word. I knew I was safe, although it was Sharon who thought I might be long on the European history. So out went Margaret of Anjou and Joan of Arc, leaving only one lady general, Boudicca, instead of three. Michael and Adrienne Romano, Donna and Fred Reynolds, Pat Lehmann, the USGA's David Fay, Oak Hill's Craig Harmon, David Barnet—they all approved. I selected only readers that would.

Jean Coe Ager, my college roommate (d. 1997), did me an enormous service by putting me in touch with Kitty Benedict, someone who would help me once the story was completed. And that was the way it happened. Kitty, a freelance editor, became my agent and guided my book to Brian Lewis's Sleeping Bear Press where Danny Freels discreetly repaired the text.

And thanks, at the end, to the philosophy of Gurdjieff, which helps me to think, and then to laugh. I learned it from Louise March, Gene Coghill (golf professional/French hornist), and my friends at the Rochester Folk Art Guild.

—S.D.D.
May 1, 2002

Contents

Illustrations

Verulam

OUTSIDE THE CLUBHOUSE WINDOWS a layer of delicate English snow outlined the mounds and hollows of the golf course. In the distance, the roofs and chimney pots of St. Albans climbed the Old London Road to the top of Holywell Hill where the great cathedral stood in a bright shaft of afternoon sunlight that spread through a break in the dark clouds. For a moment the grand old abbey looked as if it were held aloft on the shoulders of the town—the hero of the game after all.

The golf course belonged to Verulam Golf Club, where Samuel Ryder had been a cherished member. The name Verulam derived from the River Ver that flowed, before the Christian era, through the once flourishing Roman city of Verulamium where the soldier Alban died to become a saint.

Sam Ryder himself told me these and many other things while we sat in the warmth of the Verulam clubhouse and looked out at the fallen snow. But he saved the strength of his enthusiasm for the subject of golf and human behavior. Sam believed that the study of one was an aid to the understanding of the other. To his way of thinking, no matter how far afield it ranged, if the subject was golf there was something to be learned.

Just recently he told me about the benefits of playing a golf course in reverse, to give rest to overused portions of a fairway. He gave as an example the Old Course at St. Andrews which saw as much traffic as any golf course in the world. He explained that its many double putting greens made it eminently reversible, giving the grass time to recover from the countless pilgrims who inflicted their homage on the historic ground. "All things reverse themselves," he said, somewhat ominously, I thought. "Some things more than others," he added, putting on a solemn face. Then he mentioned a standard spread of fertilizer containing dried blood and bone meal that did much to make the grass grow again. Since we were speaking of fertilizers, he cautioned me to avoid the autumnal incursion of seagulls at The Jubilee, a St. Andrews course thus known for its excellent turf. Automatic scare guns and other devices had little effect against the gulls once they were determined to make their run.

Another time he expounded on my countrymen's careless regard for the *Rules of Golf* when he discovered I didn't carry them when I played. He called it a sin against God and the Masons who wrote them. He himself was never without the St. Andrews Society of Golfers' *Regulations for the Game of Golf*, May 1, 1812, a centenary edition given to him shortly after he took up the game. He pulled the copy from his pocket and waved it at me to emphasize his point.

On one of the few occasions that he strayed from his favorite subject, he warned me against sipping brandy—advice his wife Nellie had shared with their three daughters during the preparation of the Christmas pudding. He thought it was good advice, especially for a young woman from America, like me, who might not know these things. Sipped brandy, Nellie had warned her girls, did no good at all. "You must gulp it down."

"Nellie," he said absently, "was often perplexed when people laughed at her words, so we laughed with care. Our family jokes left her sweetly puzzled, for she had a literal turn of mind that missed the point almost every time."

If Sam thought there was a specific question I should examine he would put it in my mind, cross his arms over his chest, and say, "Is there something you want to ask me?" And there it would be—the question—in my head. On that snowy January afternoon in 1977, I asked him, "Why did you put Abe Mitchell's figure on top of the Ryder Cup?"

"Your neighbour Walter Hagen once asked me that," he said.

"And I asked Abe the first time I met him," I countered. "He said the figure on the Cup wasn't really him."

"Well, he was wrong." Sam spoke with surprising emphasis and then he stood up and walked around the table to the window where I was sitting. "The answer to your question goes to the very heart of why you are here in St. Albans talking to me. What do you think of that?"

The snow had begun to fall again, heavily this time, so that it obscured our view of the world outside. We watched the large flakes weave patterns toward the glass, darting this way and that. I tried to catch a single snowflake with my eye and follow it until I could see its complex design. But just at the instant of revelation, its delicate but robust symmetry vanished in a capricious swirl, as if the beauty and meaning of its brief existence were destined to remain only in my imagination.

He watched my concentration, then joined in the pursuit. All at once a single flake settled lightly on the dark brick outside the window and its tracery etched itself in my memory before it disappeared. He looked at me, his eyebrows raised in feigned surprise. When I realized what he had done I marvelled at the ease with which I accepted his presence in a world where he did not belong. It was the same ease that had bound me to him the first time we met only five months before, when we stood at this same window and watched a train roll down the tracks alongside Verulam's 1st hole, on its way to London.

~

MY JOURNEY TO VERULAM and the realm of Samuel Ryder had begun in upstate New York in February 1976, the year we Americans celebrated the bicentennial of freedom from British tyranny. I would learn in the months ahead that 1976 was also the 50th anniversary of the making of the Ryder Cup and, ironically, a tyranny of another sort. I was peeling potatoes at the kitchen sink when my husband Steve entered noisily through the back door and said, "Honey, we're going to live in England!"

"Sure, and I'm the Queen," I said.

"No, really, I'm not kidding." And he explained that out of countless unqualified candidates the company had chosen him, Stephen Winchester, to undertake an assignment to the United Kingdom. Steve had been selected for two reasons, his boss said. "One, you speak the King's English and two, with a name like Winchester you can't go wrong."

I headed for the stairs to pack my bag, but Steve grabbed my hand and said, "Hold on. First, I have to go there by myself to assess the assignment, and give the English management time to object to me. It may not work out. Therefore," he added, as if it were no problem at all, "don't tell a soul." And off he went to England, leaving me to suffer my silence. I had no way to express my joy except to shout inside my empty house, "I have news! My husband and I are going to live in England! Did you hear the news? I have something to tell you!"

I suppose I should not have been surprised at this turn of events. My neighbour read palms for party guests when she was in the mood. She had read mine and told me that someday I would live across the pond. What pond she did not know but it was my destiny and she showed me where in my hand it said so.

On the day my burden of silence was lifted, I raced next door. Before I uttered a word my neighbour said, "You have something to tell me." An unabashed Anglophile herself, she shared my anticipation and asked to see my hand again. "There it is, plain as day," she said, and she traced the line on my palm with her index finger. "I also see your *neighbours* will come to visit. Here, what's this...I don't remember this before," she said peering closely at the intersecting lines. "I wonder what it means." She frowned and sighed as she turned my hand over and patted it. "You know, I really don't know much about reading palms. We'll see eventually, won't we?"

Once Steve's assignment in England was secure he looked for a house to rent, but the few homes on the agent's list were not suitable. Houses were impossible to find, Steve was told. Within days, however, the agent called Steve to say, in stunned disbelief, that an excellent house had just been listed in the small city of St. Albans, in Hertfordshire, 45 minutes north of London by train. The man who owned it, a diplomat in Her Majesty's Foreign Service, had been called to Pretoria—quite unexpectedly, as it turned out.

Steve called me that night. "It's the perfect house!" and then he went on to describe it—a Bechstein downstairs, a bidet upstairs, and a small freezer compartment in the refrigerator, all set in a rose garden with a gardener. There were three houses on the street, a cul-de-sac that I was to call a "close," he said. He pronounced it like the adjective.

"The fellow next door, who is keeping an eye on things for the diplomat, came over while I was there. His name's Tony and he's thoroughly English. On top of that, his construction firm built the house. If anything goes wrong with the pipes, Tony will know what to do."

Steve rented the house on the spot and returned to Rochester in May to deal with absentee homeownership and international banking. In the midst of all the paperwork, the doorbell rang. It was a trusted friend who had moved away from our bitterly cold winters long ago, a bookkeeper by training. She had dropped by to say hello and announce that she was back in town, looking for a house to rent until she found one to buy. We put our heads together and struck a deal.

Within days our linens, china, and silver were packed in crates and we were ready to leave. As we said our good-byes, we asked our new tenant why she wanted to live in the North again. "I've wondered that myself," she said. "Suddenly I was fed up with warm weather and sunshine."

By Thursday, May 27, our arrangements were complete. Without a second thought I walked away from my responsibilities, left behind my cares and woes, stepped aboard an airplane for the first time in my life, and flew away. God bless corporate America, we said.

Our British Airways captain announced in a rich mumble, "If the passengers on the starboard side would care to look, they will see the coast of Wales and the Bristol Channel."

I pressed my forehead against the view. "Oh, look, Steve, look." He put his head alongside mine. We watched England pass beneath us, assorted patterns of the fairway grass, crisscrossed by hedgerows and low stone walls.

"Who mows England?" I asked.

He put his hand in mine. "Sheep, I suppose."

Heathrow was bathed in bright morning sunshine as our company Jaguar, the color of a golden bear, pulled up to the curb near a crosswalk marked in bold white paint, "Look Right." Our driver's name was Ernest and I was to sit next to him, Steve told me, to test my nerves.

Ernest sped smoothly through the traffic patterns that served Heathrow until we escaped north toward St. Albans, relentlessly on the wrong side of the road. My mind said that Ernest knew what he was doing, my heart said I was happy, but my gut feeling was that I was about to die in a head-on collision with a truck—a lorry, I was to call it.

When I mustered courage to release my eyes from oncoming traffic, I looked about the countryside and knew I was in England. If I had been blindfolded and set down in that scene I would have known it. I saw the landscape of my picture books, the landscape I painted when I let my brushes range about the canvas. I saw a ploughed field, so unlike a field in upstate New York plowed to a hillside of dense trees. My English field climbed right up and over a Chiltern hill and, beyond it, another curve of land rose to meet a lone grove of trees that looked carefully pruned by hand. "Oh, look, Steve, look," I said to the man I married, who was sitting in the back seat so that I would be the first to die. Ernest said, "That would be a copse then ma'am."

We stayed at a country inn near St. Albans until our things arrived from America, but we dropped by our house daily to enjoy the hospitality of our new neighbours. Tony and his wife Ann took over our English education, although Steve had already been schooled by his invaluable secretary Adele, a woman of such intelligence and charm that the division manager had found her insufferable and willingly passed her along. By the time we stepped off the airplane at Heathrow, my all-American husband had an entirely new vocabulary prepared for himself, and for me, and he proceeded to correct me each time I didn't get it right. He never altered his American manner of speaking—just his terminology. Suddenly boot, bonnet, and windscreen were right, and trunk, hood, and windshield were not.

Ann taught me the rules of the British road from the passenger seat of her aging Mini. Patiently she saw me through the rough stops and starts of a left-hand manual gearshift and in return for her kindness and bravery, I taught her to double-clutch, a handy maneuver in a roundabout world. I also came up with an idea whereby she could get a new Mini for almost nothing.

Tony showed us how our house worked. Steve hung onto his every word, while I only pretended to listen, although I did pay heed when he told us why the water heater was in the attic. "Not many Americans know that," Tony said with dry satisfaction as he helped me down the attic stairs. It would have been enough that he spoke in accents of Sherlock Holmes and *The Scarlet Pimpernel*, but there was his humor as well.

A recently retired Oxford don had designed our house, the first time any plan of his had been brought to fruition. The untraditional floor-length windows and gracefully curving stairway that opened onto generous hallways made our home seem bright and spacious. There was a landing on the stairway large enough for a small chair and table on which to set a vase of flowers. And a vase with flowers picked for us by Ann was there on the day we officially moved in.

The fun of fathoming the unfamiliar English phrase or product of British ingenuity was a game we never tired of. We adopted, temporarily at least, spellings, pronunciations, and definitions for our tired old American words, just as quickly as we found them. Steve's colorful assortment of American phrases appealed to Tony, while Ann became especially fond of the American term, "Yeah," said not in the round tones of a English lady but in a tone rather like my own. When Tony heard her, he looked at me sadly as if to say, "Look what you have done to her." For our part, we became especially fond of the English expression, "Bob's your uncle," as in "If you want water, turn on the tap and Bob's your uncle." Its meaning was so precise as to be a breakthrough in communication.

Tony was an avid golfer, something we did not know until our golf clubs arrived from the States. He carried a handicap of eight and belonged to Verulam Golf Club, seven minutes away, down the London Road on the southeast corner of town. He was delighted to learn that we had golf in common and encouraged us to consider a membership at his club. He wasn't nearly as delighted as I. My one reservation about moving to England had been removed.

By mid-June he offered to arrange a game with the chaps on a Saturday to suit Steve—give him a chance to play Verulam and decide if inquiries should be made about a membership. I was not invited to play. Ann was not a golfer. Tony had never played golf with women—it hadn't occurred to him.

On the appointed day, when the boys drove off to Verulam like happy children, Ann thought it was time I learned the ins-and-outs of the Saturday market. St. Albans was one of the oldest and busiest market towns in England. I might find myself a bargain for a few quid.

The city center overflowed with people speaking in jarring accents. I was jostled by the crowd, never sure which way the traffic flowed for pedestrians. Ann was forever saying, "Wait right here for a minute," and then would run off to do whatever. I saw nothing that I wanted to buy and it wasn't long before I was truly fed up. I was rude to the man that hawked pretty ribbons when he called me "Luv." That's when Ann stopped me in my tracks and put her hands on my shoulders. "Now, look here. You are determined not to enjoy yourself," she said, not unkindly. "That man, by the way, is Tony's friend. He plays golf at Verulam except on market days when he sells his ribbons to support his family and his golf. I know why you're sulking" she went on, "and I can't imagine anyone caring so much about a silly game. What's come over you?"

"What has come over me?" I said. "I'm obsessed with the wish to play golf at Verulam. I can't get it out of my head. Anyway, I'm not a good shopper, Ann. My mother, to this day, can't stand to take me shopping with her. Maybe we could visit the abbey or something."

Meanwhile, after their enjoyable game at Verulam, Steve explained to Tony that a decision about applying for membership ought to be mine as well as his, since golf meant more to me than it did to him. Without a moment's hesitation, Tony responded, "Well, then, if you're agreeable, I shall arrange for the three of us to play tomorrow after two o'clock."

I woke up early the next morning, too excited to sleep. I lay in bed wondering why there were no window screens in England and why weren't there flies or mosquitoes? Then, I started to think about my body turn and weight shift and how I would stare at a spot just behind the ball and not look up when I putted. Some of the best practicing I did was done in my head. Finally I got out of bed and walked to the long bedroom windows that overlooked the rose garden. When I saw Steve was awake I said, "Another rotten day in paradise. Do you know that it hasn't rained once since we've been here? Ann says the roses are early because it's been so warm. Do you think it's ever going to rain?" And so I rattled on while Steve looked at me and smiled.

On that beautiful day in June 1976 at 1:15 P.M. we piled our clubs into the boot of Tony's Rover and headed for Verulam where the first thing I did to celebrate my inaugural round on British soil was buy a sleeve of Dunlop 65s, so named, Tony said, to honor Henry Cotton's first-round score in the 1934 Open at Royal St. George's. Although I would not have been surprised if they were, they *weren't* whiter than the golf balls in America. In defense of the British ball, Tony said it was one-sixteenth of an inch smaller than our American ball and would go further. I liked that. He had heard that the larger ball had more maneuverability, which he imagined would only accentuate his slice. Besides, how were you ever going to get a 42.7 millimeter ball into a 4½-inch hole?

While we waited for the last of the Sunday foursomes to clear the tee, we told Tony about our casual Sunday afternoon stroke play four-ball at home during which we kept our individual scores for handicap purposes. Tony was astounded.

"Never heard of *that*," he said. "Put in a score when you aren't playing an official round? Do you mean you would handicap a player based on his practise rounds?"

"I wouldn't call it practice," Steve said defensively.

"Well, it's entirely different, isn't it—playing under pressure and playing casually? Some of us play better in competition and some of us play worse. But in either case, it's not the same."

When it was my turn on the tee, I hooked my drive over the boundary fence onto the northbound tracks of British Rail that terminated, Tony said, in Inverness. Then I calmed down and by the end of the round I knew I couldn't bear it if we were not allowed to join Verulam.

When we came off the 18th green Tony took us inside the clubhouse, introduced us to several members, and bought us drinks at the bar. The order consisted of three iceless gin and tonics, each served in a small tumbler. Tony requested ice for his American guests, and for himself. Ever since we moved in next door, Tony had come to fancy an ice cube now and then from our freezer compartment. I'm sure he thought it unnatural but he couldn't help himself. He worried that in some way he was becoming less English. The bar attendant produced a shallow dish of small cubes that disappeared shortly after they struck the gin, having absorbed the last latent heat of fusion.

"Shall I put you forward for membership then?" Tony asked Steve who looked to me, pretending there might be a question in my mind.

"There's another aspect to Verulam that may interest you," Tony said. "I should have mentioned it before. You've heard of the Ryder Cup, of course?" Steve said he thought he had, or maybe he was thinking of the Walker Cup.

"I've heard of it," I said. "Why do you ask?"

"Because the man who donated the Cup was a member here. Here, come with me." We followed Tony into the dining room, to a very large oil painting on the wall. "There he is—Samuel Ryder. He was our captain three times. Let's see," he said, looking at some plaques. "1911, 1926, and 1927. Before my time, I'm afraid. You've heard of him?"

"My first golf teacher, George Hall," I said, "was vice-president in the PGA of America back in the 1950s and he used to tell me about the Ryder Cup. But I didn't know Ryder was a person."

"When was the first Ryder Cup Match played?" Steve asked.

"1927, I believe," Tony said looking at another plaque. "Yes, 1927—at Worcester Country Club in Massachusetts."

"What kind of crazy deal is that?" Steve wanted to know. "If it was Ryder's trophy, why wasn't the first match played here in Great Britain?"

"You're right. It is odd. But whatever its beginnings, I'm afraid it hasn't much future," Tony said. "Arnold Palmer was your Ryder Cup captain last year when it was played at his own club in Latrobe, Pennsylvania. It was another disaster for our side. The contest was over before the Sunday afternoon matches began. Out of 21 Ryder Cups we have won only three times." Tony got up and took a small frame off the wall. "Here, read what Michael McDonnell had to say in the *Daily Mail*, September 22, 1975. One of our chaps had it mounted."

> THE RYDER CUP PASSED AWAY YESTERDAY. NOT JUST FOR ANOTHER TWO YEARS, BUT ALMOST CERTAINLY FOREVER. THERE IS NO FURTHER POINT TO THIS CHARADE.

Tony added, "It's really a crisis. They've tried everything—changing the number of matches, number of points, bringing in the Republic of Ireland three years ago, in 1973—does no good at all. We still lose. Even Palmer, the man who made golf a spectator sport, hasn't the magic to make the Cup a popular and financial success in America. Now there's a rumor that your PGA wants to give the operation to your PGA Tour, which doesn't want it, either. Yet, in Britain, the Ryder Cup Match is one of our most important sporting events, win or lose."

Tony beckoned us over to a glass case. "Look here. This is a Photostat of the *Deed of Trust* for the Trophy, giving ownership of the Cup to the PGA of Great Britain. It was drawn up

In witness whereof the said parties to these present have hereunto set their hands and seals the day and year first above written.

Signed Sealed and Delivered

Samuel Ryder

This Deed of Trust

is made the 9th day of December One thousand nine hundred and twenty-nine
Between Samuel Ryder of Stortford Lodge, St. Albans, Hertford Seed Merchant (herein after called the Donor) of the one part, and John Henry Taylor of Royal Mid-Surrey Golf Club Richmond Surrey, James Braid of Walton Heath Golf Club Walton-on-the Hill Tadworth Surrey, and Joshua Taylor of Richmond Park Golf Course Roehampton Gate S.W. 15 (hereinafter called the Trustees) of the other part.
Whereas the Trustees are three of the members of the present Committee of the Professional Golfers Association of Ethelburga House Nos 91 and 93 Bishopsgate in the City of London
And whereas the Donor has presented to the Trustees for and on behalf of the said Association an ornamental gold Cup which gift has been accepted by the Trustees upon the conditions and trusts and for the purposes and with and subject to the powers and provisions hereinafter expressed concerning the same (namely):

1. The Cup shall be called and always known as "The Ryder Cup".
2. The Cup shall always be and remain the absolute property of the said Association.
3. The Cup shall be competed for biennially between two teams of professional golfers, one team representing Great Britain and the other team representing the United States of America. Each team shall be composed of eight players (or such other number as shall be arranged) being professional golfers born and residing in the Country which they respectively represent and the eight players representing Great Britain shall be members of the said Association.
4. The Competitions shall take place on two consecutive days: the first of such days to be occupied in playing "Foursomes" over thirty-six holes and the second of such days in playing "Singles" over thirty-six holes. The team which shall have at the end of such two days obtained the larger number of points shall be adjudged the winners, and in the event of both teams having obtained an equal number of points at the conclusion of the second day the Cup shall remain in the possession of the team holding the same at the Commencement of the tied Competition, and for this purpose the British team shall be deemed to hold the Cup at the commencement of the Competition played in the United States of America in the year One thousand nine hundred and twenty seven.
5. Competition in compliance with this deed having been played up to and including the competition decided in Great Britain in the year One thousand nine hundred and twenty nine, the next competition shall take place in the United States of America in the year One thousand nine hundred and thirty one and so on at successive yearly periods alternately in Great Britain and the United States of America.

in late 1929 to replace and clarify a 1927 deed that had called for an *annual* match and left several matters unspecified. In the first deed there was no requirement that the teams be homebred, only that the British team belong to the PGA of Great Britain and the American team belong to the comparable association in America. The Americans decided to put on their own homebred requirements but the British did not follow suit for several years. Right here, in the 1929 deed," Tony pointed, "it describes the format for the competitions and who is eligible to play and the rest. It says, 'The Cup shall be competed for biennially between two teams of professional golfers, one team representing Great Britain and the other team representing the United States...' and further along it says 'alternately' in each country. So you can see that with such a 'home and away' schedule, it doesn't come round often.

"Let's see. What else can I show you? Sam's favourite putter, a Forgan made in 1825, hangs in the men's bar. Off limits, I'm afraid," he said to me. "Over here there's a picture of him with the first Ryder Cup team. And here is a photograph of the Cup. The figure standing on the top was Sam Ryder's friend Abe Mitchell, a golf professional noted for his long drives and his polished shoes. You know who he was, of course."

Steve and I looked blank.

For lack of anything better to say, I asked, "Why would anyone put his friend on top of a golf trophy?"

Came Down

"I USED TO WEAR MY PINK WOOLLY hat on cold January days like this," Sam Ryder said as he continued to watch the large flakes of snow melt against the glass, his hands thrust deep into the pockets of his trousers—staring at his memories, it seemed to me. After a time he sighed and turned away from the window. "Now, back to business. You asked me why I put Abe Mitchell's figure on the Ryder Cup. Well, to begin with, you need to know that Abe's likeness would not be on the lid if the Americans had won the Ryder Cup at Wentworth in 1926."

What? Hadn't Tony said that the first Ryder Cup Match was played in Massachusetts in 1927? Sam Ryder was just a spectator at the 1926 Wentworth match, not someone with a cup in his pocket. Tony had told me all about it: after the British thumped the Americans, Sam was so pleased that he invited both teams for champagne and chicken sandwiches afterward. It was during this party that it was decided to have official matches in the future for which Sam Ryder would provide a trophy. Sam knew I was confused because he knew all my thoughts. But before I could question him, he said firmly, "Another time. Right now I want to tell you about Abe and me.

"But it is a nice trophy, isn't it?" Sam walked to the wall and took down a photograph of the Ryder Cup. "My youngest daughter Joan picked it off the shelf at Mappin and Webb. She thought the Cup should be small and gold like the Havemeyer Trophy awarded to the American Amateur Champion. She had seen a news photograph of it, you see, and thought it said much more than a large silver urn. The beautiful cup had recently melted in the clubhouse fire at East Lake in Atlanta where Bobby Jones, the 1925 champion, was a member. Jones had set the trophy on a clubhouse shelf for safekeeping.

"Joan was always with me at golfing events. At 20, she was filled with her own ideas about what we should and should not do. Initially, she put professional golfers and racehorses in the same category. She bet on them and felt sorry for herself when she lost. I asked her why she didn't feel sorry for the golfer as well as herself, and she said to me, from her lofty perch, that my question made no sense. Did I feel sorry for the horse that didn't win? It was a common attitude amongst the English. After I resourcefully manoeuvred her to my way of thinking, she became as effective a champion of their cause as I."

Sam held the photograph up to the light. "It *does* look like Abe, doesn't it? Who would think a goldsmith could catch such a likeness in so small a statue? I heard that Walter Hagen was surprised we hadn't called it the Mitchell Cup," Sam said. "Abe himself liked to remind us on festive occasions that if he'd died on the eve of the 1927 Ryder Cup—as you know he nearly did—I *would* have called it the 'Mitchell Cup,' in which case, he, and not I, would have been assured a place in golf history. Considering its shaky beginning, it's a wonder the trophy survived."

"You know, don't you," I said, "that no one in America has ever heard of Abe Mitchell?"

"I suppose they've never heard of Harry Vardon, either. They should read P.G. Wodehouse's short story about Vladimir Brusiloff, the famous Russian novelist who visited England on a lecture tour. When asked how he liked England, Brusiloff replied, 'Dam' good.' 'Have you met many of our great public men?' he was asked. 'Yais-Yais-Quite a few of the nibs—Lloyd George, I meet him. But—I not meet your *real* great men—your Arbmishel and Arreevadon.' Abe's friends were sure he'd get a big head over that one, but it never fazed him. It mattered not one whit to him that he was a 'real great man.'

"Abe *was* our best British player in the mid-1920s, but besides that, he symbolized something for me personally." He walked to his chair and, with just a hint of posturing, sat down, rested his elbows, and brought his fingertips together.

"People generally believe that I hired Abe to improve my golf game. It would be more accurate to say that I had in mind to improve *his* golf game. I was 67, in poor health, and not looking for a golf tutor, although I valued his companionship on the golf course. Abe was 38, and I must admit he looked 10 years older. Then, again, so did I. It always drew a laugh when I spoke of Abe in public as "a young man who, like me, doesn't look his age." Abe, widely admired for his courteous sportsmanship and his long, accurate driving skills, was famous for having won everything in Britain *except* the Open. In late autumn of 1925, he accepted my offer of employment and I put him on a large salary as my golf consultant at Ryder Seeds. 'For the money I pay you,' I said to him, 'you can afford to stay home, polish your game for the Open Championship, and finally win it before you die.' Yes, those were my words, spoken in jest—a bad joke when he nearly *did* die a short time later, and, of course, he never won the Open. I regretted I said it, while his regret was for me.

"I wanted Abe to live and work near me for two reasons: we were coordinating plans for an international match for professionals patterned after the Walker Cup and Abe was my liaison with the British PGA and with Walter Hagen in America. The other reason was of a psychological nature that was important to both of us. I thought working for me would ease Abe's stress from a nervous condition involving noise and crowds that had its origins in the First War.

"Abe, you see, joined the Royal Artillery in 1914, just after he became a professional golfer. Amongst the immeasurable tragedies of that war were the accidents caused by artillerymen who killed their own soldiers—friendly fire, you would call it today. Ironically, too often the infantry soldiers themselves, whether from confusion, excitement, or despair, got in the way of their own artillery's creeping barrage by moving forward too quickly. Abe's younger half-brother George 'Twine' Seymour, a fine golfer in his own right, was an infantryman serving near him. Abe became obsessed with the possibility of killing his brother, and in the chaos of artillery fire, he escaped his deadly role by going off somewhere—in his mind—where he could '*see*' the action that was otherwise hidden from view. In other words, where he could '*see*' Twine. It was a refinement of consciousness he would call upon for the rest of his life. But with this gift came a burden that manifested itself in other ways."

Sam told me he first met Abe in the early 1920s, during a family holiday at Weymouth on the Dorset coast. He explained that he was a country member at Came Down Golf Club and often chatted with Ernest Whitcombe, the professional there, and his brother Charlie. Charlie, Sam said, played on the first six Ryder Cup teams and was playing captain three times. Ernest played on three teams. There was a third lad, Reggie, and, in 1935 the three brothers made up almost one-third of the team. It was from this remarkable Whitcombe family that Sam learned the plight of England's golf professionals. They could not afford to forgo their meager wages to play in the few competitions offered to professionals, and their games suffered for it. When Sam asked how he could help, Ernest suggested he talk to Britain's two top professionals, George Duncan and Abe Mitchell. With that in mind, he invited them to Came Down to play with Sam.

"On the morning of our meeting," Sam continued, "we gathered in the Whitcombes' workshop to prepare for the round. Companionship of the workshop was not usually accorded to club members, and I valued the privilege. Ernest introduced me to Abe and George, a most unlikely pair. Abe was conservative in dress and silent in manner, while George, somewhat older, was clothed in Scottish humour and costume of his native Methlick, near Aberdeen.

"It will help your understanding of these two men if I tell you about the 1920 Open at Deal. In the first two rounds of that championship Abe scored 74-73 while George scored a pair of 80s, giving Abe a 13-stroke lead over George and six over the field. In the third round George posted a 71 before Abe ever teed his ball. Then, if you can believe it, Abe lost all 13 strokes over George by scoring an 84. He never attributed his poor card to a late starting time, the cold, drizzly day, or that he was misinformed that George was in for a 69, whereas the *Times'* Bernard Darwin cited each of them as the cause of Abe's poor performance.

"Going into the fourth round then, they were tied, but in the end, as records show, George won the Open Championship with a fine 72. Abe's 76 put him fourth. It was your neighbour Walter Hagen's first Open and he took next to last place, but never mind, he would win it two years later and continue to win it time after time. Walter made his presence known in other ways that year with his chauffeured limousine prominently parked in front of the Royal Cinque Ports Golf Club—his private locker room outside the clubhouse that he, as a professional golfer, was forbidden to enter. Well, that was his wonderful way, wasn't it?"

Sam smiled a dubious smile and then went on with his story. "But to return to Came Down and the point I want to make about Abe Mitchell and me. As we approached the first tee we could hear but not see our caddies slapping themselves and stomping their shoes in the cold morning fog off the Channel. Ernest assured us that it would soon burn off.

"Then George said to me, 'Mr. Ryder, sir, we have agreed amongst us that a man of your stature would be more comfortable at foursomes with Abe as your partner. He's an Englishman who keeps his thoughts to himself, whereas I talk all the time. Isn't that right, Abe?' Abe nodded and polished the head of his driver.

" 'How about it then, Mr. Mitchell?' I said. Abe touched his cap and looked at me in a way that meant I wouldn't be sorry.

" 'Abe *is* the best, sir,' George said. 'But watch out for him—when he doesn't like a thing, he goes off somewhere in his head—and sometimes he takes his golf game with him.' While George rattled on, Abe looked pleasant and preoccupied. I could see this was a routine between two very good friends.

"Abe said, 'Mmm,' when I offered to lead off because there might be advantage to a short drive into the dense cloud. We won the toss and I topped the ball with all my acquired skill. It bounced and rolled up the steep grade to a position well within sight. Ernest's ball, on the other hand, was still rising when we last saw it. George said that I was not to worry—Abe would put me on the green. 'He is the best brassie player under the sun,' George said, shielding his eyes as he peered meaningfully into the fog.

"When it was Abe's turn to play on my feeble drive he took a rock solid stroke that ended in a low follow-through. His compact, balanced swing was the very picture of timing and latent power. I later observed that he used various swings on the brassie according to their purpose. He did, in fact, put our ball on the green, and to my astonishment I stroked it dead in the hole. Ernest also birdied for his side.

"I continued to miss my long strokes and hole challenging putts. As the game progressed George's easy banter by turns amused and annoyed me according to the shot I'd made. I tried to sort myself out, enjoy the occasion. I was usually a reliable partner, but on that day my game eluded me. By the seventh tee, when it was my turn to drive, I was mightily subdued. I took my stance, closed my eyes and swung. The ball squirted along the ground and skidded to a halt 100 yards away. George went quiet and even though the mist had cleared and the sun was out, everyone knew that it was still a grim day for Mr. Ryder.

"As we walked forward Abe surprised me by saying something. 'You closed your eyes, sir.'

"'I thought I'd try it, pretend to hit the ball with my practise swing. The sight of the ball puts me off today. Desperate times...desperate means.'

"'Perhaps you can't fool yourself,' Abe said quietly and we walked on. After he played our ball he explained matter-of-factly, 'You said it, sir, didn't you—"*hit* the ball with your practise *swing*." Well, you tried to hit the ball without the swing and it doesn't work. Take a breath, relax your muscles, loose your grip, especially at the ball, and you will regain your rhythm soon enough.'

"When it was my turn to play again, Abe stood closer to me than before. I stepped into my stance and looked at him. He gave me a brief nod, stood easily, his hands clasped behind him. When I stroked the ball it rose true and long to the murmurs of our opponents. Abe said nothing at all—just turned and strode along beside me."

Sam sat in silence for a moment to gather his thoughts. Then he looked at me to gather my thoughts as well before he proceeded. "Abe stood by me on each of my shots, sometimes closer, sometimes farther away, facing me at six to nine feet and slightly to my right. More and more I was in command of what I was doing. I had a clear picture in my mind of where I wanted the ball to go and how it was going to get there. As we walked among the ancient tumuli—the rolling Bronze Age barrows that gave Came Down its unique topography—I knew where Abe was at all times, whether he was near me or out of sight. I didn't have to hear him or see him; I just knew where he was. My dogs had this sense about me but surely it is not something given to us that have the gift of speech. In any case, there on the golf course Abe and I were on the same plane, and I had never played so well.

"We were two holes up on our opponents, so the match was nearly won by the time it was my turn to drive at the next par 3. Abe took the club my caddie had selected for me and replaced it for another with a higher loft. When I took my stance, Abe again stationed himself facing me. Then he moved his position ever so slightly, taking aim, it seemed to me, as carefully as I. When my ball came to rest one inch to the right of the hole, I looked at Abe who looked at me. Then he lowered his eyes to the tips of his shiny, brown golf shoes and moved them forward an inch. From there he sighted the flagstick, twitched his mouth, and shrugged his shoulders.

"Abe and I were as unlike as any two men could be and yet we both had the same need to examine our uncommon experience, to ask new questions and never stop searching for the answers. So, that was the beginning and basis of our close relationship and the reason Abe's figure is on the Ryder Cup. Well, there *is* another reason. You will learn of it in the months to come, and when you do, you will be the only one who knows it."

The Archway

On Monday morning, the day after our first golf game at Verulam, I stood at the front door and watched Steve drive away, my heart filled to overflowing for a man who loved few things, but I was one of them. Like any person worth his salt, Steve thought he was qualified to judge the rest of the world. Moreover, he was willing to express his strong opinions with confidence to anyone. England and I were rare exceptions to his unswerving mind-set. Perhaps because he loved us both, he kept an open mind, and almost anything we did was all right with him. He counted himself fortunate that the nature of his corporate mission allowed him to live and work alongside these agreeable people.

Weekday mornings he left the house at 7:20 and drove 20 miles north to his English factory. He followed a variety of routes, each with its challenging roundabouts. He said roundabouts and the principle of right-of-way made sense in a left-side traffic system and if he ran the zoo that is the way he would do it. "Any idiot can see that," he declared with feeling to his new English friends, as if they were the ones that needed to be persuaded.

Roundabout signs that clearly depicted where he was, where he wanted to go, and what he had to do to get to there—get on at six o'clock, get off at two o'clock—were the greatest thing since sliced bread. But there was nothing in the world to compare with the countryside—shady lanes guarded by hedgerows that stitched a tapestry of colors in secret patterns that were determined, it seemed to him, in medieval times. To catch sight of a stately manor from the corner of his eye as he sped past its gates toward a square-towered church around which houses and shops clustered like iron filings about a magnet—there was nothing like it. Unless it was the pubs. It tickled him, a former navigator, that it was the pubs that provided his geographical bearings through the farmland and villages: hard left at "The Cricketers," straight on at "The Queen's Head," past "The Crooked Chimney," right at "The Long Arm and the Short Arm," to the triple roundabout at "The Clock." By the end of his journey, he felt pieced together and right with the world.

~

TONY CALLED ME AT NOON AND said that he had arranged an interview for Steve with the captain and secretary of Verulam the following Saturday morning at eleven-thirty. His words, "Saturday next at half eleven," puzzled me but I didn't say so.

"We need to talk, however," he said. "Can you come for drinks at seven and bring your 1976 *Rules of Golf*? Also, I've been working on your scheme to get a new Mini for Ann. This morning I've been to the car hire and the British Leyland sales people and I've prepared some numbers for Steve. Your scheme seems quite a good one."

"I don't know if I'd call it a scheme," I said. I had yet to learn that their word "scheme" did not connote deception.

"Before I ring off," he said, "I hope you won't mind—I'm concerned that you are not able to play golf, so I talked to my friend Adrienne, lovely girl. She plays off—dunno, 20, perhaps. She said she'd be delighted to invite you to Verulam as her guest on Wednesday next, or Thursday, if you like. She's keen to play with you. She'll ring you. You might think about playing Batchwood. I rang them in any case and booked you in for half twelve tomorrow. If you can't do it, the number is 78721. And you may want to pop up to London one day and that will keep you busy." When I told him he was the dearest, kindest Englishman I knew, he accepted it but said, "Nonsense" all the same.

I was grateful that Tony recognized my unreasonable need to play golf. I'd been that way ever since I played the game as a child on a golf course in Clifton Springs, my hometown in the Finger Lakes region of upstate New York. When I was only nine years old I scored a 33. I didn't know it mattered that my 9-hole course was all par 3s. When I told my father about my 33, he put his hand on my head and said, "You are a *genius*—a homegrown, handpicked *genius*. And, on top of that, if you drink sulfur water from the fountains of Clifton Springs, there will be nothing in life you cannot do." I believed him. I drank the water as often as I passed the perpetually flowing fountains where they stood in the town pavilion and beneath the roof-covered sidewalks and in the parks of my village.

The curative powers attributed to the sulfur springs had caused a gigantic sanitarium to be built there in the ninteenth century, an institutional monument to the "moral and physical health of mankind." It was six stories high with a central tower that raised its overall height to 130 feet, a measurement that did not include the roof on the tower that rose upward like a bishop's hat another 20 feet.

The sanitarium was set in a park of maple trees and elms. On the rolling land outside the park, there was a golf course.

On pleasant days I liked to walk it alone, a solitary little girl in a cotton dress, carrying three clubs in a brindled canvas bag. I played my ball according to the game until I reached the sandbank on the high side of the 4th fairway where it was my routine to jump—golf clubs, dress, and all—several feet through the air to the sand below and slide smoothly downward in a warm, satisfying ride. Then I walked out the low side of the sandpit, climbed a path to the old woods that overlooked the park, circled past the Boy Scout cabin, and descended the way through the trees to the 5th tee which sat elevated over the entrance to the underground "potato house"—a cool, dark, man-made cave hollowed out beneath the 4th fairway. The potato house was used by the sanitarium for storing fruits and vegetables in the wintertime but its inventory of mysterious crates and boxes varied year-round. I never failed to try the doors after I had hit my tee shot. If they were unlocked, my game would end. But if I could not get inside, I'd head for the "outlet," the creek where I had driven my ball so that I could "jump rocks" that lay in a jumble above the gentle flow. Jumping rocks was an official sport in my town, a serious exercise that I performed with speed and confidence, and only an occasional slip of the shoe. The stream defined the northeast boundaries of the golf course so that I seldom saw the closing holes and have little memory of them except for the picture-book pond by the 9th green where I putted out under the beady-eyed gaze of two ill-tempered swans that frowned disapprovingly if my shoes were wet. Depending upon my mood and happenstance, the journey took from 45 minutes to two hours and it was never the same.

~

THAT EVENING WE ASSEMBLED with Tony and Ann on their terrace which overlooked a garden of perennials arranged in sorted colors around a fountain, birdbaths, a torchère, and creatures of stone that hid in the shrubbery and flowerbeds. The lawn, I could see, had been scraped here and there, evidence that Tony had been practicing his short game. Berry, their border collie, brought me his ball and I tossed it toward the potting shed where it hit and bounced out of his sight. When he couldn't find it, he looked to me for guidance. I motioned with my head—Ann had shown me how to behave with her wonderful dog—and off he went. Within moments he tore back to the terrace and laid the ball at my feet. Ann told him to lie down and he did.

We sat down and watched Tony pace about in front of us. First, he handed Steve a piece of paper and said, "I can get a new Mini for Ann and rent it to you for 25% less than the local car-hire monthly rates. By the time you return to the colonies you'll have bought us at least half a motorcar, and saved yourselves a penny besides. You married a very clever woman, Stephen. If you approve those figures I'll go ahead and draw up an agreement for you to sign. Very clever, indeed."

Then his tone turned dramatically ominous. Choosing his words carefully he said that despite his advocacy, Verulam Golf Club might hesitate to let us join—the secretary had been frank about it. American golfers were becoming a nuisance in the United Kingdom. Television broadcasts and visitors from the States demonstrated that there were a number of things we did, and did not do, that spoiled golf for *civilised* people. We did not favor, for example, the *games* of golf; we played at a snail's pace—taking many hours to do what could be done in half the time. Moreover, we handled the ball without the least provocation, picking it up for as little reason as rotating the letters so that they either could or could not be seen, wasting everyone's valuable time.

"I don't mean to be unkind," he added kindly, "but the British feel you set a bad example for the youth of our great nation. Unless you can convince the captain, Stephen, that you abhor this singularly American pursuit of keeping score hole by hole, I'm afraid a membership may not be on. Here. Have you your *Rules* book with you?" Tony took his 1976 R&A *Rules of Golf* from his pocket. "I want to convince you that golf is a lot more fun if you play it as it was meant to be played—as a game. Open your book to page 69, Rule 39. I don't know what page you have there. 46? Why is our book so much longer than yours I wonder? Except for the spelling, I thought they were exactly the same, subjunctive and all." We handed him our book, also a 1976 edition, and he riffled the pages. "Oh, I see. Now that is interesting. The Royal and Ancient have put their 30-page index at the beginning and the United States Golf Association have listed theirs at the end—a token attempt at individuality, I suppose." He handed our book back to us.

"*Anyway*, look at Rule 39—three stroke-play games, Par, Bogey and Stableford. I'll wager you've never played them. Rule 15 is about Threesomes and Foursomes. Rule 40 is Three-Ball, Best-Ball, and Four-Ball Match Play and then there is Rule 41—Four-Ball stroke play, and there's Rule 6 which is singles Match Play—in none of these games does one keep a running individual score. No, my friends. The game that Americans favor is described in Rule 7—individual Stroke Play where you can imagine you are Arnold Palmer with his army of fans playing the final round of the Masters. Keeping an individual score is a two-dimensional fantasy—lonely, narcissistic, and ruinous to all but the very best golfers. The traditional games of golf have many dimensions, and a man that brings something more than a golf stroke to them usually goes away satisfied. There, now."

We applauded and murmured, "Hear, hear."

~

On Saturday morning the boys went to Verulam for the interview. At 11:30, Tony, as his sponsor, escorted Steve into the unoccupied men's bar (the members were on the course), where the captain and the secretary awaited them. The "captain" was a member, elected to represent the membership; the "secretary" was an employee, but invested with significant authority. Between them they controlled the administration of almost all aspects of the club. Steve had no doubt that our future at Verulam rested in their hands.

The captain, a tall, athletic fellow, and the secretary, his stocky antithesis and something of a fixture at Verulam, both greeted Steve cordially and rather more warmly than he had anticipated. The secretary directed Steve to call him "Mac," and invited him to join them in a drink. Steve noted that he did not say, "Would you like a drink?" since that could be construed as a question to test his drinking habits, and they obviously wanted him to feel at ease. It was a little early in the day for Steve's taste, but he chose a Bloody Mary; the belt of scotch (no ice) for the others held no appeal for him. Their gentle questions were designed, it seemed to Steve, to persuade him to talk on various subjects that would reveal his character to them. Then Mac excused himself and asked Tony to join him in his office, leaving Steve at the bar with the captain.

Drinks by that time had disappeared and the captain said, "Well, while we are waiting, let's have another," and ordered two more. Steve mentioned that the secretary put him in mind of Henry Longhurst, the respected Englishman who was the Americans' personal guide to proper golf, in print and on the television screen. The captain responded that Mac and Longhurst were in fact friends, and that Longhurst played Verulam from time to time. At that point, although it hurt him to stretch the truth, Steve assured the captain that he thought of golf as a Royal and Ancient game of chance played with partners against opponents. From there the colloquy took an especially pleasant turn. Mac soon rejoined them and suggested that the captain join Tony in the office.

His glass at that point being empty, Mac said, "Well, then, let's have another." Steve could see that two things were being accomplished. First, they were comparing notes two by two (Steve predicted to himself that Tony would return shortly and relieve Mac for the final pairing of captain and secretary). Second, they were appraising Steve's barroom behavior.

At the proper time Tony reappeared, and Mac took his second turn in the office. Mercifully, Tony did not suggest that they have a drink. Whisky at lunch, Steve knew, was not Tony's cup of tea, as the English actually say.

When the captain returned he asked Steve to join Mac in his office. Mac motioned him to the visitor's chair, leaned back, smiled, and said, "Well, sir, I'm pleased to say we would be delighted to have you join Verulam Golf Club. Your membership would be of a temporary category, of course, but we can extend it as needed." There remained only the matter of writing a "cheque" for one year's dues, which Steve did.

They rejoined the others in the bar. As each man shook his hand, Steve made it clear that he was pleased to be a new member. "In honor of the occasion," he said, "at least let me now buy a round." They declined.

~

Though I averaged five rounds of golf a week, the women of Verulam would have passed me by if I had let them. At first I behaved in the forthright manner of an upstate New Yorker, only to find that the British liked their public privacy. But once I had found an indirect means to intrude upon their serious business, they responded in gracious, helpful ways that drew from a deeper well of cordiality than I had ever observed in America.

One day I waited on the 3rd tee for a woman playing behind me and asked her to join me. My invitation seemed to confuse her—she thought she had done something wrong. Once we had sorted it out, she said, "That's *very* kind."

Her name was Dorothy. I persuaded her to let my caddie pull her substantial trolley. It felt good, we agreed, to take long strides and swing our arms unburdened. Near the end of our round, after it was clear that Dorothy and I had become lasting friends, she told me that what I had done—waited for her, a stranger, and asked her to join me in that way—was probably without precedent in England.

Dorothy looked and moved like a middle-aged Peter Pan, but I was to discover, when she took me to a noontime lecture at the British Library, that by the standards of the British Labor government, she was a "senior citizen," a term with which I was not familiar. If it was used in the United States I had never heard it. At various ticket windows—the railway station, the underground, the library—she flashed a small card that let her through for considerably less money than I paid.

"What have you got there?" I asked. She handed me a card that granted her a discount to government-owned facilities that, in 1976, was almost everything including British Leyland Motors. I could see that she was genuinely pleased by it.

I said, "I never heard of such a thing. You don't need a discount."

She told me guilelessly that at 65 she felt she was finally putting one over on the British government. She was a physician and, as such, government-owned, limited in her practice and income since the inception of the National Health scheme. Furthermore, British law hindered her plans to retire and move to her family home on the Suffolk coast because she had rented it to hippies. By some legal aberration the hippies had a right to her house until she proved otherwise. It had been tied up in court for well over a year and she couldn't afford to stop working.

"I used to think it was amusing but I don't anymore," she said. "I was a Socialist at one time, so I shouldn't whine about it. At Oxford, my friends and I joined a sports club that fought the Loyalists in the Spanish Civil War in August and skied the Alps in March. I hope we were Socialists and not Fascists—it was hard to tell. Mother would have fought for the Fascist side, but perhaps I misjudge her. She was an opera singer, drawn to the Wagnerian madness of Bayreuth in the summertime."

Dorothy's slender build, her blunt-cut graying hair, the pleasant features of her smooth face that had never worn disguise—they appealed to me. She was a psychiatrist attached to a small pediatric hospital near London but had worked in other fields of medicine, although she had seldom been called upon to use the extent of her training.

She was terribly shy about her golf which she had undertaken only recently in order to occupy her time in her retirement. She took three golf lessons a week from Denis, our Verulam professional, a young man with so much sex appeal that he was worthless as a teacher. I had taken one lesson from him and near the end of the hour he said to me, "This is possibly the most important thing I, or anyone, will ever tell you about the golf swing." I waited to hear what it was but apparently he had told me while I watched his face.

Dorothy followed each lesson by playing Verulam's first four holes. There she quit in order to take a convenient path back to the clubhouse nearby. She said she planned to play the other holes someday.

"Do you know the archway?" I asked her. She told me she did not. She had never walked from the 8th green across Cottonmill Lane to the 9th tee, had never passed through the old Palladian entrance to nowhere. The arch with its iron gate was so crowded by blackthorn and lime that there was no way around it. The Verulam golfer was forced to walk through. At my urging she agreed to keep playing. After we putted out on the 8th green, I coolly led the way and she followed.

"Good heavens!" she said. "Isn't this wonderful. I had no idea it was here, yet I often drive along Cottonmill Lane." She turned around and walked through the archway again, her head tilted in an aspect of scientific inquiry.

"I thought I felt a vibration, a sensation in my chest."

"When I enter the gate," I said, "I have the notion that I'm walking along beside myself. I keep the feeling for a time but then it fades. Do you know what I mean?"

"Mmm. Yes, I do, in fact, although I've never experienced it myself. But I've observed this separation in some of my patients. It can be a godsend—and may well be, for that matter. One of my children in hospital—we thought he had died but he hadn't—told me he had watched himself from the far corner of the hospital room and saw far more than he could possibly have seen from his hospital bed. He wasn't the least afraid and I believe that is what saved him. I think some children do it quite easily—slip out of themselves—but then they are told they mustn't do it, only because adults can't explain it. I think we must recognize it as a human possibility and endeavor to develop it, not suppress it. What a pity to lose something that is part of our humanity. But isn't it curious that the sick child saw *more* than was visible to the eye?"

After that Dorothy and I often played golf together, sharing our questions and insights. I concluded that she and I had retained some of what we were as children and this was the reason I recognized myself in her. Our wisdom was the confident wisdom of little girls and we saw no need to discard or disguise it as we grew into an adult world that made no sense at all.

~

Every day was warm and sunny. The parched fairways were like concrete, the Thames riverbed had sprung a leak, the Queen had stopped watering her rose garden, and a straight ball at Verulam rolled unimaginable lengths. On Thursday, the twenty-second day of July, I took 38 strokes on the front nine. It was the first time I had scored less than 40 strokes for nine holes since I left my little golf course in Clifton Springs.

I had a disappointing 42 on the back nine, but still, Dorothy thought my 38 was worth a gin. While she went ahead to change her shoes I circled the lounge, drink in hand, looking at the photographs. Then I headed toward the women's locker room, a route that took me through the dining room where Sam Ryder's large oil portrait hung on the wall. I glanced up at him and said, "I hit it as far as Abe Mitchell today, Sam." I often talked to portraits, being a portrait artist myself, but they seldom talked back.

He looked right at me and responded sternly, "I beg your pardon..." It was chilling. At least that's what I told Dorothy when I reached the locker room.

"There you are, you see," she laughed. "Comparisons to Abe Mitchell from women sipping gin are not on. You'll have to apologise, won't you? Samuel Ryder's oldest daughter Marjorie—lives in Harpenden—just recently gave that portrait to the club. He's a nice-looking man, isn't he? Well... except for that *dreadful* mustache."

Seeds

The day following my first words with Samuel Ryder's portrait I purposefully passed through the dining room again. Sunshine poured through the large windows, lighting the artist's strokes. I gazed into Sam's clear, dark brown eyes and soberly apologized for my previous remark about Abe Mitchell. He remained silent. His black hair waved pleasantly across his forehead but I agreed with Dorothy—his otherwise nice face was all but destroyed by a long, droopy mustache. I inspected a rendering of white embroidery at his neck and wrists that I hadn't seen before. He was wearing ceremonial robes of some sort. The painting had darkened with age and its details were not clear, although I could detect pretty red bows at the shoulders of a long, fur-edged cape. The medallions that hung about his chest and other trappings of office were explained by words and Roman numerals painted on the canvas, "Mayor of Saint Albans AD MDCCCCVI," a fact that was news to me. Apparently Sam had done more than get rich, play golf, and donate the Ryder Cup. Tony knew everything—he would satisfy my curiosity.

That evening I saw my neighbour trimming the beech hedge between our gardens and went out to him. "Howdy, pahtna," he said as I approached.

"Pardnerr," I said.

"Howdy, pardnerr. What's up?"

"You and Ann—can you come sit in the garden when you're through? I'd like to talk about Sam Ryder. You didn't tell us he had been Mayor of St. Albans."

"Can we do without Ann? She and Berry are at obedience class for dogs and people in Luton. She thinks Berry is clever enough, or Berry thinks *Ann* is clever enough, to do agility training, so they're off learning a new sport."

Tony leaned over and picked up a piece of fluted glass that lay next to his handclippers. "See what I've found! On *your* side of the hedge, too." I didn't believe him for a moment and said so. "It looks to be the top half of a vial, clear enough to be from Roman times. Put it with the ones you are collecting for your mother. When will she be here, by the way? We must plan a party."

I had implied deceptively to Tony that it was my mother, not I, that liked broken bits of glass. "She arrives Southampton August thirteenth. She's very excited about the visit but it's the getting here and getting back that's her first priority. She likes to float across oceans slowly in the grand style. What's disappointing is that she will be here such a short time. I wish it were longer, but she says she doesn't want to get in our hair."

He held out the piece of bottle with its small decorative neck intact. "Here, it's yours." When I took it under protest, he said, "The look on your face is my reward."

I had learned early on that if I pulled a weed in my rose garden I was sure to find a glass shard among the strange stones in the soil. The stones were called flints, the same flints, when flaked, that sparked a flintlock gun. My flints were whole or broken into large chunks, some looking like baked potatoes, halved and ready for butter and sour cream. Flints were quartz deposits inside a thin covering of chalk, the result of water erosion on the limestone bedrock of southeast England. Given a sharp rap with a knapping hammer the hard quartz rock broke evenly, revealing a smooth translucent interior in shades from oyster white to slate-black edged in cream. The rough skin of limestone, rich in iron, came in shades of tan, often tinged with rust. Knapped flints were so serviceable and gleamed so pleasantly, rain or shine, that they were decoratively applied to exterior walls all over the region.

Until Tony informed me otherwise I had assumed that all Hertfordshire soil contained shards and flints, but he said that I had more than anybody. My garden had been the site of the former landowner's collection of glass, some of it from the Roman city of Verulamium buried beneath a part of St. Albans. While our houses were being built the shed was vandalized. Glass was strewn hopelessly about and eventually turned into the diplomat's soil.

"I'll be over shortly," Tony said gathering his tools. "Just let me find one or two things about Ryder."

The entrance to our garden, except by a service gate, was through the French doors of our dining room and Tony soon strode through, a small refreshment in each hand, one for him and one for me, made by Steve who was packing his bag for a meeting in Stuttgart. We sat in the diplomat's tattered sling-back canvas lawn chairs and watched the amber glow of the evening sky change nature's colors to the sentimental shades shunned by careful artists everywhere.

Tony began by saying that he didn't know a helluva lot about Sam Ryder—Tony had learned "helluva" from Steve—except that Sam was a devout Nonconformist, and in a cathedral town that was not a good thing. He was largely forgotten. Yet buildings stood today in St. Albans because of him—the imposing Trinity Congregational Church on Victoria Street, his office building in Holywell Hill which was now the main post office. Other than that, there was just his name on a plaque here and there about town, and a tombstone in the Hatfield Road cemetery. Nowadays only Verulam golfers remembered him and told tales, brought to mind, Tony supposed, by Ryder's old Forgan putter in the bar. Tony's favorite story was from a club report in 1920: Birtwhistle complained that his opponent Ryder foozled his tee shots into serious trouble on Birtwhistle's two stroke-holes, yet diabolically managed to win them. Birtwhistle wanted to know, "What can one do against such a man?"

"But here, start with this short history I found tucked inside an old Ryder Cup brochure," Tony said and he handed me a booklet of facts that I wasn't really interested in. It told how Sam Ryder, at age 37, moved his family to St. Albans in 1895 to start a mail-order firm that packaged and sold excellent flower and vegetable seeds at a price anyone could afford —a penny a packet. Apparently, gardening experts thought it was a terrible idea at the time. Nevertheless, thousands and thousands of customers materialized overnight and he was in business.

"Born 24 March 1858, Preston, Lancashire," Tony read, "died 2 January 1936, age 77, of pneumonia, Langham Hotel, London. Father: Samuel Ryder, Wesleyan lay-preacher and market gardener; mother: Elizabeth Martin, dressmaker. Five older sisters, two younger brothers."

"Yes but what was he *like*?"

"All right, then. Sam was a straight stick, at his father's side in business and religious affairs. He was educated—went to Owens College, now Manchester University, excelled at mathematics and cricket, and that's about all I know of his youth. What I do know is that when he was over 60 years old he began to help professional golfers in every way he could find because American professionals were beginning to dominate the game. Sam blamed the repressive attitude of the British toward their own professionals for this rise in mediocrity. In the 1920s he, with his brother James, organized challenge matches and exhibitions at Verulam and other courses where he had country memberships or friends who would help him with his crusade. He provided substantial cash prizes to the winners, but, to the point, he ensured the field a starting fee, travel expenses, room and board. In other words, he offered 'appearance money' not so that they *would* appear, but so that they *could* appear."

I was skeptical. "Don't you think he was just using the professional golfers to promote his seed business, Tony? Besides, he was so religious—I can't abide golfers who expect God to sink their putts for them. It puts God in an awful position. And then, really, that portrait of the mayor. Why did he want to be mayor, anyway? It's my guess he was pompous, pious, and morose. Look at the photographs—he couldn't have had a sense of humor. And I think he was just lucky the business didn't fold. I can't imagine Steve risking everything we have on such an uncertain scheme."

Tony looked at me somewhat dismayed. "I don't mean to be presumptuous, but if you feel that way about him, why do you care?"

I was silent. For once in my life I had no words. Bewildered, I said slowly, "I don't know, Tony, I *don't* know."

"Here now. It's all right." Tony said it with great kindness. "Tell you what. I'll check the lot with the chaps at Verulam. They seem to have fond memories of him. It's been discovered that Sam quietly paid the club deficit every year."

~

WITHIN DAYS TONY WAS AGAIN pacing about my garden, eagerly allaying my doubts about Sam Ryder's character. I watched his professional presentation from the diplomat's tattered lawn chair. "To begin with, Sam's daughter Marjorie—lives in Harpenden—says emphatically that her father was not pious. She also says he wasn't morose—he just liked to look that way. It was part of his humour. What man would move to Folly Lane to start a new business and not have a sense of humour? So, there's that.

"As for the portrait, Salisbury was an aspiring young local artist and Sam was helping him financially. Salisbury hadn't yet painted the royal family, or Churchill, or Franklin Roosevelt. He did a charming piece of Sam's three daughters called 'Playmates,' the first of Salisbury's paintings to hang at the Royal Academy."

Tony looked at me, paused and said out of the corner of his mouth, "How'm I doin'?" I laughed, more at his twisted face than at his American twang. He did not approve of my flattened vowels and Cornish "r"s, so when he did his imitations I had the notion he hoped I would recognize myself in his sounds and do something about it.

Then Tony told me he'd found an interview of Mayor Ryder in *The Hertfordshire Gazette* from 1906. In it Sam described why he came to St. Albans, saying that over the many years he'd managed his father's seed catalogue firm near Manchester, which sold expensive seed to gentry, he had come upon a commercial principle. But to implement his plan, Sam needed to find the perfect distribution center and St. Albans, in 1895, was it. Sam called it "the centre of the Kingdom," a cathedral town of 7,000, small, convenient, with cheap rents and rates, connected to the rest of the world by three train stations and postal service to every corner of England and, therefore, the British Empire. In such a place he could sell a packet of the finest seed, by postal-order catalogue, for only a penny and still make enough profit to keep going.

He prepared himself well, traveled widely to learn all

aspects of the trade, and at the end of it, moved to St. Albans, with the best flower and vegetable seeds from wholesale suppliers. Then he printed catalogues—250 of them, knowing they would be shared. He copied out names and addresses of people in the poorer parts of a town (information found in a library) and mailed the catalogues at ha'penny apiece.

Tony sat next to me to finish off his story, the better to share his enthusiasm. "I surmise that Ryder knew the history of eighteenth-century farmworkers who moved to industrialized cities, how they kept their hands in the soil by growing their favourite flowers—primrose, anemone, hyacinth, ranunculus, pinks, sweet william, and pansy—all compact enough to be grown in pots in their tiny rowhouse gardens. They became plant scientists of sorts, competing with one another in their home laboratories, learning secrets of cultivation that eventually passed into horticultural textbooks.

"Every English gardener knows the success stories of the eighteenth-century 'Florists'—the fierce rivalry and secret formulas among the millhands and weavers of Lancashire. There were florists' clubs, shows, and competitions, even a magazine. But by the middle of the nineteenth-century the cities had grown dark with smoke; the heart went out of their inspiration and the movement faded.

"In Ryder's day Manchester was the industrial centre of the world. It was a black, crowded, unhealthy city to live in. The workers, disproportionately women and children, had income, some education, shelter, but if they had light enough to grow anything in their tiny cottage gardens it was to another purpose than beauty: it was to grow the largest gooseberry or the heaviest leek in town. Sam and his wife wanted to restore the gardener's soul to any factory worker who had a bit of earth and sunshine and a penny to spare.

"The story goes that after he bought seeds, printed and posted the catalogues, paid the rent and provided a fortnight's keep, he had half-a-crown left, which he put in the Sunday collection plate. Such was his faith in God and himself. And it was justified. The business almost drowned in the orders. But he soon had it efficiently organized and became a wealthy man." Tony stopped, smiled at me broadly, and went on. "But that is *entirely* beside the point. When he and Mrs. Ryder took on their venture, they had in mind the spiritual welfare of mankind, no more, no less; they simply wanted everyone to have a flower garden!"

Tony sat back in his canvas chair and looked satisfied. "You believe me—I can see you do. It came to me whilst I looked at your roses just now. I'm sure it is the truth. Sam never intended to get rich." After a pause, he added, "As for the other thing, I haven't a clue why he wanted to be mayor."

I felt an unexpected urge to return to the portrait, not to pursue my dialogue but to see if the painting would tell me more about the man. When I shared my intention with Tony, I added inscrutably, "Maybe the picture will talk to me." He suggested gently that if Mr. Samuel Ryder should, indeed, speak to me, and I, in turn, should speak to him, I might try to do so without the glottal constrictions that impeded the round tones so pleasing to a gentleman's ear. I decided not to tell Tony that I also had an unaccountable need to make a pencil sketch of the overgrown archway in Cottonmill Lane and take it to the portrait.

Tony stood up and helped me to my feet. "These chairs are dangerous. Has your mother had word from Cunard since the fire?"

Within hours after our last meeting in the garden on July 22, the 66,851-ton *Queen Elizabeth 2*, the only British luxury liner still making the transatlantic run, had caught fire 80 miles west of the Isles of Scilly on her way to New York. The *QE2* was forced to return to her home port of Southampton with 1,200 passengers aboard.

"Yes," I answered. "She called yesterday. The tentative plan is for the ship to cancel at least one crossing—make two crossings out of three or something of the sort, which means Mother will arrive later but stay longer. We're delighted."

"Just a few days ago you wished she could stay longer," Tony mused. "And now here you are."

The Sketch

AFTER TONY'S GLOWING REPORT of Mr. Ryder's character I worked up a pencil sketch of the old archway and, on the following Sunday, I took it to Verulam for a private audience with the Right Worshipful Mayor, never once wondering why I felt compelled to do such a thing. But first I had a foursomes match at 1:30 P.M., by special invitation of the lady club champion. Since my stellar round with Dorothy, I had become known as the second best woman golfer in the club, the designation of a loser that was to be mine for years to come, at home and abroad. But in this case I felt privileged and pleased to be noticed by the champion.

The 1st tee was reserved for foursomes from noon to two o'clock on Saturdays and Sundays. If the golf committee back home tried that they would be lynched. Red-blooded Americans disliked four*somes* because they hit the ball only *some* of the time. Hence, this traditional way of playing golf, so much a part of international matches, had degenerated into something called a Friday night "Scotch," a 9-hole social event staged primarily to appease weekend golf widows. It was played before, and even during, the "happy hour."

I set my prejudice aside when I saw who was waiting for the women's champion and me on the 1st tee. There was Denis our club professional and another young man. I was relieved that Denis was not to be my partner because he simply paralyzed me with his stunning face. Rather, I was to have the other nice-looking young man, a teenaged professional named Nick from the nearby town of Welwyn Garden City.

A small gallery gathered at the tee as Denis and Nick drove it out of sight. One bystander confided to me that he had bet a quid on my side and wished me well. As we walked to his drive I asked Nick about the betting. He said that some of the blokes had started it just for fun and I wasn't to concern myself. When he said that the odds were even, I realized what a good golfer he must be and why much of the gallery was still with us.

It did not take me long to see that my prejudice toward foursomes was just that. It proved to be a fast-moving, intense ballet choreographed by unseen forces of synergy and God's will. As it turned out, Denis did mention God on two occasions.

From time to time I was an asset when a dead straight ball was required to avoid the wicked bounces off the concrete-hard surface toward the boundaries of the course. I was especially proud of my drive at the 8th hole with its domed fairway poised to kick the ball left into the verge of Cottonmill Lane or right toward the River Ver. Our opponent had put her drive beyond recovery and, in my turn, I placed my drive dead center, 100 yards short of the green. The three of them, and the few spectators that remained with us, were pleased that I, a David by any standards, had brought down Goliath—our lady champion. They were so effusive, in fact, that I was forced to admit they had spied my shortcomings.

The match fluctuated very little. Each side had its share of lucky breaks and ridiculous disasters; it was hard to take it seriously. We were 2-up at the 317-yard 13th, a dogleg left where Abe Mitchell, I had been told many times, liked to hit a towering fade over the trees onto the green. When Nick tried it that day his ball flew over the treetops and never reappeared. "My God, Faldo!" Denis said. We lost that hole, but won the next two holes so that Nick and I were dormie on the 16th tee.

I drove it neatly to the center of the fairway on the 527-yard hole. Nick then put our ball just short of the green, and I in turn holed it to win the match. "Good God!" Denis said. In my excitement at having pitched it in the hole, I gave each of them a hug and kiss—*not* acceptable behavior among casual acquaintances in England even in the circumstances, to judge by their startled looks. Back home I had a reputation for rewarding partners and bystanders with unsolicited kisses in moments of euphoria. This time my warm feelings of fellowship had a marked cooling effect upon my companions.

The match over, we started to walk in, bypassing the short 17th hole over Cottonmill Lane. It was a long walk down the 18th hole to the clubhouse so we each threw down a ball and played it. My third shot, a solid 3-wood, was snatched from the air by the high lip of a deep fairway bunker. My three "pals" gathered round to watch the show—a comedy as it turned out when I failed to extricate myself again and again. I considered picking up, but *damn it...*

I looked up at Nick. "I wish I knew how to do this," I said. He entered the bunker, dropped several balls on the sand, took my club in his strong, capable hands and for three minutes gave me a superb lesson on how to play out of unusually deep bunkers to full advantage. I did what he said with amazing results. "How can I thank you?" I said, overtaken by another attack of uncontrollable goodwill, whereupon he covered his head with his arms to ward off another kiss. The gesture was funny, and kind. We all laughed. As we climbed out of the sand Nick patted my shoulder, Denis gave me a hand up, and I was forgiven my impulsive behavior.

~

THE VERULAM CLUBHOUSE WAS deserted by the time we finished a drink in the bar and I had stored my shoes in the locker room. I wandered casually into the dining room and approached the painting in a businesslike manner. Samuel Ryder was holding notes in his right hand and looked as if he had just risen from his mayoral chair to address the council chamber.

"Hi," I said disruptively, placing my sketch of the archway on a table in front of him. Then I examined his face. I don't know what I expected, but surely I was playing to a dead audience. His mustache still drooped and yet, now that I knew more about him, I thought I detected humor in his seriousness.

"Over here, young lady." I didn't breathe. "By the windows," he added encouragingly when I didn't move. I turned enough to see a man standing in the afternoon sunlight, his back to me. He wore a summer tweed and his hair was no longer black. I inhaled deeply, as if to acknowledge that I had brought this upon myself. Then I crossed the room and stood beside him. Together we looked out the window at the fairways of Verulam. To our left at the 1st hole we watched a freight train roll silently toward London.

"Like Troon," he sighed, "we have our railroad."

To our right a Sunday stroller with his dog and two children moved, at some risk to themselves, close to the line of play at the 18th hole. "And public footpaths, like St. Andrews," I said and sighed as well.

He looked down at me and smiled. "Hmh," he said, pleased at our joke. British golf courses, famous or otherwise, usually had railroads at their boundaries and public footpaths that crossed their fairways. "Not every golf course, however," he said, directing his head toward the left, "has a large brick macaroni factory alongside the 1st tee." I had hoped he hadn't seen Avery's Pasta Ltd., the largest manufacturer of macaroni in the world, so I had heard.

Abruptly he turned around and looked across the room to my small picture where it sat facing his portrait. "On the other hand, how many golf courses have an eighteenth-century archway through which to make one's way?"

Under his watchful eye I fetched the drawing. I was so keenly aware of his attention that I lost my natural stride and bumped into a chair. He looked away then until I returned. I hesitated to hand the sketch to him directly and looked around for a place to set it. He smiled at my dilemma and with a lift of his chin he beckoned me to hand it to him as if it were the most natural thing in the world. Reluctantly I gave him the picture, fully prepared to hear the sound of breaking glass as it crashed to the floor.

"There, you see," he said pleasantly and turned the frame toward the light. For more than a minute he studied the scene and studied me. Then, just as I had hoped, he followed the way through the gates to the other side. When he looked at me again it was with a texture of kindness that I cannot describe or ever forget. Without a word my doubts and uneasiness vanished.

He set the picture on the table. In a business-like manner, he pulled away two chairs and motioned for me to sit beside him. Clearly, I had been interviewed and got the job.

"You have captured the meaning of the old archway," he said. "Golf can be a passage to other levels of consciousness, a gateway to human possibilities that lie fallow in everyone."

I said the old gate's meaning was clearer to him than it was to me and that he gave me credit for knowledge I did not have.

He nodded his understanding. "I used to pass through the archway and not even know it was there, so intent was I to make my next stroke. No ball at rest was safe from my relentless attempts to get it airborne. I had known others who formed attachments to golf, but mine was a serious addiction bordering on madness. The way my spirit soared when I hit a proper shot put me in touch with something inside myself that I did not know was there. I became obsessed with the notion that if the clubhead met the ball in precisely the right way, the ball could escape its earthly tether, rise beyond this dimension and never return. Well, I was feverish most of the time, you see, and apt to confuse a golf ball with my soul."

He smiled at himself and cleared his throat. "Then one day—it was the strangest thing—I crossed Cottonmill Lane and entered the archway. Just as I stepped through, a man much like myself fell in step beside me. He said that we had met once before, that he had come to my bedside when I was about to die and said, 'What's your hurry, Sam? Hang about.' And I did. This time, at the gate, he asked me how I was getting on. I told him I was dissatisfied with a number of things and he gave me bit of advice. 'Stop thinking,' he said. After that he showed up from time to time. Oh, I knew what he was from the start, yet he was very real to me. My companions dubbed him 'Old Bill,' when they caught me audibly taking his advice. 'What does Old Bill have to say about your stroke today, Ryder?' they would query me whenever my game was not up to snuff." Mr. Ryder was pensive for a moment and then added, "Old Bill was more apt to appear on cold days when I wore my pink woollen hat than at any other time.

"Looking back," he continued, "it seems to me that I was forever getting out of my deathbed to get things done. I had a weak chest, they said. Always had. Even as a young man I was disposed toward every respiratory ailment, yet I was a champion swimmer, a fair enough slow bowler on the cricket fields around Manchester, and a rugby player. My poor body was kicked and bruised in every part.

"By the time I was 50—1908, that would have been—I had put my hand to a lot of things and done them with my might, as the Bible says. It was the surprise of my life that I found myself with discretionary use of large sums of money. My first inclination was to give it all to God. My second inclination was to play God myself—so said my wife. 'You can't change people, Samuel,' Nellie would say. But the good Lord knows I tried. I played too many roles at once: patriarch, businessman, politician, councillor, deacon and church-builder, regional Sunday schools principal, mayor. The role I liked best was Justice of the Peace. It was the one civil job I never relinquished.

"But it was all too much. I completely collapsed from overwork. To help me recover, our Congregational minister and friend Frank Wheeler suggested I try golf for its fresh air and simple exercise. My sport of choice had been cricket; I always had an ill-defined contempt for golf, as most cricketers do, but Frank finally persuaded me to go with him to a small five-hole course in St. Albans, Cunningham Hill, and hit balls. 'Divine guidance,' Frank mused years later, and it may be so. I was convinced that golf was God's gift to me, that it had saved my life, and I was more than willing to repay a gift of such magnitude. I believe golf helped me to understand my religion, although I never did know where I stood in the scheme of things. Pragmatic soul that I was, and not sure of the evermore, I had my mashie placed in my coffin. Well, just in case, you see.

"When I became possessed of the game, Frank gave me a small book entitled *The Complete Golfer* in which Harry Vardon advised the beginner to place himself unreservedly in the expert hands of a professional teacher, to forswear matches and even, at the very first, to forswear golf balls until he had learnt the habit of a good, natural golf swing. 'No matter what he has been told about the way to swing,' Vardon wrote, 'he will forget it the moment he sees the ball. Even the very best players find they can swing much better without a ball than with one.' Vardon was 35 years old and at the top of his long, magnificent career when his book was published in 1905.

"I made a golf hole at my home where I had a paddock that extended more than 200 yards to Sweetbrier Lane—Victoria Street, it is now. It was my routine to drive the length, then pitch over a hedge onto a lawn with holes cut in for putting. I hired John Hill, a local professional, to coach me..."

I had heard this story from Tony and cut in. "And every day, but not on Sundays, you practiced for an hour at your stately mansion, Marlborough House."

"Marlborough House wasn't mine. I rented it. And it was not a mansion." He frowned at me as he said this, and I knew I had been discourteous. I had interrupted an Englishman. Tony had warned me that I was deluded if I thought he wanted to hear what I had to say before he had finished what he had to say.

I offered Mr. Ryder a humorous gesture of contrition but, nevertheless, I helplessly resumed the story. "You practiced in this way for a year until you became proficient enough to allow the Reverend Wheeler to put your name forward at Verulam Golf Club. It was 1909 or so, about the time the new clubhouse was built." I had been looking out the window while I spoke, but now I looked at him. "With some of your money, I suppose?" He did not respond. "Anyway, you were required to play a round with one or two of the club officers, the first such formal round of golf you had ever played, and you returned a score to justify a handicap of six."

"Well, it's true, you know," he said. "I followed Harry Vardon's advice to the letter. I didn't play on a golf course until I had systematically practised my golf strokes. Within a year, a short time really, I was a remarkably able player—not a six, however. That's someone's exaggeration. Handicapping has always been an inexact science but back then it was a friendly estimate amongst one's peers. We had one woolly thinking secretary who reckoned that since I was the best player at Verulam I should play off scratch." His mustache (a shorter, more flattering version than the mustache in the portrait) lifted at the corners as he added, "I am proud to say that on three separate occasions my ball was carried off to London in a goods wagon.

"And it's true," he continued, "I was invited to play a three-ball match with the Verulam secretary and captain, both excellent golfers, in order to test my ability and behavior on the golf course. In my day the underlying principle of all golf games was: two sides and two balls. I remember that there was discussion at the time of the efficacy of playing a three-ball—whether or not it might not take up too much of our time to play three balls in three separate matches. In the event, it didn't take up much of my time. I was roundly beaten by each of them and walked in after 14 holes, but their match was all-square and they were keen to carry on, and undoubtedly settle the matter of my membership as well.

"Unlike most of my countrymen, it wasn't the games and companionship I sought at golf. Rather it was what it exacted from me as a human being. There is an element of suffering intentionally when one strides off to a golf course to spend a few hours striving to do what cannot be done. The perfect game is better played if that is not your purpose. But more of that later.

"In any case, the captain and the secretary must have found me acceptable for I was invited to join, for the considerable sum of four guineas, I might add. Most of the members were 'professional' men—officers in His Majesty's Forces, clergymen, barristers, physicians. They were just getting used to merchants in golf clubs in those days—wouldn't consider asking you to join if you worked for someone else. I don't mind telling you that I put that right within a short time after I became captain, starting with the manager of my own firm."

"I had heard Abe Mitchell was your golf coach, not this John Hill," I said.

"No, I didn't meet Abe for at least another 10 years. But I had heard of him because he had become the centre of a deplorable controversy amongst amateur golfers. It was Abe's predicament that first called my attention to British professional golf. You see, he was an artisan golfer, a member of a workingmen's golf club called the Cantelupe Golf Club that played over the Royal Ashdown Forest course. He was such a marvelous young player that he was selected several times to play on the English amateur team in the annual international match with Scotland, from 1910 through 1912, the first artisan golfer ever invited to represent his country. His fine play was the theme of universal admiration. In 1910, he reached the semifinal in the British Amateur. No one seemed to mind that this labourer was playing in the amateur ranks until he won the *Golf Illustrated's* Gold Vase a short time later. Immediately, nasty letters appeared in the press from amateurs and sports writers questioning Mr. Mitchell's right to call himself an 'amateur' since any hired workman who played as well as Mitchell would surely have it in mind to turn professional—tomorrow or next year, it didn't matter. They argued, moreover, that entry into the Gold Vase competition required 'only members of recognised clubs.' When Abe's critics questioned whether the Cantelupe Golf Club was a 'real' golf club, its patron club Royal Ashdown Forest Golf Club fought back with a campaign of its own."

Here Mr. Ryder took a clipping from his wallet, unfolded it and read it to me. It was a letter written to *Golf Illustrated* magazine by one of Mitchell's defenders:

> It is lamentable that some responsible writers on sports are guilty of flagrant breaches of good taste. Mr. Mitchell is a man of unimpeachable character and to say that he is practically a professional, or suggest that he is about to become one, is simply the grossest impertinence. His intentions for the future have nothing whatsoever to do with his present status as an amateur golfer. They are nobody's business but his own. I know that Mr. Mitchell has at present no intention of becoming a professional golfer and has

> no desire to be one. Such statements that have been made must inevitably prejudice him in the eyes of other amateur golfers and deprive him of the full enjoyment of his amateur status.

"This is the part that caught my eye," he said, before he continued.

> It is a serious thing for a man to become a professional golfer. The step once taken is irrevocable. It is a case of once a professional always a professional. It is not, therefore, surprising that a man in Mr. Mitchell's position should prefer to remain as he is. The professional golfer's career is not so attractive as many people think. There are a great many more blanks than prizes in it, and success is at best comparatively short-lived. We have all known cases of men who became professionals and who have bitterly repented it, having lost their means of livelihood and their status at their favourite recreation.

"Until I read this letter I had thought that professional golfers generally attained the universal respect enjoyed by Harry Vardon, J. H. Taylor, and James Braid. I never thought about what lay beneath the top rung of...Is something wrong, my dear?"

Mr. Ryder had begun to disappear before my eyes while he was speaking. I was alarmed and moved my hand toward him. "Wait, don't go..." He became alarmed himself. We did not move, either of us. Instinctively, I thought that if I were quiet within myself I might bring him back. "Tomorrow. At first light. The archway." The soft words hung in the air after he faded from the room.

The River Ver

"It's Jake with me," Steve said, after I told him that I planned to meet someone at the golf course very early the next morning. He assumed I intended to play golf and that he was included. Several times we had put the bargain days of that English summer to good use—two sunlit rounds of golf for the price of only one day.

"How early is 'very early' and who are we going to meet?" he wanted to know, whereupon I embarked upon a prize-winning, befogged, but true, explanation that nobody in his right mind would have believed, much less a sensible man like Steve. Although I saw a flicker of disappointment cross his face when he realized he wasn't invited, he remained remarkably calm while he listened. If I hadn't known better, I would have said he understood.

"I must be at the gate at 'first light.' What time would that be?" I asked him. Steve liked questions about latitudes and longitudes and the retrograde motion of the superior planets and transits of the sun by the inferior planets. He knew where everything was at any given time from any given point. I had been amazed by a notice in the *Times* on June 17 that said, "Motorcar lights may be extinguished at 3:45 A.M." I showed it to Steve who wasn't the least amazed because he knew where he was in the solar system. I did not. I had no idea that the sun wasn't the same for everyone except the Eskimos. To confuse me further, he added that without B.S.T., British Summer Time, car lights could be extinguished at 2:45 A.M.

"How early is 'first light'?" he began rhetorically, as I readied myself. He invariably gave me more answer than I looked for. I knew if I listened I would learn something, but my mind impatiently sought the answer and not the logic behind it.

"Let's see. At this latitude at this time of year twilight lasts about half an hour longer than it does back home, and, I might add, over twice as long as it does at the equator. Sunrise tomorrow is at 5:20, so by 4:20 we should be able to see where we are going." He added that considering the early hour he would accompany me for at least part of the way.

At 4:00 the next morning we drove our separate cars down the London Road to Verulam Golf Club. I parked my new bright blue Mini next to his golden brown Jaguar. It was indeed just barely light. Steve took my hand and we headed down the hill to the 5th hole that ran along the northwest boundary of the course. Already a kestrel hovered overhead, his imperceptible movements aerodynamically perfect, waiting to fall upon his prey in the unmown fescue through which we walked.

Just at the back of the 5th green there was a wall and culvert made of smooth, dark brick that stopped golf balls from rolling into the River Ver. The structure was sturdy enough to hold back an Atlantic storm, but its only purpose was to carry off surface water to the river. The wall, with thick bushes planted at each end, curved concentrically with the collar of the green so that a player lucky enough to have his ball stopped by the wall, was unluckily near the bricks. The player's only relief not nearer the hole was in the bushes at either end, where his ball would be unplayable.

The first time my ball encountered the wall I was Tony's partner in the Wednesday Night Stableford. I picked up my ball and Tony asked me what I intended to do with it. I told him that the wall was artificial and I intended to invoke the Obstruction Rule and take *free* relief. I looked for a place to drop the ball that wasn't nearer the hole or in the bushes and couldn't find one. Tony said I must charge myself a stroke for moving my ball by picking it up, and I must put it back or charge myself another stroke. With the ball still in my hand I declared the Rules were stupid. He laughed at me. He said that one purpose of the Rules was to get us out of trouble without unfair advantage.

"How are the Rules going to get me out of this one?" I asked him tossing my ball back and forth from one hand to the other.

"Well," he said, "you still have the right, under the Obstruction Rule, to drop your ball in the bushes *without* penalty. Then, if you wish, you may declare it unplayable. Under the "Ball Unplayable" Rule, you can then exercise the only relief option available to you in the circumstances; that is, go back to where you played the stroke that put you up against the wall in the first place and, under penalty of one stroke, try again. But if you don't do something soon, the committee will be after us for undue delay."

Several days later I observed that when Tony's ball was near the wall he didn't pick it up, as I had done, but rather he punched it with a 5-iron at the wall where it struck the bricks and rebounded onto the green, without penalty or harm to himself or his club. After he performed this clever maneuver he turned to me and said, "As your partner last Wednesday evening I could have advised you to do the same thing, but you had lifted your ball before I had a chance. In England, we do not lift the ball unless we know what we are going to do with it."

Steve and I leaned over the brickwork, still warm from yesterday's sunshine, and peered down into the beautifully engineered culvert to the Ver below. I thought of the ancient rivers of England. "Steve," I said, "if the River Dart flows into the sea at Dartmouth, and the Fal at Falmouth and the Plym at Plymouth, where does the Ver flow into the sea?"

He groaned and said it was too early for jokes like that.

We walked along the once important river toward the 6th green. A ribbon of mist hung just above the surface of the narrow stream where it bordered the fairway. The water barely moved and the air was motionless in the valley. It would be another hot day.

"So tell me—what's he like?"

"Well, he's a nice man, as I told you yesterday when I tried to explain all this. He's older than you by 10 or 15 years. He has your slender build, although he's not so tall, five eleven, maybe six feet—quite like your father, in fact. He spoke like an educated man with some local accent. I think you would like him." Then I stopped walking and faced Steve. "Steve, he knows my thoughts. There is a communication between us that has nothing to do with words. And it seems so right to me. Human beings must be able to learn this. Other animals do it; why can't we? You and I, close as we are, hardly understand each other half the time, even in practical matters. If I see a thing as black and you see it as white, shouldn't we, by some exchange between us, see it in a third way? Besides begetting, maybe that's what pairs are for. Separately we miss the beauty and the truth of a thing because we cannot perceive the whole." I looked into his face and saw an apology forming between his eyebrows. I'd done it again—hurt his feelings.

"It's very hard to explain," I said, my voice trailing off.

Poor man—I was sure there were times he would have

liked to trade me in. Yet he was patient with me. How I wished he knew what I was talking about.

I returned to his side, took his hand and we continued on. Beyond the 6th green we climbed to a plateau beside the river that was the 7th tee. We stopped and stared. I felt the pressure of his hand in mine increase as we stood side by side and looked out upon a scene of breathtaking beauty. The river appeared to have widened into a broad curve where it met the stillness of the watercress beds. It was a flawless landscape of reeds and willows reflected in the muted colors of early morning light. The moment was exquisite and timeless and truly shared. Slowly he brought my hand to his cheek.

"You wished for it, didn't you?" he said.

"Why do you say that?"

"Because I know you did."

Then he urged me on my way. "I'll stay here and watch until you've cleared the bunkers up there. Oh, and give my regards to the old man." He smiled as though he had made a fine joke.

As I looked around at the natural beauty of the 7th hole, I realized that I had never seen this view before—the view from the men's teeing ground next to the Ver. The route to the women's 7th tee led away from the river to the far left side of the hole, dangerously close to a dense forest of mature trees and undergrowth that extended the length of the hole. When James Braid, designer of Gleneagles and five-time Open champion, drew up his plans for the new Verulam in 1910, he designed a single tee at each hole, knowing full well that both men and women were going to play his course. He would be astonished to see the women sidelined in this manner so that one must aim her drive somewhat sideways to find a fairway. If she wasn't blessed with a draw or fade, appropriate to the shot, a good player driving diagonally to the fairway could easily cross into the rough opposite.

As I walked toward the 7th green I thought about the first time I played Verulam on that Sunday afternoon almost two months before—and the spectacle of the pasta factory only yards from the 1st tee. It took some getting used to, that and the Doppler effect from the trains on British Rail that ran alongside the first two holes. I had been silent with doubt until the golf course turned away from the tracks. I was not prepared for a distant view of chimney pots gathered round the old St. Albans Cathedral, or a walk beside the River Ver. By some law of opposites I should not have been surprised that bluebells grew beside the shady pathways from green to tee, that there was a stone arched entrance to nowhere that stood oddly in a lane called Cottonmill, that there were farmers' fields and grazing cattle and a cream-colored manor house named Sopwell, once the home of Edward Strong, master mason of St. Paul's Cathedral and Blenheim Palace.

I remembered that inaugural Sunday round for other reasons. Not only did I cement relations with the golf course, I cemented relations with Tony. He took genuine pleasure in watching me play. There was no doubt in my mind that I added dimension to the way he thought about golf and his expectations for himself. For my part, I found Tony to be a perfect golfing companion after whom to pattern myself. He allowed himself a few quiet phrases when he thought the rare comment was called for. "Rrrubbish," he'd say, or "I liked that," "bad luck," "jolly good," and "never mind." He displayed a consistent, outward calm that I could only hope reflected an inner tranquility, but I had learned that things were seldom as they seemed.

I climbed the hill until I came face to face with a carefully tended wall of sand that guarded the elevated 7th green. The bunker was tidy, as always, as if no balls but mine ever penetrated the surface, and no shoes but mine ever left footprints. I wondered if Samuel Ryder had been fooled by the elevation of this maddening hole. I never adjusted my instincts to my experience. The better I drove the ball, the more likely I was to misjudge the relationship between the distance and trajectory required to fly the bunker. James Braid had made nice use of local topography when he designed our playing field to test our patience with hidden greens that sloped away, and bunker faces that rose up from the line of play like baseball mitts to catch the descending ball on its sure way to the target. His small jewel would be preserved as long as there was no money to change it.

When I reached the top of the hill, I turned and looked back at Steve. He was already waving farewell. I raised my hand to him, then waited until he was out of sight. As I turned toward Cottonmill Lane I saw a man making his solitary way across the 8th fairway. He was dressed in a rough belted jacket with his cap pulled over his eyes. I recognized him by the large wooden rake he carried against his shoulder. I had thought him to be a miracle of quiet ubiquity until Tony told me that what I saw was not one man, but two, almost identical brothers that lived in a stone cottage covered with moss at the edge of the golf course. I never once saw them together or near their tiny house but, sure enough, as soon as I blasted out of a bunker, one of them would materialize like the Grim Reaper and rake rhythmic patterns over all evidence that I had ever existed.

Private golf courses in England sometimes did not have bunker rakes and ball washers, while benches, if there were any at all, were sturdy concrete structures anchored to the ground alongside public footpaths. I asked Tony about this during a Wednesday Night Stableford. He pointed to a thingamajig tied to his golf bag, a shallow rubber cup with a bit of soft sponge tucked in its center (Steve and I had not asked Tony the purpose of this curious British device in case its use was of a personal nature). This, he said, was his ball washer. Such movable obstructions as washers and rakes were apt to come up missing, he said, because of a recent change in attitude toward the private sector by the public on the footpaths. He added that golfers need not sit about on benches, and perhaps we should mind our game.

Tony had inquired about my participation in the Wednesday Stableford before he signed me up as his partner. Since the matter of gender had never been addressed for this normally all male function, there was no rule against it and no one, to our knowledge, objected. If he was alarmed that we nearly won it, he never let on.

I found it charming that Tony thought there were restrictions for English men and women that did not apply to me. He was rather permissive about my language as well. Whereas he might say, "Rrrubbish!" to the odd sclaffed wedge, I was more likely to utter "Damn!" with apologies. "Quite all right," he would say. "Ladies in America say it but I don't believe Ann would do." *Maybe she would if she played the bloody game*, I thought to myself. Tony and Ann would not have recognized the foul-mouthed person inside me that burst her seams from time to time. I had liked to play alone when I was a youngster just so I could give vent to "Shit" when I was out of earshot. When I shouted the word it was between God and me, and I thought at the time He understood. But over the years it had lost its punch. Perhaps I had tested its strength too often. I read somewhere there were no words in other languages that struck home with quite the satisfaction as our English four-letter words. "Shit!" dissipated my anger but it was not to be squandered, according to my father, who told me when I was five that it should be saved for special occasions.

I often thought if I had Ann's tall, athletic build, I could be a world famous golfer. What a waste it was that she could not abide the game. It made her uncomfortable that we talked about it incessantly. Golf on television was equally tedious for her, but she tolerated it simply because she was polite. Our game was not her game.

She had shown one spark of interest in golf. It was caused by her accidental presence in front of the television set when Severiano Ballesteros changed the face of golf during the Open at Royal Birkdale. Ann had just returned from her tennis game and joined us as we watched the final hole. The youngster from Pedreña on the northern coast of Spain was about to play a golf shot to the 18th green that would announce to the world that there was a new and exciting golfer on the scene.

For three days I had watched BBC close-ups of Ballesteros. The picture resolution on British television made our view of him as clear as a Kodak transparency. Over and over he ripped it bravely off the tee, raised his arms in triumph, and marched toward me from the television screen to save himself yet again from disaster. Just as everyone did who watched BBC coverage that year, I fell in love with the Spanish boy with the appropriate name. He had led the Open for three days, but on the final day, leading the field by two strokes and paired with the eventual champion Johnny Miller, he lost his magic. It appeared he had blown himself out of the championship and broken our hearts. When things could not have seemed worse, Ballesteros regained his touch and suddenly a third place finish, tied with Raymond Floyd, was in sight. His new British fans were ecstatic. When he eagled the 17th hole, a second place tie with Jack Nicklaus became a possibility if he could birdie the par-5 18th hole. His second shot landed short and left of the green, the most difficult angle to the flagstick that day. We were riveted as he stroked a delicate 9-iron pitch onto a grassless knoll near the greenside bunker. The ball dropped just short of the crest, and then meandered through a secret passage beside the bunker and finally onto the green, ending only four feet past the hole. With the wind at his back and the hole cut a mere seven paces from the front of the hard green surface, it was the only way he could have stopped his ball near the hole from where he was. No one believed the audacity and imagination of this young man from Spain. It brought European and American watchers right out of their chairs. Ann admitted, as she watched Ballesteros roll his putt into the hole to tie for second place, there might be something to golf after all.

The Crossover

As I stepped through the gateway I saw Mr. Ryder sitting on a stump at the side of the path, his hands resting easily on his knees and a walking stick caught beneath his arm. With no expression of greeting on his face he took me in as I approached. He leveled an even gaze at me and I returned it with confidence. When he spoke after a long silence I found that my mind was cleared of its senseless noise and associative thoughts which only minutes before had led me from Ryder to rakes, ball washers to Ballesteros, in a bewildering swirl of inner chatter. I was aware only of a lime-scented breeze that rustled the linden leaves and stirred my hair, and the sight of my new friend before me.

"Come," he said and stood up. "We will walk to the crossover," and off we went as if it were our daily exercise.

I had no sense of wonder or unease as we climbed the gentle slope of the 11th hole to its intersection with the 16th fairway. This crossing of fairways created a loop of some of the cleverest holes on the course. Invariably, when I approached the crossover from the other direction after my drive from the

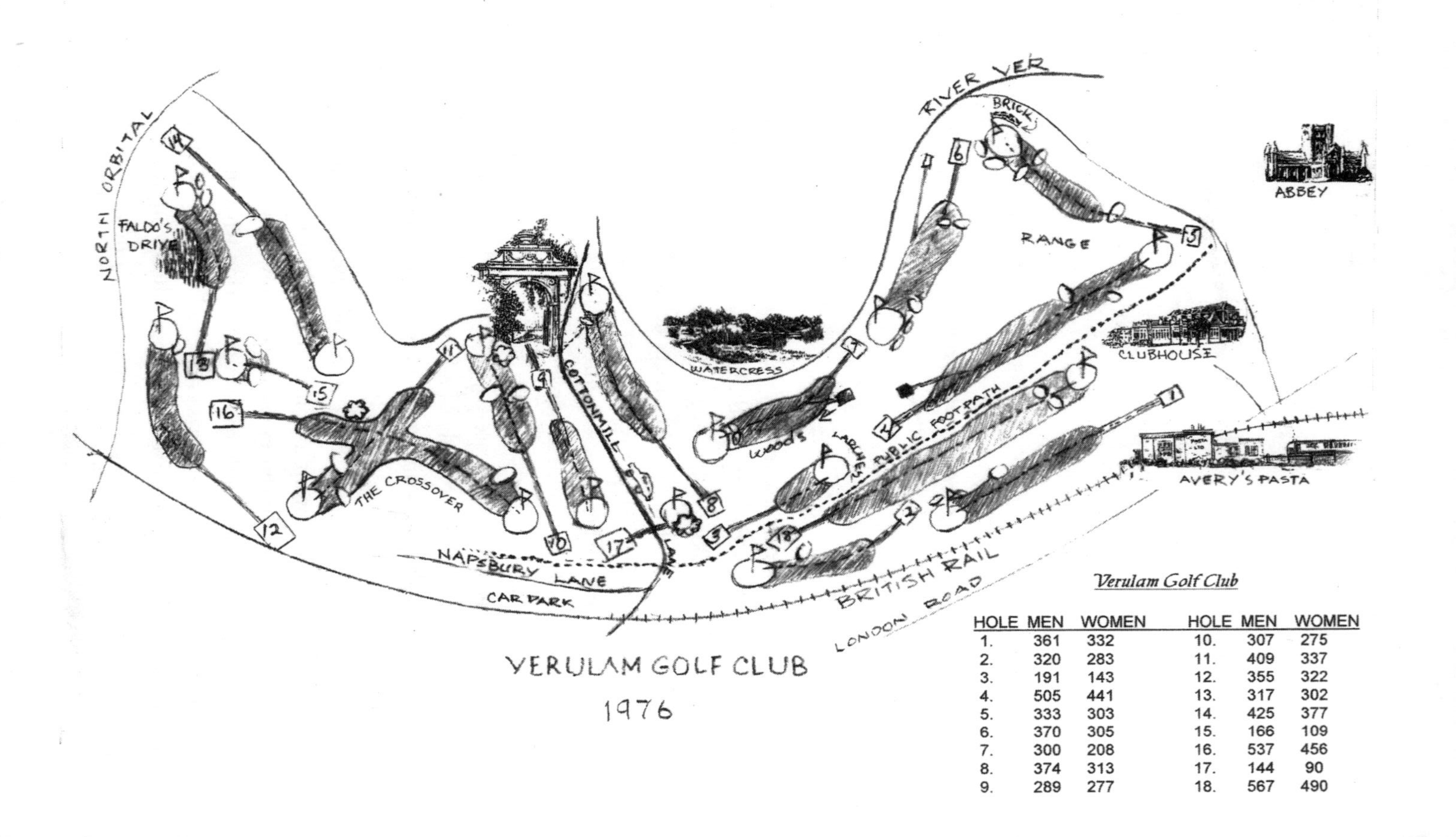

Verulam Golf Club

HOLE	MEN	WOMEN	HOLE	MEN	WOMEN
1.	361	332	10.	307	275
2.	320	283	11.	409	337
3.	191	143	12.	355	322
4.	505	441	13.	317	302
5.	333	303	14.	425	377
6.	370	305	15.	166	109
7.	300	208	16.	537	456
8.	374	313	17.	144	90
9.	289	277	18.	567	490

16th tee, I would begin to think how I would play the loop if I had a second chance. "If only," I'd say to myself, "if only I hadn't aimed over the bunkers." "If only I had cut the corner." "*If only*." Yet, there had been a time in my life when my inner voice said "if only" once too often, and on that occasion I recognized the possibility that if I didn't do a certain thing, it was actually because I couldn't. I was so pleased with my insight that I made a cardboard sign and taped it to the wall outside my bedroom door. It read: *If I didn't do it, I couldn't have done it*. The words were so simple and clear to me that I never understood why no one else knew what I meant by them.

"Your motto means more than you think. It's not a simple matter," Mr. Ryder said. I wondered if I had been thinking aloud. "You meant that it was a waste of time to regret something you failed to do, when you could not have done it differently at the time. However, your insight, if it is true—and I believe it is—also means there is no such thing as 'free will.'"

I nodded and said, "I guess."

"Abe Mitchell and I wanted to play these holes over again, too. He insisted we do it—although I suspect it was the fact that he could drive the 317-yard 13th hole that gave him the idea. He said we deceived ourselves by thinking there was any good in having a second chance, and he wanted to prove it. So 'round we'd play—have another go. We observed that it didn't matter how many times we went 'round the loop, we still wanted another chance. We also observed that we never once brought to our strokes the things we were going to do if we had a second chance. The reason was simple enough, we decided: a stroke is basically an instinctive movement. A man's instinctive movement at the ball is tempered by thoughts and feelings. Since our moods fluctuate and our thoughts do not speak the quick language of body movement, Abe and I might as well have been different people for our lack of continuity.

We were unable to *do* anything on purpose or even remember what it was that we wanted to do. We could see for ourselves that a second chance is a deceptive and useless concept—nothing but a daydream.

"Yet, it need not be that way. A man need not live his short life on this primitive level of consciousness, in a helpless state, unable to *do* and shape his own life. But first, he must see it for himself and then, he must wish to change it.

"Nothing makes fools of us better than golf. It's a godsend and that is why it is the only game He is interested in. The Royal and Ancient Game can bring man to wish for higher consciousness, a possibility for which he is designed and on which our universe depends for reciprocal maintenance." I glanced at him to see if he was serious.

He looked back at me, his eyes moving up and down my face as if he were wondering if he had hired the right girl. "Mmm? Well, take my word then: golf is the only game that God is interested in. This brings us to the subject I want to discuss with you—the future of the Ryder Cup Match." Clearly, if there had been any summoning to the dining room the day before, it was not by me.

"I am aware," Mr. Ryder continued, "of Ryder Cup history and the preponderance of talent on the American side. In the beginning, you know, it was the British who were embarrassingly dominant. But that quickly changed. The time has come to reassess the situation and perhaps look to other options provided for in the Cup's *Deed of Trust* if no good purpose is served the way it is."

At the crossover we turned toward the 16th tee. He led us to the old oak tree beside the fairway and invited me to sit beside him among the exposed roots that lay bench-like at its base, and where more than once I had declared my ball unplayable. He leaned back against a sturdy root at shoulder height and stretched one arm along it away from me. I, too, leaned back. The sun had risen and a dusty light shone through the trees, casting long shadows that accentuated the subtle contours of the golf course. The two of us had effectively blended into the scene so that no one could have detected us. Mr. Ryder sat relaxed and unfocused. In fact, I had the distinct impression that he had vacated his figure, drifted off somewhere. In this space, I could not avoid wondering what in heaven's name I was doing there and what was going on.

Within moments he turned toward me and said, with undisguised enthusiasm, as if he were about to embark upon his favorite subject, "Yes. Let's talk about it. What *is* happening between us?" Before he continued he leaned forward slightly, placed his hands over his knees and gazed down at them. I did the same.

He spoke slowly and clearly. "I am as real as you are. In fact, there is more reality to me than there is to you. Neither of us exists in the way you think of it. Our universe, all universes, you and I, are solely and completely energy organized from a vast sea of pulsing charges. You and I are, and always have been, waves of energy, but my energy is organized in a way not available to you. There is some permanence to me but not to you. Having said that," he smiled wryly, "I admit to a certain weakness in my present state. Making a visible form for you to see and bringing you temporarily to a frequency to perceive it, puts a strain on my abilities. As you know from yesterday I tend to lose clarity after a time, but I'll get better at it. It's not what I do, you know—come back to Verulam, hover about the old golf course. Reverting to one's previous existence to attend to dead issues, so to say, is not good use of cosmic resources. In this case, however, genuine good may come of it."

He looked up from his hands and turned toward me. "The answer I have given you is simple and true, but don't try to understand it now. It will come." Again, the same texture of kindness that I had experienced the day before was in his voice when he said, "What is important for you to know as we work together in the coming months is that the persona I have created for you is my own. You can trust it on your own terms."

With that he straightened up and seemed to wait for me to respond. Then, he changed his mind. "Well, you will want to sort it out, won't you?"

What about form and substance, I wanted to ask him, but he lifted his hand to stop me. "Hello," he said. "We have a visitor—handsome chap—just over the rise there near the 16th green. He's looking toward the gate. Do you suppose that he is looking for you? I believe he is. You will be on your way, then."

I had been about to learn the secret of life that might never be proffered again. I ignored what he said and made no move to go. He looked at me solemnly then and I understood he'd run out of steam again. With a quick nod in Steve's direction, he gestured that I should be on my way.

"We will meet in three days as we did this morning. Meanwhile, give some thought to what might be done to make the Ryder Cup Match more competitive. I understand that the people in America have so little interest in the event that the PGA there wants to divest itself of it. With that in mind, what do you say to Ireland and Great Britain versus Continental Europe *instead* of the United States?"

"That's a terrible idea," I exclaimed, forgetting my place.

"Think about it. Now run along."

George Hall, my old golf coach, wouldn't like it, I thought, as I walked the 16th fairway to the crossing and up the slope that had blocked my view, but apparently not Mr. Ryder's, of Steve. There was a small public car park near the green where gypsies sometimes parked their caravans for weeks on end. I could see Steve had turned in that direction but I caught his eye when he glanced back at the golf course one last time to see if I was in sight. As he faced me, I detected a rise and fall of his shoulders as if to indicate either a sigh of relief, or impatience. He stood relaxed, his thumb hooked in his pants pocket, a finger curled around his sunglasses, the planes of his pelvis, shoulders, and head counterbalanced in an S-curve, in the manner of Praxiteles. Steve's startling good looks had evolved at such a slow pace that I had thought it had been only of my own beholding. I was always surprised and pleased when others, as in Mr. Ryder's case, saw it too.

Steve hadn't always been a "handsome chap." When I first saw him he was only 15 and had "a ways to go," as I said back then. I was 12 and only recently removed from my beloved Clifton Springs to Steve's hometown, which I mistook for a religious community until I realized the spires and steeples were the ivied towers of a great university. My potato house days were over, wrestling with boys took on another meaning, and golf became a full-size game with restrictions that addressed every aspect of my behavior.

The quiet brook that whispered through the fairways of my new Tillinghast course contained not rocks to jump, but a season-long supply of watercress in its bed. My father's ball found the watercress and he picked it for my mother who favored the piquant leaves in her sandwiches. On another day his ball found a fragile patch of pigweed at the edge of the woods. He picked the glabrous leaves, brought them home and tossed them lightly in a hot pan with crumbled bacon. As he served us he proclaimed it was the sweetest green of all.

Not all the men in my life were golfers. My father did not like the game, although he bravely pursued it three times a year—on Memorial Day, the Fourth of July, and Labor Day, always with the initial optimism that this time he would discover why he shouldn't be fishing instead. My mother, on the other hand, liked to play. Her game never improved over the many years I played with her. Then, again, it never faltered. She played to her handicap, which made her an invaluable member of any team. Everyone who watched her golf swing agreed with my father that if she hadn't had such a splendid bosom her game would have improved, a comment without merit but funny all the same, even to Mother, whose humor was splendid besides.

Mother set my moral code on the golf course by saying, whenever I shortchanged the rules by adjusting the ball or reporting fewer strokes than I had taken, "You are only hurting yourself." I didn't know just what she meant, but she meant it. She could have said that lying about one's golf game was tantamount to lying to oneself, but I doubt that I would have understood that, either.

Steve first caught my eye when he was caddying for his older brother Hugh in the club championship. Hugh was a favorite to win and if he had not been so old I would have attached myself to him. Instead, I attached myself to Steve, putting him fourth on my list of lifetime attachments, heroes of the fictions I dreamed before I went to sleep at night. My brief chronology of men and boys began with Felix the tuba player in the Clifton Springs Memorial Day Parade that marched past my house on Broad Street when I was four years old. We met three times a year, Felix and I, for there were the Fourth of July and Labor Day parades as well. I would have loved him on other days but without his shiny horn, gold braid, and epaulets, I didn't know who he was.

The second man on my list was my brother, and the third was an ear specialist who found his way through my left eustachian tube to save me from certain death, I was told. He brought me home from the hospital in his pale yellow Cord convertible.

Steve was four grades ahead of me in school, about to enter the university. While he was mature of mind I was mature of body and I saw no reason to believe he loved me for anything else, but he assured me it was not so, even as he corrected my grammar, my spelling, and my village voice—no more fishin' in the crick and turnin' on the spickets. I told him that I loved him for his genes, *and* his older brother. When I found out their father, in his younger days, had been one of the best golfers in town, I knew that Steve was the boy for me.

Steve's dad had been a professor of Latin at the university for more than 40 years by the time I arrived on the scene. When he died at age 77, he was extolled with such passion by the university president that it was a wonder the institution survived without him. "Orator, teacher, scholar, counselor, administrator, linguist, politician, ambassador to alumni..." There was never a mention of golf. But one obituary, at least, lamented that the "professor has walked out on us and joined the old foursome. [He] could have knocked off the present course in the low 70s in his prime." Steve's dad would have been pleased to hear that, and also to know what his younger colleague had to say: "With his boyish geniality he was the undergraduates' delight."

When I asked Steve to introduce me, he took me to his father's office in the university hall that was the centerpiece of the campus. It was summer break and the empty building echoed with our footsteps. His father was not in his neatly cluttered office, so Steve guided me through the classrooms and lecture halls, coloring our tour with stories about the faculty. Steve had his father's sonorous eloquence and his voice resounded through the marble corridors giving it a vibrant ring. When we came to the main stairwell he began Cicero's *First Oration Against Catiline*, "Quo usque tandem abutere, Catilina...?...O tempora! O mores!...," at the top of his lungs. I liked to think the sound remained among the marble slabs.

The tour finally brought us to what I realized had been Steve's underlying destination all along—the museum of casts, the largest collection of Hellenistic nakedness of its kind, he said. The plaster reproductions, mutilated and smudged here and there by generations of students, were otherwise unrelentingly white. I was unprepared for Steve's latest treat for me, but in no time I was taking a closer look at things. I interrupted his perusal of Aphrodite to ask several questions about male anatomy which he answered readily enough. Then he led me to a statue of the Greek God of Sunlight and pointed to a crack in the plaster that showed that the penis of Apollo had once been broken. He explained that some time ago a cleaning woman had heedlessly knocked it off with her broom handle. She chased it as it clattered across the marble floor, picked it up and looked around. Then, seeing no one about, she reattached it with her chewing gum. A professor, a passing witness to the tragedy, came forward and observed to her that perhaps she had reattached it upside down, to which she replied that it was the only way she'd seen 'em, sir.

Eventually we sat outside on the front steps and leaned against a pillar in the sunshine. Miles to the west, beyond the curious geometrical shapes that were the university's oldest buildings, we could see the hills on the far side of the lake. All at once there was a sound, a reverberation from the patterns of light and shade beneath the old elm trees.

"Stephen. Wait there."

It came from nowhere and everywhere. "It's Dad. He's learned to project his voice."

Across the way a slender man wearing a trilby hat descended the steps of an old stone building and walked toward us. I had the notion as I watched his easy, athletic stride that he was leading a parade of caesars across the quadrangle to ovations from a throng that lined the way. As he approached he gave us a low greeting with his right hand, which he then extended to me as he came up the steps.

When Steve introduced me, his father said heartily "Well,

well, now. What have you been doing, what have you been doing?"

In fact, Steve and I had been long-kissing inside the front doors, behind the once dismembered Apollo. I had planned to win his father's favor by talk of golf, but my loose behavior embarrassed me and made me silent. I hoped the professor was proverbially absent-minded, and I would have another opportunity to meet him for the first time. He smiled kindly at my shyness, which I'm sure he mistook for innocence. After a brief exchange with Steve, he expressed his pleasure at meeting me, lit a cigarette and was on his way. As he strode off I saw that his suit coat and trousers did not match, remnants of a time when he had been the best dressed member of the faculty, a status he gladly traded for a large family he could barely support on the low salary paid uniformly to America's most respected segment of society.

"He's 68," Steve said pensively as he watched his father round the corner of the building to go in the back door. "He's a crack shot with a pistol and was a deputy sheriff. Maybe he still is. I'll have to ask him. He speaks street Italian, Greek, and Vulgar Latin fluently, and learns a new language every year. He teaches as if the Romans were still alive and killing each other in the senate. He plays the piano like a professional. He could have been a great sports announcer, but I'll bet you knew that already. On Saturday afternoons, students and faculty used to crowd into the Concert Hall to watch him announce 'away' football games as the plays came over the telegraph wire. They say he made a one-yard gain seem like a touchdown. But he could have just as successfully rolled out the Steinway and played Chopin études for them."

It was impossible to live near the university and not hear tales of this colorful fixture. My father told me, with unmistakable envy, that the professor was a Savage, a member of the Savage Club—a society of people who could have made careers in the performing arts, but chose other vocations instead. It was no secret to me that Dad hoped to be invited to join the Savages once he had perfected his rousing baritone rendition of "The Road to Mandalay," a song of such fulsome chords and commanding beat that, if played loud enough by me, could cloud the issue. We practiced every day.

Anecdotes about the professor were often ones he told on himself. "Sometimes," Steve said, "they circle back with another name and university attached but they are still his tales of academe. Dad hopes he will be remembered for the wit, charm, and piercing logic that persuaded several ladies of the Women's Christian Temperance Union to vote for him—even though he asked them not to, on principle—when he ran for Congress on the prohibition-repeal Democrat ticket in 1924."

George Hall told me the professor and golf arrived at the university at the same time, in the late 1890s. He learned to play on the campus quadrangle and, from the first, was known to have the knack. When the lively new Haskell wound rubber-core ball found the campus windows, the professor and his friends moved into the countryside where they made a club for everyone—men and women, students, faculty, and the townspeople.

"Until two or three years ago," Steve said, "Dad practiced golf regularly. I would take the shag bag out to a precise distance and he would fire shots straight at me with his 'spoon.' I'd hold the bag open and catch the balls after one bounce, scarcely moving off the spot to reach a ball. One day he was so accurate he seemed to shine. But the range was hot and sunny—so who knows? I can still see it though—Dad, me, and the flying golf balls that connected us somehow. I'll never forget it—that, and the time he came tearing out the front of the house with his .32 caliber Smith and Wesson revolver and shot a rat big as a cat by the kitchen door. That I will never forget, either. Remind me to show you the copper golf mug Dad keeps on the library shelf. It's engraved with his name and total of the best score he made at each hole over the summer."

C.L. WINCHESTER
1913 RINGER CONTEST
24 + 25 = 49

Watling Street

When I arrived at the 16th green Steve smiled pleasantly at me as if we did this sort of thing all the time. I could see he required no explanation, so I slipped my arm around his waist and we walked to his car. But I was puzzled. While I easily accepted the illogical events of the day, I wondered why Steve accepted them. Ordinarily, if he thought I was up to something that had no merit he spoke his mind. "What the Sam Hill!" he would declare at the drop of a hat. Now he was all cooperation, as happy as I with the inconsistencies of our daily routine.

As was so often the case, gypsy caravans were parked nearby. We waved to a small child watching us with serious eyes from the doorstep of her home. Then she disappeared like a soap bubble into the darkness behind her. There was a special drawer in my head for gypsies. The English, according to Tony, were not the least keen for them. They lived by deception, scoffed the laws, and were the devil to be rid of. I told Tony that I thought his opinions sounded like the prejudices of others. In Clifton Springs "us kids" had welcomed these mysterious nomads with their tragic tales. We suspended judgment in case they knew secrets about life that everyone else had forgotten. What secrets? Tony wanted to know. I said that I had heard that with gypsies, telecommunications took on a whole new meaning. Although he smiled when he said it, he called my views poppycock and childish nonsense and said he was delighted for my sake that I wasn't bothered by the mess they made in the Napsbury Lane car park at the 16th green—the site, I should know, of the original Verulam clubhouse.

When we were in the car Steve explained his unscheduled return to the golf course. "I couldn't help myself," he said. "I made breakfast, read the *Times*, did the crossword, looked at the mail—there's a letter from your mother—and started for the office in entirely the wrong direction. I turned at the London Road instead of going straight on. Next thing I knew I pulled in here and parked. I got out and saw at once where I was, so I looked for you." He wanted to say more but thought better of it. Instead, he expressed a sigh through his nostrils. Then he put his hand over mine and looked at me as if I was the cutest girl in town—his smitten look, I called it. "I'll drive you to your Mini," he said.

There it was again, Steve's blithe acceptance of our abnormal behavior. Steve hadn't come because he was worried about me, although, truth to tell, he rarely worried about me. He might caution me about the sharpness of the paring knife in my hand or call to my attention the position of the cupboard door in relation to my head if he were standing next to me in the kitchen, but he didn't fuss. What's more, on the few occasions he didn't know where I'd gone or when I would be back, he didn't burden me with a self-indulgent concern when there was no need.

He drove to the clubhouse where we had parked our cars "at first light," and pulled to a stop but left the engine running while we both looked straight ahead. As if he had an inkling of irrationality, he turned his head to study my face, his eyes searching for something amiss. "Is everything all right?" he asked. Before I answered I thought about it and got a lump in my throat. I gave him a kiss and said gently, "Yes, it is." I got out quickly and watched him drive away.

The clubhouse driveway encircled a practice putting green. I couldn't resist getting my putter and a few balls from the Mini. It was my routine to riffle through the dozen or so time-tested putting clues filed away for quick reference. From experience I knew that an insight applied to a golf stroke lasted an alarmingly short time, and that the mark of a successful golfer was the ability to counter the entropy of degradation with the charge of a fresh idea.

This time I focused on a way to avoid decelerating the clubhead at the ball on "pressure" putts. One way around this pitiable defect was to pretend that the putterhead was passing through thick soup as I stroked the ball. I tried to feel the steady resistance to forward movement on the slotted spoon that stirred the chili, the pressure required to move a stick through honey. Such imagery provided several things: smooth acceleration of the clubhead, excellent "roll" on the ball, complete follow-through down the line of the putt, and something positive to think about under the stress of anxiety.

For this worthwhile advice I was indebted to a French horn player, composer, philosopher, and gifted golf professional from upstate New York. He'd had a serious brush with death that made him wonder if he'd got it right about life. So he began to search, and before long he thought he had discovered a path to follow to find the answers he sought. Unintentionally, I believe, he wove his insights into my golf lessons. So discreetly did he share his philosophy that I didn't realize until it was too late that he was asking me to consider a point of view about mankind that was not the one I had learned. I had accepted that the meaning of life was for the human brain and spirit to evolve toward a state of perfection, slowly, over countless generations, and it was my job to do my best with what I "got." Not so, said my golf teacher as he adjusted my grip and corrected my swing plane. Not so, he said—the meaning of life was much more complex and practical than that. Man was a powerhouse of possibilities ready and waiting to evolve in his own lifetime, but the body of knowledge that recognized that kind of human evolution had not survived the "Age of Enlightenment" of Western Civilization. Western thought no longer contemplated our real possibilities. I surmised these were the same "God-given human possibilities" that Mr. Ryder had referred to when he saw my drawing of the old Palladian archway.

~

As usual when I had time, I took the long way home. I turned to the right out of the Verulam driveway onto the London Road, joined the morning traffic on the North Orbital and got off at Watling Street—an authentic Road to Rome laid out in the First Century A.D. by the invaders from the Italian peninsula. I wondered if Steve's father knew about Watling Street, the straight road from the English Channel to North Wales that passed through Verulamium, an ancient Roman city buried beneath the gardens and churchyards at the western edge of St. Albans.

"Though not at all but ruines now I bee,
And lye in mine own ashes as ye see:
Verlame I was; what bootes it that I was
Sith now I am but weedes and wastfull grass."

— *Edmund Spenser* —

Verulamium—"settlement by the marsh"—was the earliest municipium in Britain, where the dwellers were Roman citizens, a status that gave them certain rights not available to others. One such right would have a far-reaching effect upon the spread of Christianity. The city boasted sophisticated homes with hypocausts (I savored the perfect word) that warmed mosaic floors, city buildings, and the only Roman theater in Britain. It seated 1,600 people and had a proper stage, and an orchestra that was large enough for a show of wild beasts and competitive pastimes. There was a world of history and prehistory within blocks of my house in St. Albans, and I soaked it up like a dampened sponge.

We had been introduced to Roman Hertfordshire by Ann while we were sitting on her terrace in the early evening sun. Tony had handed me another piece of pretty glass and said he was sure it had belonged to Julius Caesar. Steve said the campaigns of Julius Caesar had been his bedtime stories.

"Did you *know* then," Ann said with the nonchalance of someone who had just struck oil, "Caesar began his final march to victory within sight of here?"

And so we learned from Ann why and how Julius Caesar conquered Britain. "This has nothing to do with golf, mind you," she said, and we assured her that was okay. "I'll tell it fast then." She explained that before the Christian era, Caesar conquered the three parts of Gaul, but soon discovered that the Celts in Gaul were getting arms from their Celtic cousins across the English Channel. Caesar realized that to keep the one region, he would have to conquer the other. In 55 B.C., he crossed the narrow straits to have a look, but soon departed.

He returned a year later, she said, and battled his way across the Thames at Weybridge in pursuit of the head Briton Cassivelaunus, leader to thousands of chariot-riding Celtic warriors. Cassivelaunus was not easy to find, but find him Caesar did—at Wheathampstead, only a few miles from where we were sitting.

"Just down the hill, there," Ann said pointing, "is a very deep ditch made by our Celts. 'Beech Bottom Ditch,' we call it. It's a convenient place to walk, out of sight, out of the cold wind, much like our English lanes today, come to think of it. We speculate that Caesar's troops followed the ditch to Wheathampstead and won the day. The Celtic stronghold was disbanded and the refugees moved to Ver'lam.

"Caesar negotiated a treaty stipulating that an annual tribute be paid to Rome. Then he returned to Gaul with a few hostages, leaving as many Romans behind. The Britons paid the tribute until they realized nothing would come of it if they didn't. Things went on as before except that Ver'lam prospered by its new association with Rome.

"And that was that, for almost 100 years. Then Emperor Claudius, back in Italy, decided to reinvade Britain. Why? Because Gaul had complained that their British cousins, who had helped them a century before, were now encroaching on their shores. Claudius then sent his legions to Ver'lam where Romans were welcome after generations of intermingling. Ver'lam was proclaimed a *municipium*, renamed Verulamium, and Watling Street was constructed to pass right through the town centre.

"The conquest of southern Britain went apace until the Romans unwisely terrorized the Iceni tribe who lived to the northeast of Verulamium. Now, are you chaps listening? Boudicca..."

Tony leaned over to Steve: "Whom we refer to as the Goddess of Obscure References."

Ann frowned and began again. "Boudicca, the recently widowed Iceni queen, revolted against the Romans and their supporters, furiously burning everything in sight, leaving much of southeast Britain in ashes, including Colchester, London, and Verulamium. When the Roman soldiers finally caught her chariots on Watling Street they slaughtered her army, as well as their families who had come to watch the wonderful fires. Boudicca and her daughters committed suicide.

"Rome rebuilt Verulamium into an imposing centre for commerce. Then another fire, accidental, swept *it* away. Again it was built, this time as a centre for regional administration with mansions that rivaled the villas of Tuscany. But it, too, did not last. Nowadays, although Watling Street can still be traced through the countryside, scarcely a single Roman brick remains in place.

"Citizen Alban of Verulamium, by legend a centurion, hastened his city's demise by giving shelter to a Christian priest, a saintly thing to do in a Roman world that was losing its grip. The priest converted Alban to Christianity and that's when the trouble began. It was okay for Alban to worship Jesus as long as he worshiped the Roman Emperor, too, and this Alban refused to do, even though the magistrate in charge of his case assured Alban that the Emperor was legally a god. But Alban stuck to his guns and was sentenced to be torn apart by wild animals in the orchestra of the theatre. Luckily, a clerk reminded the judge that as a Roman citizen Alban had certain rights, and one of them was to die with dignity. Alban was entitled to be beheaded, and so it was done. But best of all, he was axed on the highest hill, commanding the broadest view. The time and place could not have been surpassed and Britain had its first martyr. His hilltop grave became a centre of Christian worship for all Western Europe, and an abbey administered from Rome became as rich and powerful as Roman Verulamium itself.

"As Christian pilgrims filled the coffers, Saxon kings moved in and built churches. When William the Conqueror arrived from Normandy, with his Gothic builders, the abbey reached its finest hour. Having possession of the bones of a saint was a limitless financial asset, good for everyone but the man who was declared one in his lifetime. Pagan bricks from the Roman city were carried up the hill to build the Christian cathedral. Verulamium, a hometown to our ancestors, became a popular dumping area and gradually disappeared under a heap of trash."

The Gardener

Watling Street had become an imaginary line by the time I drove past Verulamium on my way home from the golf course, so I turned toward the town center to get a sticky-bun at the bake shop at the top of the hill where Alban died. I followed the narrow lane called Fishpool Street, past crooked walls of houses and shops that tilted precariously over my car as it wound upward to Romeland, named not for the ancient capital, but for the rooms available to visitors to the abbey shrine.

When I arrived home I ate the sticky-bun and read Mother's letter. According to the July 26 *New York Times*, trouble in the starboard generator had caused the explosion and fire aboard the *QE2*, forcing the ship into long repair at Southampton. Mother had been notified of a new date of departure from New York. She would arrive in Southampton in early September and stay with us five weeks, two weeks longer than her original plans called for. She added, with some authority, that the explosion hadn't surprised her, since she'd read in the same *New York Times* report that the huge ocean liner had been running guns and ammunition for the Irish

Republican Army, something the old *Queen Elizabeth* would never have done.

Though it was hardly 8:00 I wanted to crawl into bed, ponder the world Mr. Ryder had described as we sat beneath the old oak tree beside the 16th fairway, examine some unfamiliar emotions in my heart, and go to sleep. I often took a nap when I didn't need one. Back home in America there was a sign taped to my bedroom door that read, "I have so much to do, I am going to bed." I was a dedicated clothes-off, under-the-covers napper. My mom and dad had napped back in Clifton Springs, but their short snoozes were not comparable to my Broadway productions. The difference was that they were professional people with office hours and I was an unstructured lazy person.

In England I did not nap without guilt, however. I had an uneasy notion that I should be on a train to London, on my way to the British Museum, The Tate, Trafalgar Square, Wimpole Street, Waterloo Bridge, Elephant and Castle, and the Old Curiosity Shop. To ease this burden, I rationalized that I could visit London as a tourist for the rest of my life but I was unlikely ever again to be a legitimate part of the community of St. Albans.

I climbed the stairs, lay on the bed, and looked at the ceiling. Then I got up, took off my clothes, and slid between the sheets. I tossed and turned, lively as a freshly charged battery. For a while I focused my attention on our resident thrush whose clear melodic line, to my untrained ear, never repeated itself. Then I recognized the sounds of Jim Nairn setting about his work beneath my open window, getting an early start on a hot day.

Jim had become a gardener in his retirement. He watched over the 28 varieties of roses entrusted to us by our landlord, the diplomat whose fortuitous departure to Pretoria was foremost on our list of wonders.

Gardening was not new to me. Back home I was known as the "rhubarb queen," an undisputed title as far as I knew. I was the champion grower of the biggest, most succulent petioles east of the Genesee River. The rhubarb had not been planted by me, nor was I even aware of its presence in my garden until months after we moved into our home at the very edge of the city, so deeply did this large, shapely plant draw itself into the ground for the winter months. Nevertheless, it flourished under my neglect and became a rich source of satisfaction to the discriminating among my circle of friends who savored the taste of spring rhubarb done up in a hot, juicy pie. No one has, but if someone were to ask me for my expert advice, I would say this: "When one has charge of growing things, be it plants or children, play it cool, act as if you know what you are doing, and be consistent." This advice, however, was not appropriate to the landlord's rose garden, which had more to do with science and engineering than nature ever intended.

Jim Nairn was a comfort to me, as I'm sure he was to the roses in our garden. The plants had recently been purchased in St. Albans at the Display and Trial Grounds of the National Rose Society, a part of the largest horticultural society on earth, at least in 1976, and the young bushes were unsure of themselves. One floribunda was seeing the light of day for the first time without an intervening ceiling of glass, while a new variety of silvery blue hybrid tea rose was the first of its kind to be grown in a private garden. It was best that I stayed out of it and let Jim pretend he knew what he was doing.

Before he retired Jim had been greenkeeper at Batchwood Municipal Golf Course, St. Albans' manorly 18-hole layout (with bunker rakes and benches, I might add, because the public didn't steal what was already theirs) set within the imposing grounds of Batchwood Hall. Born on the Moray Firth in 1902, Jim had been a scratch golfer in his day. He told me these things in a soft Scottish burr, grudgingly, for he did not talk to me easily. He was tall, slender and straight, and invariably came to work in pressed trousers and faded blue V-neck golf sweater. With his worn tweed sports jacket hooked on his thumb, he put me in mind of a slightly tattered 007.

Although Jim was happy to show me the proper way to cut blossoms for my table, he resisted my attempts to put him at ease until the day I asked him to prepare a patch of soil at the bottom of the garden for a few zucchini plants I had purchased in St. Peter's Street on market day. My purpose was to show our neighbours that large zucchini was as delicious as courgette, a diminutive form of zucchini, picked wastefully, I thought, before its time. Jim offered to put them in the ground for me. When I handed him the three plants, he looked at them, and then at me, astonished. After several false starts he said, essentially, that the Queen of England would not put them in *her* rose garden. When I tried to explain the miracle of zucchini to him, he said that the plants he held were not zucchini, but marrow—a seedy gourd grown for its potential of prize-winning size, a national pastime with amateur gardeners "hereaboot." With suppressed amusement he looked at me hesitantly, fearing perhaps that he had been too direct in his comment. "Dunna be embarrassed, M'um," he said, and wondered would I mind if he told the lads at "The Cricketeers."

After that, Jim and I often chatted about greenkeeping and the game. He had worked for a time at St. Andrews under John Campbell, links supervisor there. Mr. Campbell, he said, had been captured at Dunkirk and held by the Germans for five years, and he counted himself privileged that for most of his life the village of St. Andrews trusted their famous golf courses to him.

"Years ago," Jim said, "the grasses on St. Andrews were red fescue and chewing fescue, but later on, a German mix from Bavaria was brought in. 'Colonial' you called it in America. It was the grass of our old classic courses. Ryder and Son, here in St. Albans, was one of the distributors. There was an old poster on the wall of our maintenance shed that said, 'Grass seeds for putting greens and fairways are a Ryder Specialty.'"

"Did you know Mr. Ryder?" I asked.

"Me? Noo. He was gone by my time. But I do know one thing about him—he was the greenman's friend. They said he served on his green committee for 20 years just to make sure no one changed James Braid's golf course. It's very easy for green committee secretaries to want to leave their 'marks'—at no cost to themselves.

"I worked on my own to find better turf grasses, using the German mix of creeping bents, velvets, and other colourful varieties that made the fairways look like gingham. I selected consistent patches and matching sod and stolons to see how each performed.

"I found two kinds of bents, a velvet bent good to putt on and a creeping bent that took a shorter cut and grew a playable surface quickly. That was years ago when a close cropped surface was a quarter inch. Did you know that the greens on the Old Course were cut with a scythe in the 1920s? Then rolled, of course.

"A nice chap from the British Golf Union's St. Ives Research Station in Yorkshire at Bingley offered me a bit of money if I'd keep at my experiments. I suppose everyone has to do something but I couldn't see myself watching grass grow the rest of my life.

"Taking care of God's belongings, 'tis a serious job for a greenkeeper. Seein' now't comes t' harm—that is a real man's task, since most men disregard our natural world. But as long as we play golf we won't have paved the entire Garden o' Eden, will we?"

If he was still in the garden snipping and pruning and "tickling" the flower beds with his hoe when I returned from my daily round, he would ask me politely how I had got on. Then he would listen politely while I told him more than he wanted to know, in the weak manner of golfers. On one occasion he said to me, "I should imagine your ladyship plays off single figgurs." He said it without sarcasm. I had no idea what he meant but I worked it out and was charmed that he thought my handicap was below ten. Years later, when I did achieve a single number, I felt that he had given me the goal to shoot for.

I wondered if Jim thought the Ryder Cup Match should be changed. I wanted to get out of bed and ask him but just then he started the engine of our Atco greens mower with which he cut our grass to 5⁄32 of an inch, a dangerous height in times of drought but he simply refused to be talked out of it. I was sure that on Mondays and Thursdays our lawn had a Stimpmeter reading of 8½ to 9 feet. The changing tones of the smooth engine sound as the mower moved back and forth across the lawn soon put me into the deep sleep I wished for. When I awoke Jim had gone for the day, leaving behind him the soft scent of cut grass.

~

"The next time you want to go to the archway at 'first light'," Steve said as we did the dishes that night, "I'll drive you there from the clubhouse so I won't have to get up so early." I had found him asleep in his chair with a coffee mug in his hand just before dinnertime. When he was tired, Steve could sleep anywhere and he was convinced that it was coffee that did it. Most nights he retired to bed sipping from a full hot cup that he rested on his stomach, at some risk to the bedcovers, while he read. I read, watched the cup and took it gently from his hand when he fell asleep.

On our honeymoon in the mountains of New York State, after a full day that included 27 holes of golf, I found him at bedtime standing at the back of the closet beneath a bright overhead light in his starkers ostensibly reading our scorecard, but he was, in fact, sound asleep. He said, and would always say when I woke him from an unintentional snooze, "I was thinking of something else." The other side of the coin was that he was able to come awake with a smile from any sleep. I supposed it had to do with the Navy. I could not turn my switches off and on in such a way. I seemed to leave some circuits on that sapped my energy while I slept.

Tony was trimming the wisteria on their pergola when I carried a dishpan of soapy water to my roses that evening. The *Times* had assured me that English flowers would accept any moisture and even preferred a bit of soap from time to time. I apportioned the sudsy water to the most needy plants and then called to Tony. I told him that I wanted to know some Ryder Cup history to see if the teams were as unbalanced as they seemed. Could I consult a reference book in his library, a dog-eared summary of facts used to settle disagreements. He said, "I'll bring it over—I've found something I want to show you. Just let me put these tools in the gardenhouse and clean up a bit."

When we were seated in my freshly mowed garden, he handed me the book. Then, with a flourish and a smart American *ta da*, he drew a brochure from his pocket. It was a "programme" and pairings sheet, dated 20 September 1969, from the Ryder Cup Match at Royal Birkdale. Jack Nicklaus had inscribed his name for Tony on the front fold. I was to "guard it with my life."

He told me that he and other Verulam chaps had been part of the gallery that thronged the final holes of the final match of that meeting. It was Tony Jacklin against Jack Nicklaus and the winning or losing of the Cup rode on every shot. Thirty-one matches had been decided and Britain and the United States were all square at 15½ points. Tony had never known such excitement. Jacklin, of course, had just won the Open in July, the first British golfer to win the home championship in 28 years. Jack Nicklaus, who had won every major championship, some several times, had never played in a Ryder Cup before.

"Some of the lads from Verulam and I were there to support St. Albans' native son and Verulam golfer Peter Townsend, a member of the British team. Townsend, partnered with Jacklin on the first day, did indeed comport himself well, winning both morning and afternoon foursomes, first against Tommy Aaron and Dave Hill, and then against Billy Casper and Frank Beard. When he won again the next morning at four-ball, this time partnered with Christy O'Connor against Dave Hill and Dale Douglass, we reflected over drinks later in the day that Townsend would have made Princess Margaret a fine husband and that Buckingham Palace had missed its chance to have a proper golfer in the family.

"Going into the last day the two sides were all square. The third day comprised eight singles matches in the morning and eight more in the afternoon. Our spirits soared when our team stood two points in the lead after the last morning match which was between Jacklin and Nicklaus, Jacklin winning 4 and 3. In the afternoon Nicklaus and Jacklin were again paired last."

Here, Tony moved his lawn chair closer so that I could follow along as he read the outcome of each match as he had recorded it on the back of the brochure in 1969. In the first match Dave Hill beat Brian Barnes but Bernard Gallacher won over Lee Trevino. Miller Barber beat Maurice Bembridge in the third match; Peter Butler won the next over Dale Douglass in the fourth. Then the American side picked up two points when Dan Sikes beat Neil Coles and Gene Littler won over Christy O'Connor. The teams were all square once more. That left two groups on the course, Brian Huggett and Billy

Casper playing just ahead of Nicklaus and Jacklin. Huggett, facing a four-foot putt on the 18th green to halve his match, heard a roar from the 17th green and mistakenly thought Jacklin had won his match. Huggett sank his putt to halve his match and leapt for joy thinking Britain had won the Cup. But it wasn't as he thought. Jacklin and Nicklaus had been all square after 15 holes. Nicklaus won the 16th to go 1-up. The roar that Huggett heard had erupted when Jacklin sank an incredible 45-foot putt for an eagle on the 17th to pull back all square. The 32nd and final match was not over.

Both players were on the par-5 18th hole in two strokes. My neighbour said he'd heard that as Nicklaus and Jacklin approached the green they admitted to each other that they were petrified. Nicklaus left his second shot 25 feet short of the hole while Jacklin's had settled at the back of the green. Jacklin putted first to within 20 inches of the hole. Then Nicklaus boldly stroked his eagle putt five feet past. If he sank his next putt it would be good for a half and the United States would not lose the Cup because Britain needed an outright win for the trophy to change hands. He sank his putt, and then, unforgettably, he conceded Jacklin's putt for the half, saying words to the effect, "I know you can make it, but I'm not prepared to see you miss." It was the first tie in Ryder Cup history. Jack Nicklaus, 29 years old, had a transcendent sense of occasion.

The Lesson

Without questioning the sense of it, Steve and I again drove off to Verulam at first light in separate cars for my next meeting with Mr. Ryder. I parked in the Verulam driveway and Steve drove me to Cottonmill Lane. He stopped the Jaguar well short of the archway and let me out. I took my golf clubs from the back seat and waved a kiss in his direction as he drove off. The bag with a few clubs in it had been Steve's idea. It would give purpose to my presence on the golf course at that ungodly hour.

With the sheepskin-covered strap over my shoulder I supported the golf bag across my lower back, letting my arms hang loosely over each end. I never tired of carrying my bag in this fashion. I felt young and buoyant as I strode down the lane toward the gate, mindlessly ill-prepared for what lay ahead. I craved to be with Mr. Ryder, to partake of our strange companionship. At the archway I placed my clubs in some undergrowth near the path, and walked through to the other side. He was resting against the stump as before, but I knew at once he wasn't there. I fought to stay calm—I had, after all, felt his brief absence while we sat among the tree roots three days before. But this time I became confused and stood helplessly in the middle of the pathway. Slowly a profound desolation crept over me, so frightening that I covered my face to hide my eyes. I turned away and dropped to my knees in the grass.

Within moments Mr. Ryder was kneeling beside me. "This was not supposed to happen," he said. Then with some urgency he added, "What you imagine and what is real are two different things, my dear. Do not concern yourself. Put it out of your mind." I uncovered my eyes and hugged my chest, rocking back and forth. He brought his head low as if to make me to look at him but I wouldn't do it. He said, almost comically, "It's an order." The mock sternness of his tone was intended, I believed, to grasp my usually responsive nature but I wanted none of it. I wanted to get away. I started to rise but had no energy to move. He spread his hands to quiet me and so we stayed, but I could not erase the dreadful woe that lay like a rock in the center of my chest. Then all at once I felt it ease, dissolve and go away, with no effort at all. I breathed a great sigh and he said, "All right?"

"Yes, all right," I said.

He stood up with effort and stretched out his hand to me. Without thinking I took it and he pulled me to my feet.

Whoa, I thought. Aloud, I said, "What's this?" looking at our clasped hands. His hand was as warm and as firm as mine.

"Why not?" he answered with a tired laugh and seemed relieved when I laughed, too.

He retrieved my golf clubs from the weeds and motioned for me to follow. I asked him brightly if we had broken a universal law by going backward out of the gate—by going against the natural progression of the course.

"Please—," he said.

I bounced with good feelings, delighted to be alive. I loved the world, and Mr. Ryder. He looked at me and sighed. As we proceeded across Cottonmill Lane toward the 8th green I could see that he was very tired.

"Here," he said. "let me see you hit some chip shots. It will put you back on an even keel. I will give you one of Abe Mitchell's lessons. That way you can do your own work on yourself and I'll not have to do it for you."

Mr. Ryder handed me three golf balls from my bag. "When you run out of golf balls, imagine your favourite brand," he said, and then he sat on the grass to watch me. He directed me to hit the balls with my niblick off a tight lie over a deep greenside bunker onto the firm putting surface that sloped away toward a small herd of lovely Friesians that grazed beyond the red bunting at the top of the flagstick. They were pastured on lands bordered by the River Ver where it curved toward the Colne and the Thames. The land, and undoubtedly the Friesians, were owned by the Earl of Verulam. The Earl owned nearly everything in sight including the golf course and was, in fact, president of the Verulam club which leased the land from him. It occurred to me as I looked back down the river that Mr. Ryder and I were at the farthest margin of the view reflected in the watercress beds—the scene that Steve and I had so truly shared on our morning stroll three days before.

I heard Mr. Ryder clear his throat. The look on his face was a mixture of sorrows. I regret to say that I said, "I'm sorry."

"No," he said, with the impatience of a weary man. "You are not 'sorry.' Are you asking me to forgive you? No, of course not. This 'I'm sorry' is your indulgence and my burden. It's said carelessly and without thought. Consider it objectively and you will never say it again—at least not to me, eh?" he added with a smile that belied the intensity of his words.

In no time I focused my attention on the golf stroke. My euphoria and despair were replaced by a worthy challenge—a delicate pitch over a severe obstacle, a "hero shot." Instantly, without thinking, I visualized myself making the stroke. Without an inner word, I looked and saw what I had to do, and with a measure of intestinal fortitude, I did it. I hit five or six balls, slowly and rhythmically, one after the other, remaining lightly alert to myself, externally assessing my strokes, trying to get it better each time. Then I felt it: *snick*, the perfect meeting of the clubface, ball, and grass. All parts of me were under the benevolent and wise control of whatever it was inside me that put these things together. It seemed to me that Señor Ballesteros could not have stroked it better.

"You *are* very good," he said.

I stubbed the next two shots into the bunker. I bladed another over the green. I made a fourth ugly shot and quit. I thought to myself it must be time for Abe Mitchell's lesson before I realized I had just had it.

"A little flattery to overload the circuit of self-love will put a player into disarray every time," he said. "Your second foozle was the result of fluster; anxiety caused the third, and the fourth—anger, perhaps? Now I see we have remorse. 'Pride goeth before destruction...' and so forth. Your inner boss must have thought it was time for her nap." Then he looked me over as if weighing my readiness for what was to come.

"That's Abe's lesson: '...and an haughty spirit before a fall.' The most difficult stroke for a player to master is the one that follows the stroke that has pleased him most. As it is in golf, so it is in life. For every one thing there is its opposite. For every positive there is a negative. There are exactly as many positive charges as there are negative charges in the universe. Even God has an opposite. 'As above, so below.' A godly man is equal parts devil. It's the law and it applies to everything, even Abe's lesson. Snick, then foozle. You were so pleased with yourself that you dreamed of winning the women's amateur. I nudged you along, but you were ready to destroy yourself without my help. The moment of learning lies just there, *after* the tragic strokes. And if you are angry, all the better.

"There is no one minding the shop within you, no one to warn you away from the shoals of self-satisfaction. You must 'keep the watch,' such as is done on ships, and not let things to chance, otherwise you will never break the chain of your reactions, never attain the equilibrium that lets you see things as they are. You will sleep your life away, never knowing who you are, never *doing* as long as you live, and certainly not after you die."

I received the lesson easily, straight up, undiluted, channeled straight into me without buffers to alter its meaning. It was as if it were something I had always known but had forgotten. He must have bypassed my carefully guarded personality, penetrated my facade, for I looked for no excuses outside myself for my missed strokes. The origins of my disaster had not come from British Rail, a stiff wind, a bad back, or even the grazing cattle. But especially I sensed from his manner that even though he had bothered with Abe's lesson because he needed me for something, it would please him to instill in me the wish to be more than I am.

"Isn't it remarkable," he said, "that the Royal and Ancient Game can teach us as much about ourselves as that great cathedral up there in the town?" We both looked at St. Albans Abbey on top of the hill in the middle of the city. It was an impressive sight. "Best not tell anyone I said that about the abbey, although I consider it true of my own chapel as well. The real meaning of my religion didn't occur to me until after I started to play golf.

"Religions," he continued, "begin as schools to teach us ways to find the universe within ourselves so that we can reach the universe around us—literally, reach for the stars. But real knowledge that is the seed of religions cannot flourish against Nature with its powerful agenda unrelated to our own lofty purpose. Truths upon which religious movements are founded quickly lose their evolutionary meaning. They become secrets of temple art and religious ceremony. We are left with words and symbols, but the understanding of them is lost or labeled 'hidden' when, in truth, nothing is hidden."

This was not the man that Tony and I had imagined for ourselves in my garden. Where was our devout churchman? Mr. Ryder seemed to be saying that it was a darned good thing that the Christian soldiers who spread "the gospel" also spread golf when they settled throughout the British Empire.

"Right!" he said rather loudly, scattering my thoughts. "Shall we gather up your golf balls, then?" He picked up my bag and waited until I joined him. Then we started back toward the archway. I was looking down at the uneven pathway as we walked through the gate so that the first thing I saw of Abe Mitchell was a pair of immaculately shined golf shoes. He was resting on Mr. Ryder's stump, one foot planted firmly on a rock beside the path. I stopped in my tracks and took in the sight of him. Dressed in matching plus fours, jacket, and cap, he was a picture of manly grace, his strong forearms resting lightly on his thighs, his large hands folded gently at his knees.

As Mr. Ryder approached, Abe rose to his feet and removed his cap. He looked closely at Mr. Ryder and quickly took my clubs from him and put them under his arm. "I have her now, sir." And, just as it had happened in the clubhouse dining room a few days before, Mr. Ryder's image faded. I heard him say, "See that she is fit..." And then he was gone.

The Cantelupe

ABE LOOKED AT THE ARCHWAY and shook his head as if to clear his mind. "It sounds like a battlefield here," he said, breaking the silence. "Let's move away." He looped the strap of my bag over his shoulder and I followed him toward the large sycamore tree by the 10th green. He paused and waited for me to catch up. As I came alongside he asked me politely what had happened.

"Well, I entered the gate and walked up to Mr. Ryder," I answered. "After that, nothing is clear. I knew he wasn't there—that part of it was all right—but as I stood on the path I began to have an unbearable realization, but I can't remember what it was. Only moments later, or so it seemed, I heard Mr. Ryder speak to me. I remember the urgency in his voice. I think he said something that meant I had not understood what I'd seen and I wasn't to think about it." I looked up at Abe questioningly.

At the tree Abe sighed with relief. "That's better," he said. "Quieter here." He took off his jacket, spread it in the shade and invited me to sit. I had heard that Abe's wardrobe was among the best of Britain's conservatively dressed professionals. His tailored coat was finely woven and I hesitated to use it. The white shirt, coat, vest, and tie worn by amateurs in the early days of golf had been adopted by professionals. I had read somewhere that when professionals began dressing like gentlemen, amateurs began dressing like the hired help: it wouldn't have done to confuse the two.

"How do you feel now?" Abe asked.

"Okay, I guess—tired maybe."

Abe mulled me over in his mind for so long I began to worry. "I'm going to tell you what happened. That's best, I think. It will help you know yourself and the more you know yourself, the more you can help us. But you must try to keep your thoughts on what I'm saying and not wander off." He relaxed the knot of his tie and smoothed it down in one easy motion. Then he crouched beside me on his heels, his right knee resting on my golf bag, heel raised slightly to support the bulk of his weight, hands clasped lightly in front of him. He was as sturdy as the sycamore beside us. His calf muscles strained the knitted pattern of his knee-length stockings and provoked my silent admiration.

He cleared his throat and waited for me to wander back to our subject before he said, "The arch, you see, acts as a shock for some people. Many stone archways have this power and some people are electrically wired, in a manner of speaking, to respond to its energy. What it does is wake you momentarily so that for a second or two you see things as they really are. Well, you said it, didn't you? You had a 'realization.'

"You walked through the arch and came upon the empty figure of Mr. Ryder. For some reason—perhaps it was an accident—you entered right into the void and took it on as your own. Delusions, half-truths, self-deceptions peeled away like onion skins, leaving you with a clear view inside yourself, and what you saw is what all of us fear is there—nothing."

He resettled himself on his other heel as if to emphasize what he was about to tell me. "There was a time in my life," he said in a quieter tone, "when I was haunted by this idea. I used to dream I played a game of golf that did not end until the sun had set on a course that was armed with all the joys and sorrows known to man. I strived to play every hole as I found it, do the best I could and not complain, but when the round was over and I looked at my card, there was nothing on it, no marks to show that I had played the game at all.

"My dream meant to me that at the end of the day when I went to tally up what was in my soul, there would be nothing recorded there, nothing for me or anyone else to attest to. There would be nothing to define that I ever existed. *It was as if I had not got the point of the game in the first place*. Whilst I played within the bounds of the fair green, over harebells and heather and sparkling streams, in and out of watery filth and sandy depths, I played for the wrong reasons. And, of course, that's just it, isn't it?

"We live our lives in the wrong way for the wrong reasons. For a moment you saw the frightful truth of it. What you failed to see was that you carry the powerful seed of your own evolution inside you and you don't even know it is there. It can transform you from the ordinary person you are into the person you are able to be. But you need a sustained wish to wake up, a wish to be conscious enough to do the job you are designed for. If you have no such wish, then when you die you will add no more to the maintenance of the universe than any other animal your size. Man has no idea what people are for. He doesn't know the significance of his life, the nature of his mortality, or the structure of his universe.

"In any case, the frightful situation blew your circuits and scattered enough electrical charges to start a small planet, as we say. Mr. Ryder feared that you were harmed. Therefore he gave you much of his own energy—more than he was able to handle, in fact, so I have come. Now, do you understand all that?"

"I confess I have no idea what you are talking about," I said. "My thoughts are skipping about like drops of water on a hot stove. I am not the person you think I am."

"Of course you are. We didn't win you in a lottery, you know." I frowned at his joke and he frowned right back. I thought to myself that he was a very nice man.

"That's better. I *am* a very nice man. As I say, we didn't win you in the lottery. Mr. Ryder and I know that something has crystallised in you, some energy has organised that will outlast the great recycling process of Mother Nature—something begun in your childhood perhaps and surely strengthened by golf."

It was probably all that sulfur water I drank as a kid, I thought.

"Imagine that! You think that's funny, don't you?" Abe was about to say more, but decided against it.

He moved my golf bag so that he could sit on the grass. "We'll rest here quietly for a spell and not think. Put your hands so. Now try to feel the air around you and the weight of your body as you relax."

We sat for a long while, it seemed to me. During that time two men played past us down the 10th hole, a short par 4, measured by the Ladies Golf Union at 275 yards. Just the week before, I had driven the full length and over. My ball had bounced along the parched turf, skidded between two of Verulam's deepest bunkers, skipped past the flagstick, and come to rest near a boundary stake 25 yards beyond the green. The hole sloped downhill all the way. It should have been the easiest hole on the course but the putting green fell so steeply toward the back that for me, in normal conditions, it was a drive, then a wedge off a hanging lie from which the ball sped hell-bent down the green.

The early morning golfers replaced the flagstick and

moved toward the 11th tee with their golf bags thrown easily across their backs. I imagined their companionship, their good moments and bad moments silently shared—the very grounds for friendship. Players that identified excessively with their own fortunes were too full of themselves for companionship, I mused.

Then, for the first time in my life I realized that I was daydreaming. I saw myself seeing the players and I saw my undirected thoughts—associating, pushing mechanically in an endless stream through my head, but I did not try to stop them. I knew I was sitting on the silk lining of Abe's jacket. I knew I was breathing in and out, that my face was relaxed and I was hungry. Abe said quietly, "Yes, that's it. Notice how your machine runs all the time, with or without you. If you pay attention you can begin to see what goes on, how your energy flows. Transforming energy is a function of human life. Maybe, before you are through, you will transform yourself into something of real value to the universe."

Abe observed me briefly before he gave me a look of satisfaction that I took to mean I was fit again. He stood up and moved to the tree trunk, leaned against it, and lit a cigarette. I watched the harmony with which he went about his business without an awkward step. He had a natural ease that Mr. Ryder did not have, as if he drew comfort from his environment. He would have been comfortable anywhere, I thought, even in the Queen's apartments.

"Why is your figure on the Ryder Cup?"

"Oh, I don't think it is, really," he said.

"Of course it is. I've seen pictures. It looks just like you."

"Well, there is a reason, but not a very good one. However, I *did* do something significant—without knowing it at the time. I upset a group of amateur golfers who thought I should not be allowed into their ranks, even though I never intended to be a professional. After a few years of controversy I looked to the other side, the professional side. What I saw were simple, honest men I would rather play golf with. So, I joined them and was never sorry.

"And," he added, "I did win a National Open Championship, you know—the Irish Open in 1929." Something in his voice made me look up at him. He was grinning at me, forcing his cheek muscles to form deep dimples. It brightened the man entirely and I knew at once why everyone liked him.

Abe's eyes followed the golfers walking up the 11th fairway. "Those two men are Artisan golfers. I don't believe you have Artisan golf clubs in America. Do you know what it means?

I admitted that I had never heard of artisans in reference to golf.

"Well, I've seen several definitions but the most telling one said, 'An Artisan player either cannot afford to be, or is not acceptable to be, a full member of a golf club, probably because of working-class origins. Some English clubs may allow a limited form of membership with restricted playing times.'

"I was the first Artisan golfer to break into the lofty ranks of English amateur golf. I entered for and won the *Golf Illustrated* Gold Vase, played at Sunningdale, Thursday, June 30, 1910. The entry form had read, 'Members of recognised golf clubs who are rated at scratch or better in their own clubs are alone eligible to compete.' The amateurs asked two questions: are Artisan clubs 'recognised,' and would not an Artisan golfer of my caliber have it in mind to become professional? Letters poured into the press from sportswriters and amateurs. I had no idea what they were on about. I feared they would take away my prize. At 23, I was a yokel, as you say in America."

Abe watched the men approach the crossover. "My brothers and I belonged to the Cantelupe Golf Club, one of the very earliest Artisan golf clubs. The Cantelupe was created for our use by the members of the Royal Ashdown Forest Golf Club."

His eyes narrowed as he drew on his cigarette. "It's a nice story." I said I would like to hear it.

"Well, then. About 90 years ago some wealthy men made a golf course on our land—common land, not far south of London, where my people had lived for centuries. This 10 square mile region was a part of Ashdown Forest, which itself was originally a section of the Forest of Anderida, a vast cover of trees that crossed southern England in an arc from Kent to Hampshire, almost 150 miles. The part where I lived rose out of the forest valley. The weald, as it is now called, was owned by the Crown and was home and hiding place to outlaws—some say it still is. Six centuries ago it was so dense with thieves that Edward III needed the protection of a small army to get him safely to the south coast on his way to fight in France, where he had just started the Hundred Years War. He was safer at Poitiers than he was in the trees of his own hunting park.

"In the 1600s, King Charles II had used this land to grant favours in exchange for loyalty. The permanent dwellers of Ashdown Forest so resisted the newcomers' fences and walls that the matter was referred to a Royal Commission who decided that, though the new lords owned the land, a portion of Ashdown Forest, 6,400 acres, must be set aside, in perpetuity, for the use and enjoyment of its indigenous people.

"Successive centuries of kings, noblemen, men of industry, and even the simple people that lived there, treated the land badly. It took 2,500 fully-grown oak trees to supply the English navy with a single man o' war. And there was iron in the earth besides. Charcoal from oak was used to smelt the iron until the day came when there wasn't a proper tree left standing. Then the foundries moved north to the Midlands; the air cleared of black smoke, but what remained was a rugged, uneven landscape, woolly surfaced and moor-like, called by one nineteenth-century traveller, William Cobbett, 'the most villainously ugly spot I ever saw in England.'

"For a century after industry moved away, my ancestors remained relatively untouched by England's vast commercial changes. They seemed caught in a lifestream eddy, biding their time, as if nothing in their experience had any more meaning for them than what they were already doing.

"Then in 1888, a year after I was born, the wealthy people I mentioned, 'toffs' we called them, formed a club and prepared a golf course around our small cottages, on our bracken hills. Although no one tried to evict us, they tried to contravene our traditional rights of cutting litter—bracken, that is—taking peat for firing, and grazing our animals. When we showed our opposition, a Board of Conservators looked at the matter and told the aspiring golfers and the Earl de la Warr, who owned the land, that they had no right to do what they were doing. The gentry, in their wisdom, then found a way to silence our objections. They resolved everyone's needs by putting golf clubs in our hands and teaching us to play.

"Well. You would have thought the kettle had boiled over, the way we came out at dawn to swing sticks of our own making at balls we 'found' at the edges of our newly graded fields. Mr. Ryder once compared us to what he saw in Africa collecting seeds: the brightest flowers, he said, grew in the driest regions of the desert, once the rain began to fall. Soon entire families played golf, made golf clubs and worked at new livelihoods around the golf course. It only made sense for the Golf Club to trade some of our work on the course for playing privileges. My stepfather Mark Seymour for the Foresters, and the Archdeacon Scott for the toffs, arranged for us to form our own golf club in 1892. It would be called The Cantelupe Golf Club, named for Viscount Cantelupe, the oldest son of the Earl de la Warr, president of Ashdown Forest Golf Club.

"Our patrons supported our enthusiasm, competed with us, took pride in our achievements, and bought our finely crafted golf clubs. Cantelupers became top-notch club professionals and players for England. My younger brother, the junior Mark Seymour, and Alf Padgham—we all won national and international titles. Jack Smith hit it further than any of us. Alf's cousin Hector Padgham was professional at Royal Ashdown for 41 years. My sister Sophe could beat most any man—playing from his ground, too. And there was my brother Twine, who never recovered from the war and died not long after."

Abe explained that the term "Artisan Golfer" became official in 1921, under King George's patronage, but that in Scotland there was no need of such an association. Golf in Scotland was the most democratic of games, played on public land, open to all. Royalty and workingmen played together. Massive private clubhouses of Masonic origin, including the Royal and Ancient clubhouse, sat side by side around a tract of the public land that was open to all comers.

"I was eight," Abe continued, "when I first played for the Cantelupe. When my long drives drew the attention of the toffs and the envy of my playmates, my brother Frank Mitchell decided to bring me down a peg by informing me that he was *not* my brother but my uncle, that I was the son of his sister and like some other Forest youngsters, a bastard. The news went a long way toward explaining a few things, but I kept hitting golf balls and got on with it. When I thought about my new status, I saw it made no difference one way or another. If that was the way it was, then it was right for me. It was a fact of life that wherever Forest children put down their heads at night was where they belonged. More often than not I put down my head in Mark Seymour's house because he married my mother Mary Mitchell.

"My mum—everyone called her Polly—came at life from the bright side, so we had a good laugh when she told me why I was the only Mitchell in the large Seymour household. It seemed that while she was betrothed to Mark Seymour, a dark, handsome stranger had come her way. When I unexpectedly came her way as well, both Mark and the stranger went theirs. We were absorbed into the household of her parents, George and Sophie Mitchell. I was christened Henry Abraham William Mitchell at the Church of St. Richard de Wych. Some 60 Mitchells were born and baptised in the area in those Victorian times and I was lost in the crowd.

"She said that Mark Seymour proposed to her again when I was three years old, not because he liked her but because he liked *me*. My stepfather was a good man, looked out for other people, like Mr. Ryder. I wasn't like that. I never looked this way or that except to wonder at times that so much had come from so joyful a thing as playing golf."

Abe paused in his story and looked thoughtful. I asked him if he'd ever wondered why the Ashdown Forest community was so suited for golf. He said he *had* thought about it and decided that, isolated as they were, his people were never taught to curb their other brain.

"There is a brain here," he said, drawing his fist down his front, tracing a line with his thumb from the knot in his necktie, over the buttons of his vest to the crotch of his plus fours. "It knows how to feel, think, and do things without being taught, yet it can learn and remember. It is an independent system that consists of the same circuitry, transmitters, and components that are here in the head. It's fast and sure. Nothing is surer or takes less time than gut feeling. Yet 'civilised' adults condemn its usefulness, and its chores are inadequately taken over by the sophisticated but plodding mechanisms in our heads.

"This brain directs our movement with thoughts that take no time. It walks unerringly through darkness toward an unseen goal. It understands love, nurturing, and the structure and language of the universe. Its senses are keen, as are its perceptions of mood and danger. It has a strong sense of loyalty and ownership. It knows fear but not anger. It lives in the present tense, does not know how to be false, and does not recognize ruse or disguise. It is altogether lost in the face of logic..."

And does it chase sticks, then? I thought. I couldn't help myself.

He flicked his cigarette and pushed himself away from the tree trunk. "Time for you to go home."

He didn't mind my impertinence, I could tell. He was the soul of patience. I stood up with his jacket in my hand. As I brushed off the dry grass he lifted my bag and placed the strap over my shoulder.

"Abe," I said, handing him his coat, "should I be suspicious because you and Mr. Ryder are exactly the way I want you to be?"

"'Suspicious' is not the word. Rather, you should surmise that what you see is in response to yourself, our reaction to you. In other words we are simply interacting with you in a way you are used to. There are other ways for people to interact that don't waste so much energy."

"What did Mr. Ryder mean when he said that the persona he had created for me was his own and I could trust it on my own terms?"

"Well, you see, he has created a mask for you to relate to in your own way, as you would relate to anyone in your dimension. But he wants to assure you that the mask is of himself. The man you are getting to know has knowledge of a higher consciousness but otherwise he is a dead ringer for Mr. Ryder. It's true for me as well. That does not make us any less real than you."

"And did you get to keep the Gold Vase?"

"Another time."

The Vicar

As I turned to leave, Abe said casually, "Avoid the archway and get a good rest," as if my recent drama were everyday procedure with Samuel Ryder and Abe Mitchell. I signaled that I had heard him, then cut through the rough toward the 9th fairway, bypassing the arch, on my way to the 17th tee so that I could lob a wedge over the early morning traffic in Cottonmill Lane. It was only a short hundred yards from the forward tee to the green 20 feet below, but it was long on moral implications. The 17th hole could brighten anyone's day, or make newspaper headlines. James Braid must have been befuddled when he designed it, or Cottonmill Lane was just a cowpath in those days.

The branches of a large tree obscured the right side of the green, effectively reducing the size of the target. It was often heartlessly necessary to play a 'provisional ball' in case the original ball had been imperfectly struck and came to rest out-of-bounds in the lane, or was lost. A ball deflected off the tree, or a Deux Chevaux, usually lodged deep within the hedge at the side of the road. A well-directed ball, on the other hand, would find a soft landing on a high-backed, two-tiered green, proof that Braid was a good-natured fellow after all. The trick was not to think about repercussions, but get on with it. It was my favorite hole.

I made par in regulation and played down the 18th hole toward the clubhouse, more or less keeping pace with a bearded Englishman and his dog, a black and white border collie with a pretty face and low sweeping tail that dusted the public footpath. She swept along sedately with her fine, sharp nose in the air, as if to cover for her master's activities. He carried a broad-bladed golf club with which he poked about the bushes and clumps of long grass alongside the path in search of golf balls. More than once I had purchased back my American-size Titleists from the Verulam golf shop bulk bin at a reduced rate. Nigel, my caddie, a 15-year-old Hertfordshire lad, was particularly adept at knowing just where balls were likely to collect. I had seen him come away with a handful of good balls gathered from the hedge in Cottonmill Lane.

Nigel had been my caddie ever since I injured my back in Paris on the Fourth of July, 1976. Steve and I had gone to Paris at the invitation of our American friend Bill, a journalist for the *New York Times*, who had said, "Where better to celebrate the Fourth than with the French?"

Paris was crowded, hot, and dusty and the most marvelous place I had ever been. To guard against heat exhaustion and dry throat it was necessary to sit in sidewalk cafes and order seltzer and Martini *verde*, a combination of fluids that quenched our thirsts but baffled our waiters who refused on principle to understand our accents. I have a photograph that shows me sitting beneath a green striped awning on a tree-lined boulevard sipping my drink. "Take my picture," I had said.

The air remained warm and still throughout the evening. In our hotel room Steve and I pulled the mattress across the sill of the French doors, partially onto our third floor balcony. There we slept naked behind a very large American flag we had brought with us for Independence Day. We had attached it to the balcony railing with the expectation that one or two Parisians would be amused. "Look," they might say, "some Americans have come to our city to celebrate their freedom, based on our own *philosophes*!"

To this day, I will not believe that the French meant anything by ignoring our Old Glory. Surely, I would not have been bored if the countrymen of Nicolas Chauvin visited America and draped the Tricolor for display on Bastille Day. Perhaps the French had more important things on their minds than a light-hearted celebration of liberty, such as sharing their expensive city with the vanquished and victorious of the world as they came and went from sidewalk cafes in accordance with their moment in political history.

After a night on the doorsill I could no longer comfortably carry a full set of clubs or pull a trolley, so Nigel helped me play golf. I shared him with the Vicar of St. Botolph's to whom he was committed on Wednesday afternoons and Saturday mornings. The Vicar and I had become acquainted when Nigel told him about me, the American lady who liked to hole out and make a score at every hole and add it all up at the end. The Vicar harbored a guilty wish to do the same. "It may be tedious," he said to me one day, "but it's good discipline for the soul."

Before long he invited me to play on a weekday, when he was not shepherding at St. Botolph's. He suggested that Nigel carry both our bags and that we mark each other's cards. It seemed a simple proposal. But this was England and it was not simple at all.

In England, making a score for handicap purposes was serious business. For me it entailed entering my name in a leather-bound book in the women's lounge labeled "Extra Day

Scores." A light covering of dust told me the book was rarely used. It was nailed to the wall with a length of chain so that it could lie open on a Chippendale desk. I was startled to see that the last entry had been made nearly two months earlier, on Wednesday, May 19, by Peggy Coyne, a former lady captain who, as a young girl, had gone to public school in Scotland, a girls' school for traditional studies with a special curriculum in golf. This wonderful woman had known Dr. Stableford and played at Wallasey, his golf course. A "Wallasey," she explained to me in an unforgettable moment during the captain's tea in the Verulam dining room on a Thursday afternoon, was the name given to a variation of the Stableford competition. When I told Tony what I had learned from Peggy, he said, "Not many Americans know that, nor Englishmen either."

Also on the Chippendale table alongside various lists and charts was a recent edition of the *Ladies Golf Union System of Handicapping*, which explained the "LGU Scratch Score Scheme." These items were the preserve of the Verulam lady handicapping secretary, a bird-like creature with a strong heart and discerning eye who performed her vital record keeping in the strict but kindly manner that such a sensitive operation required. A golf handicap was, after all, a reflection of oneself.

I hesitated before I wrote my name and date on the line below Peggy Coyne's entry. By this act I declared it was my official intention to make an "extra day score" for handicap purposes. I had no idea what "extra day score" meant until I looked it up in the Lady Golfer's Handbook. An extra score, it said, is one that is not returned in competition. Under the Ladies Golf Union 1976 Handicap Scheme only two official scores were required annually. Handicaps were fixed once a year, and once fixed did not rise, but would be adjusted downward if a player revealed a fat handicap by winning a medal competition by too many strokes. The logic of the scheme made sense to me, especially since British golf was primarily a match play game in which the number of strokes taken on a hole reflected your opponent's play as much as your own.

The Vicar, Nigel, and I walked to the first tee. The Vicar mentioned how much he had looked forward to our inaugural round and wasn't it nice to be doing this without a care in the world. I confided that I had never been so nervous in my life, what with the awesome responsibility of making an "extra day score." He said, "No, no, my dear—we will just *pretend* to do it. The ladies are not allowed to put in extra day cards in the summertime. Cards may only be returned under 'normal' spring and autumn conditions of wind and weather." For a moment I thought I was through the looking glass until I remembered that, unlike the men, women did tend to nudge their handicaps downward. No wonder the book was as dusty as the dry fairways.

The Vicar and I were a successful union of holy Briton and "failed Colonial," as he called me. As we walked away from the 4th green with birdies, the Vicar said, "Since we are both in such high spirits, it might be a good time for me to confess that I had an ulterior motive for inviting you to play. I wanted to talk to you, you see." Then he sighed, clearly uncomfortable. "A quid is simply too much to pay young Nigel for caddying." I admitted I had already been told that by the lady captain.

"The point is, my dear, you might bring down the existing wage structure for all the golf clubs in England. 50p will suffice." Fifty pence was a tenth of what I had paid a caddie in upstate New York and the reason why I had seldom hired one. Each time I settled up with Nigel I could not bring myself to give him less than a pound note, worth on that day exactly $1.7235. The Vicar and I discussed it and we settled the dispute amicably, although I did not make it clear to him that I had an alternative payment in mind for Nigel. He gave me many of the golf balls he found if they were my brand and size. From now on I would buy them from him.

That settled the Vicar's problem but I also had a dilemma with Nigel. We desperately needed an interpreter. Nigel had an 'Artfu'sheer accent the likes of which I had never heard. He cut his words in half at the back of his throat with grunts and noises that I simply could not decipher. Time and again he would say something that brought me to a halt while I tried to piece together his sounds. And when I caught him looking to me for visual clues, I knew that I was equally incomprehensible to him. Nigel would say, "Yr bu unh uhr u ghrunh." To my further confusion, he would repeat himself. Finally, from the Vicar, "He says your ball went over the green."

It didn't seem to bother my new Anglican friend that I drove the ball as far as he did. He was used to being outdriven by the chaps at the club. It was his amazing sense of what it took to run a ball 60 yards to within inches of the hole that was enviable and the reason he played off 12. He was unabashedly keen to beat me, which made me unabashedly keen to beat *him*. In fact, we had a great time together, on the course and in the clubhouse lounge after the game was over. Mrs. Sutherland, the steward's wife, served us drinks and small sandwiches in her quiet, invisible way while we settled our wagers. The Vicar assigned me a handicap that he thought best suited my game and inasmuch as he was handicapping secretary for the men, I did not question it. I had been handicap chairman at my club in America for as long as I could remember and because I knew the United States Golf Association's system so well, I could appreciate the logic of the LGU's scheme all the more.

The subject we most frequently addressed, however, was the relationship between Samuel Ryder and Abe Mitchell. The Vicar had known them personally and now was making a study of their lives. Careless assumptions disturbed him and he intended someday to set the record straight.

~

THE TANGLED SEQUENCE OF MY THOUGHTS disappeared as I approached and prepared to play my ball to the 18th green. The pretty collie and her master were long gone by the time I neared the clubhouse. I strained to see through the dining room windows, wishing with all my heart that Mr. Ryder was standing there. I wondered when I would see him again. He hadn't said. As I started to putt out, an unnatural weariness swept over me so that I had to steady myself. Without warning I was drained of energy, exhausted, and on the verge of tears.

"Good morning!"

I looked up surprised and relieved to see the Vicar. "You're out early."

"Yes, I am. Couldn't sleep, you know. Tried to write but it wasn't on. I like to think that on some days God would rather see me walking the golf course than at my desk. Thought I'd play a few holes before the heat of the day. I say! You aren't well. Here..." Quickly he laid down his clubs, came around behind me and walked me to a weathered teakwood bench below the clubhouse windows.

"Why, it's a lucky thing I came along." He looked at me with great concern. "You wait right here. I'll just bring my car round the circle and drive you home. It will only take me a moment. Dear me." He hurried off.

The next I knew I was in Ann's guest room bed, the doctor had been called, and Steve was on his way. And then I slept happily for hours and hours until I heard the sound of tinkling glass as Ann entered the bedroom. She carried a silver tray held high above the commotion at her knees. Berry had pushed her aside, his long tail banging back and forth as if to say, "I'm here! I'm here! Where's the patient? Where's the patient?" He placed one paw and his handsome snout on my

blanket, and with soulful eyes he addressed my case in his polished bedside manner.

"Lie down, Berry," Ann said. On the tray was a crystal goblet of steaming hot water. Over the rim of the glass was a small coverlet of crocheted netting anchored by eight seashells of various shapes stitched to points at the edge of the pattern. The shells dangled so that the least movement of the goblet made them ring against the glass, an altogether cheery Victorian device.

"Hot water, a slice of lime and a sprig of fresh mint to tickle your nose," Ann said. "My mother served it to me when I was sick and she said a little poem:

Look upon the pretty shells
That *sound* against the cup.
Smell the mint
Taste the lime
Feel the heat, drink up!

"She said it was food for the senses, as nourishing and vital as the air we breathe and the food we eat."

Ann looked at me hard. "What *are* you up to on the golf course, anyway? And how should you ever get along without the Vicar? Never mind. The doctor says you'll be right as rain in a few days. Meanwhile, you'll stay here where I can keep an eye on you."

She handed me the glass. "Now. While it's hot." She watched expectantly as I removed the netting. After I examined the seashells I took a sip and my eyebrows shot up.

"The gin was my idea," she smiled proudly.

"What's wrong with me, anyway?"

"The doctor said your blood pressure was unusually low. He said you had 'run out of petrol,' probably from anaphylactic shock. He assured us that you were only sleeping and not unconscious and he gave you a shot of epinephrine. Said he'd call in later.

"Now listen," she continued. "It's been decided. The four of us are going to take a brief holiday as soon as you feel up to it. It was Steve's idea. We thought we'd go to York since you fancy Roman history—check out the Wall and the Minster, that sort of thing. No golf, no cooking, nothing to worry about. How does that sound?"

Just then the Vicar tapped on the door and walked in. Berry immediately abandoned me and nudged him toward my bed.

"You're looking much, much better, my dear," the Vicar said as he took my hand. "I have never seen anyone so wan and helpless as you were this morning. You know, when I think about it, it *was* strange that I went to the golf course at that early hour. I cannot but wonder at myself. You don't suppose I'm becoming clairvoyant, do you?"

He looked at Ann. "I've just popped in to tell you that rooms for visiting dignitaries to the Minster have been set aside for you anytime you wish to go to York. Is there anything else I can do? No? I'll be on my way then. You take good care of her," he said to Berry who had resumed his place beside my bed.

"I'd better go, too," Ann said. "Check on you later, then. Steve will be here for lunch. Try to go back to sleep. Come, Berry." Berry held me in his serious gaze until Ann said, "Oh, she'll be all right. Come."

I sat up and took a gulp of my medicine. As the warm gin coursed through me, I wondered at the circumstances that had landed me in bed. Were Mr. Ryder and Abe simply a pair of inept guardian angels? If they were, they should go to angel school, I thought, knocking back my drink and setting the glass on the bedside table. The alcohol was making me silly and sentimental.

I heard Mr. Ryder's voice before I saw him. "I haven't seen one of these in years—keeps the bugs out," he said holding the netting across his palm. He raised the goblet and tenderly arranged the shells over the rim. He held the stem, three fingers gracefully extended so they wouldn't damp the resonance of the crystal as he rocked the glass.

"Impressions," he said watching the seashells move back and forth. "Do you know that if you are deprived of impressions you will die? You receive impressions through your senses and process them in your head *but*," he emphasized, "only to the extent you are *awake*. If you are not conscious of a sound, there is no sound for you. If you are only partially conscious of a sound, your impression of it is incomplete, inaccurate—wasted, shall we say. Oddly enough, this apparent selfish preoccupation with one's own processing is where human communication and understanding begin."

To cover my lack of comprehension, I gave him my intelligent look, a ploy that worked so well with the rest of the world that there had been times when I was the only person not to be told something important because everyone thought I already knew it. But naturally it did not work with him. With a quick nod he encouraged me to say my question.

"What am I then? If I'm not awake, not asleep—what am I? Sometimes I'm too busy thinking of other things to notice everything at once."

"Just so. It's a knack, this processing of impressions that are 'food for thought.' Understanding how to be sensitive to your universe is a very practical matter and I want you to take it seriously. If you only think, and not feel, your thought will be isolated, cut off from the rest of your mentation. You will say it is forgotten, but it is there, lost in the wrong drawer. Impressions are a vital material of our universe. Impressions feed the body, change its chemistry. If you live your life awake, everything will come to you. Finally, you will be able to do what you never thought possible."

"What could I do?"

"You could become a Christian. Christianity, like any true religion, is a physical condition."

"It's too late for me."

"Perhaps you are right. But you could learn to be objective enough to write an honest account of the origins of the Ryder Cup."

"Really. I think you should hire the Vicar and not me. He has a keen interest in you and Abe Mitchell and the Ryder Cup."

"The story must come from an American because certain revelations might sound self-serving if told by an Englishman. The Ryder Cup, as an international match, is about to die of neglect. We know that. Arnold Palmer said it when first he was captain, in 1963. He suggested that we include the rest of Europe but, back then, there were precious few Europeans to choose from. But now that is changing. With immediate attention the Ryder Cup will survive and grow to unbelievable popularity. Television, keen competition and the new status of the modern golf professional will drive it over the top, to the point of derailment. That's when you write your history about the Cup's shaky and controversial beginnings, in the hope that someone who reads it will be inspired to save the Cup from itself."

"I don't write."

"You will, and you will know what you are talking about."

Sam paced back and forth, glancing at me frequently, telling me what was in store and how I must see for myself the possibility of my own evolution. Suddenly, he stopped and, in the silence, gave me one of his dear, patented looks. It was a magic moment for me. It lifted me right up. I don't know why the word "brave" was in my mind, but I felt "brave."

Purposefully he pulled a chair over beside my bed and sat down. His eyes searched my face, his lips compressed and pushed beneath his mustache. Something was on his mind but I couldn't read it, not usually the case with us. I knew what he thought most of the time. He looked down at the covers and for a moment I thought he was going to take my hand. Instead, he stood up and left as though he'd never been there.

The Rover

WE MILLED ABOUT OUR NEIGHBOUR'S driveway getting in Ann's way as we prepared for our brief holiday in York, which Steve reminded us was "Eboracum" in Roman times. Ann reminded us that our purpose was to get there. She herded us into a semblance of order, much as Berry might have done if he'd had sheep to care for. Only occasionally did Ann lose patience with our questions designed, she accused us, to impede her progress.

In the boot of Tony's old Rover we packed tinned paté and a blue Stilton from the cheese shop at the top of St. Peters Street, only a few doors from the 300-year-old Pemberton Almshouses erected by a penitent Roger Pemberton after he accidentally killed a poor widow with his bow and arrow. Flaky biscuits and creamy butter for the cheese were stored in wicker baskets alongside a good wine "for the countryside," selected by Tony, our sommelier. Steve contributed a handful of England's latest road maps and an ordnance survey map of the Yorkshire Dales, tightly squeezed by a good American rubber band.

Steve wondered if we wanted to water our horses one last time. We hadn't until he brought it up. When we returned, Tony was wiping the windscreen with the *Times*, unarguably a better glass cleaner than the *Guardian*, he said. As I watched him bring up a perfect shine, I asked, "How does it *do* that?" He said he had no idea. It was a trick he had learned from his father, a military man who had served in Egypt.

We stood around the Rover while Steve discussed the merits of riding "Moline style" so that he could navigate from the front seat while Tony drove. Solemnly Ann and I climbed in the back, sinking into the fine leather cushions, long worked and softened to everyone's comfort. Then, to our dismay, we watched our boys disappear inside to do the ritual things that keep the home fires from burning anything in our absence.

At high noon the Rover sped out of town and didn't stop until it rolled into Sandridge where it was suddenly a good idea to have lunch at "The Queen's Head" by the church. Tony and Ann introduced us to their friend Peter the publican who told us, as he told nearly everyone, that the citizens of St. Albans were not nearly so *English* as the citizens of Sandridge. The few miles that separated the two communities made all the difference, Peter said. It was a matter of old families and new riches, putting the right value on things. The people of St. Albans had no idea of what really mattered.

Despite our shortcomings, he would not let us pay for our drinks. Steve watched the proceedings closely. Each pub had its protocol and unless he knew it by heart he was not easy. I could not convince him the British would be happy to guide him. "That's not the point," he would say.

Ann found us a tiny table in a room of tiny tables where we leisurely went about the sober business of eating and drinking the noontime away, elbow to elbow with a lively crowd of people and several large dogs. It was Tony who finally admitted that our travel plans had so deteriorated that we couldn't possibly make it to York. In 1976, the highways that bypassed towns at lunatic speeds were rare. The Great North Road, an ancient woodland track, had in recent years become a wide, paved surface called an "A" road and labeled the A1. The A1, destined for an uncertain future in a full-fledged Motorway system, was now in its chrysalis stage, called the A1(M), and would remain so, since "M1" had already been appropriated for use elsewhere.

Tony proposed instead that we proceed laterally toward Stratford-on-Avon and find a night's lodging in a honeystone Cotswold cottage. That way we could visit another of Samuel Ryder's golf courses the following morning. Ryder and his family, he explained, were subscribers to Shakespeare performances and attended on such a regular basis that Ryder had become a country member of the Stratford-on-Avon Golf Club. He was elected its captain in 1927 and 1928, and even vice-president before he died, despite his less than full-member status.

"He was captain at our club at the same time," Tony said. "I heard he stepped in and took over when financial matters at Verulam were a bit dicey in 1927. That man—70 years old and he still thought he was the only person with enough sense to put things right for everyone. Self-confident chap." I asked Tony where he'd got that idea and he answered that he had a surprise for me, but—not now.

At two o'clock closing time Peter urged us on our way. It was the law, he said. Steve announced he was off to drain the swamp and he invited us to do the same. Ten minutes later we sauntered to the Rover. Tony tossed the car keys to Ann and said that she would have to drive us to the Cotswalds inasmuch as he and Stephen had consumed much of our beer as well as their own. The guys crawled into the back seat to sleep.

Ann's route to Stratford took us north through Wheathampstead and then by the least traveled single lane roads she could find. She dodged in and out of strategic widenings in shady lanes not designed for two-lane traffic, while she entertained me with a running commentary. I had become unreservedly fond of our neighbour. It made no difference that she was half a generation younger than I. Her good nature and loving heart were refreshing, and if something displeased her, she did not display it like a precious jewel the way I did.

Her energy found its escape on the accelerator pedal as we whizzed along the deep, winding, expensive roadbed, excavated and maintained well below the farmers' fields and hedgerows, so that no signs of traffic could be detected except an occasional flash of color through a broken hedgerow.

"That was George Bernard Shaw's house," she told me, too late, as we sped through the small village of Ayot St. Lawrence. "Well, you can come back another time," she said when I complained. "The village is nearly a thousand years old and listed in the Domesday Book. Ayot, or Ayete as it was spelled back then, means island between two rivers." She glanced at me, lifted her chin and said, "Not many Americans know that."

When the Rover briefly broached a high ground I asked Ann why the lanes were below ground level.

"They are? I never noticed, or rather I never thought about it. Now that you mention it...well, I'm not sure really. Worn away by wagon wheels, horses hooves? But it's nice, isn't it, having the traffic out of sight, although it does cut off our view."

This reminded Ann of the eighteenth-century landscape architects, Lancelot "Capability" Brown, Humphry Repton, and their sort, who had redesigned Britain to please and fool the eye, meticulously improving upon nature, in much the same way, she supposed, golf course architects did today. England had attractions for the discerning eye around every bend in the road, fabricated vistas as sweeping as any in the world, the far reaches of which were only minutes away—

forests removed and planted elsewhere, rivers rerouted, moors kept barren, sun-streaked downs of color-shaded vegetation apportioned by stone walls and hedgerows, crisscrossing at angles that purposely described a broad perspective—a painting already composed for the artist.

"And the clouds? Were they arranged, too?"

"You might well ask" she said. "Only the odd 'folly' gives away an underlying theme—the half-built tower, the bridge to nowhere, an unfinished battlement beyond the hill. These eccentric notions scattered about the countryside are rich men's jokes that give another perspective to time as well as to space."

An hour had passed as we drove through place names like Peter's Green, East Hyde, Slip End, Kensworth. We were less than 10 miles from St. Albans, but now, Ann promised, we were truly on our way. At the next roundabout there was a sign for Whipsnade, and below Whipsnade there was a small brown sign decorated with an elephant. "Zoo," it said.

"You mean there really is a Whipsnade Zoo?" I asked. Ann went around the circle again and took the exit for Whipsnade. Within a short distance we were at the gates. Whipsnade Zoo. It rolled off my tongue with a familiarity that surprised me. I must have known it from my childhood. Whatever it was, it had made me giggle. As the Rover proceeded slowly through the gate I tapped Steve's knee.

"Steve," I whispered, "we're inside Whipsnade Zoo."

It took him a moment. "Seriously? You mean there really is a Whipsnade Zoo—the home of free love, the largest breeding place in the world? You're sure this is it?" he asked, looking at a large sign that said so.

We got out of the Rover at the visitors' center so Steve and Tony could shake hands with the mayor after all that beer. When Tony returned Ann and I were sitting by a tree with the basket of cheese and biscuits. He sat down between us, started to speak, but hesitated as if he didn't know how to say it. He took one of our hands in each of his, folded them all together on his knee and said, "Ever since we drove away from the house today, I've had the distinct feeling that we should not make this journey. Do you mind if we go home...?"

"I felt it, too, when I drove away from 'The Queen's Head,'" Ann responded quickly. Steve and I had no idea what our friends were on about, but by this time it only made sense to abandon the trip, at least for now.

By 4:00 we were on Batchwood Drive, almost home. We had been away four hours. As Tony slowed the car to turn into our street, he said to me, "Remember, I have a surprise..."

That's when it happened. There was a terrifying crack and tearing of metal at the front end of the car that sent us all flying forward. It was as if the Rover had run into a rockpile at high speed, but, in fact, we had been going slowly. Steve's door was partially jammed and he had to kick it open to get out to see what had happened.

"Holy Moses, Tony, I think the front wheel has fallen off!" And, indeed, it had—it had snapped spontaneously. Later, it was found that the ball joint that supported the left front wheel had sheared from the front suspension. Slowly it dawned on us that it could have happened anywhere—on a Cotswold curve or speeding down a highway or, God forbid, on a roundabout.

We stood around and made bad jokes about the Rover's unladylike positioning and our almost permanent departure from this world. "Who needs to get away?" we quipped and then laughed like children. Tony went home, only two doors away, to call a service garage. I sat on the curb doing nothing while Steve and Ann unpacked the car. When Tony returned he sat on the curb beside me. He put his arm around my shoulders.

"Will you ring the Vicar and explain?" I think Tony just wanted to give me something to do.

The Rover, empty now, looked pitiful, lurched forward and tilted on its broken wheel, the bonnet torn from its latch. The others wondered at our good luck while I wondered about Mr. Ryder—had he led us through this foolish afternoon to safety?

Before long a red repair vehicle arrived and attached its rig. The Rover's once dignified nose was carefully lifted off the rough surface of the road by a chain hooked to the undercarriage. Resting on her rear wheels she glided smoothly and sedately away.

"The old girl tried to tell us, didn't she?" Tony said, remembering his reluctance to drive away in the first place. "Now, tell you what. Give me half an hour and then come over to our terrace. We'll have our surprise."

~

I SAT ON A LOW STONE WALL and stared trancelike at our neighbours' beautiful flower garden until Berry came barreling out the French doors and onto the terrace. Ann had fetched him from the kennel and he was ready to play. We did our tricks until Ann came to my rescue. "Lie down, Berry," she said.

Tony soon arrived carrying a sheaf of papers in one hand and a tabletop bookstand from his library in the other. He wore a white pleated dress-shirt with ruffles. About his shoulders and chest hung an assortment of very large horse brasses that clanked noisily as he arranged the lectern and papers on the glasstop table at the center of the terrace. We placed our chairs in front of him, for he was obviously going to lecture us. He took several cards from the papers, held them up one by one so that we, in turn, could read, "laughter," "applause," "hear, hear," "the sewage farm," "pocket bureau," then he replaced them at the ready. Finally, he pressed a long-haired mustache beneath his nose.

He pulled a fresh white handkerchief from his sleeve and patted perspiration from his brow. In doing so he dislodged a black curl from his neatly combed hair. His dark eyes, bright with fever, bristled at us as he looked into our faces with a mixture of fatherly concern and youthful determination, but clearly he was not in robust condition. He raised his fist toward his mouth and cleared his throat, before he clasped the sides of the lectern, and began to speak.

> Thank you for your kind words. I do not lightly undertake these duties. The reason which guides me is that I might do something for the city of St. Albans. I should have liked more years on the Council before becoming Mayor, especially in a growing city like this one.

He paused, shuffled his papers, lifted one up and waved it.

> Already I see that the engagements I must meet are enormous (we laugh on cue and he looks pleased). I had no idea there were so many institutions and people deserving of my time (we laugh again). Even while I have rejoiced in being your Mayor-elect, or "Mr. To Be," I have been told about the work I must do and the time I must give. I will do what I can, but you must try to be reasonable. I am not the strongest man in St. Albans.

Again, he grasped the sides of the lectern and seemed to examine his audience one by one.

> While I am Mayor, I will be no politician (hear, hear). In ordinary life I am, as every thoughtful man should be, a keen politician, but as your Mayor, I will represent no political party. Nor will I represent any religious denomination. (Applause) But I will not be

good at the trivial and graceful things that Mayors do.

I want my year of office to be a working man's year. I am not easy that our debt is £45,000, and our income is spent before we raise it, so that we are, in a sense, debt collectors. It seems wrong and I do not understand it. And expenses loom ahead for us. The Government may demand at any time that we extend our hospital accommodation and buy a dust destructor, and we would not get that for nothing.

He stood up straight and crossed his arms.

Any man who looks upon the conditions of the poor in this country knows that this question must be dealt with. Personally, I have the greatest sympathy with the poor. I have, in the course of my work with the children of the city, gone into their homes, and two or three things have struck me—first, the poor people are much better people than we thought they were. (Unsolicited, I applaud the kindness implicit in his sarcasm.) You would be surprised at the cleanliness in those simple cottages in Sopwell-lane. They are honest people, and from their ranks our soldiers and sailors are recruited. Their homes should be right, and they *are not right.* A working man told me the other day that all the money that came into his house was the 24s. he earned per week and that he paid 8s. per week in rent, while he had five children to keep. That is the position in which we place the poor of this rich country, and if we do not put it right, one of these days the poor will make demands which will surprise us.

He took several paces sideways and then returned to the lectern, hands clasped behind his back as if he were thinking.

As a young man on the council, I have tried to take an unbiased viewpoint. I am not short of audacity —some people have called it by another name—and I am going to be audacious on this occasion. In what I am going to say, I have not consulted a single member of the Council.

We have an excellent set of *officials*. Our officials really do the work of the Council. I am proud of our officials—all of them. And our *Council* is quite the smartest, keenest, and cleverest business body I have ever been on. (Ann is directed to laugh while we say, "Hear, hear.") I have been on *committees* since my youth, and I have never found any committee so expeditious in doing their business, so courteous and clever as is the Urban Committee; the best work they do, concerning the health of the city, is quite the best work that is done. (Ann calls out, "the sewage farm" and laughs.)

He stepped from behind the table so that he was nearer to us. His black eyes gleamed and we could tell he was getting to the point.

But the Council have grievous faults. It is getting old, so I ask you to make the Council young again by enlarging it. It ought to be extended to 24 members, and the city should be divided into wards. It is an unpopular proposal, I know, but whether it is carried now or later, it *will* be carried because it is right. (Steve shouts, "A pocket borough!")

To mask his annoyance, the Mayor was suddenly overcome with patience. He put his hands in his pockets and for a few moments looked down at the floor while his tongue searched his back teeth.

> Alderman Hurlock, Sir, it is difficult for me to speak from the fact that I have left my bed to be present today, and I must ask Councillors not to interrupt because I cannot go on if they do.

He stepped behind the lectern again and rearranged his papers.

> I know it grieves you that I say you are not a perfect Council (a laugh). Nevertheless, you are not perfect. An association should be judged worthy by the results of their work. Ten years ago, after I came into this city, I went to the Corn Exchange one evening and heard an election appeal for *baths*—if they returned the candidate they would have *baths.* I was told that the same thing had been said twenty years before (laughter). At any rate, it took ten years to decide to erect baths, and then the Council did not erect them. The credit of those baths belongs to my friend, Councillor Slade. It was not the Council that said, "We shall have baths," it was a strong man who said, "This thing shall be settled." And he settled it.
>
> Take the electric light. The electric light was proposed ten years ago. Four years ago, when I appealed to the burgesses to elect me on the Council, I made what I thought were sensible remarks about the electric lighting, and I charged the Council with dallying. An Alderman rose from the crowd and said that the electric light question was settled and lying for signature the next week. *I saw at once I had lost the election!* (laughter) Now, four years have passed, and whenever the Council finish early, we ask the Town Clerk how the electric light is going on. And a very good thing it is to have such humour on hand.

> After I visit other towns and am shown round, I say, "Come to St. Albans. I will show you our place." But if they came, my heart would sink. Where should I take them—to the Council Chamber, which belongs to someone else ("no, no"), to the Gasworks which belongs to a private company ("a good job, too"), to some Waterworks which belongs to someone else? The fact is that the only swell thing we have is a sewage farm. (Pause) *There is something wrong with our government, and there has been for years.*
>
> Our Council is a comfortable, happy place to spend an evening—sleepy and easy-going. Frankly, the Council is not doing its work. Yet there is not a Council in the kingdom so self-satisfied. And considering the future, we ought to give it new life by reconstituting it. I am confident that when it is considered, the decision will be that the Council shall extend as I suggest. (applause)

The speech was over. In my mind's eye I saw his daughter Joan, a toddler, run down the aisle of the Council chamber to her father. When he saw her coming he leaned over and scooped her up in his arms and carried her back to the podium so that he could say a few more words to the Council.

> I ask the Councillors who will be speaking to the resolution to follow, not to refer to the subjects I have discussed. I think it would be out of order. You should have time to consider these matters, and I think it would be wrong to discuss them now. If anyone does I will call him to order (from Steve, "Oh, lor!").

Tony carefully removed his mustache and looked at me. He knew he'd made a hit. I was mesmerized. He said quietly and with surprising emotion for Tony, "Well, now we know him."

"Yes," I said.

"Sam Ryder made that speech in the Council Chamber of the Town Hall on November 9, 1905, at noon. He was 48 years old and had lived in St. Albans for 10 years. As he mentioned in his speech he had stood for election unsuccessfully in 1902, but was unable to electioneer because he'd had whooping cough for six months and hadn't sufficiently recovered. However, two years later he stood again for Councillor and received a record 1,342 votes."

Steve said, "He was a flaming liberal but I would have voted for him anyway."

Gorhambury

"YOU'RE ALL DOLLED UP THIS MORNING," Steve said as I traded his briefcase for a kiss at the front door. *Dolled up?* I thought, after he had gone. I raced back upstairs, changed into khaki slacks and light blue L.L. Bean oxford cloth shirt with a button-down collar, and caught my loose hair in a ponytail. I looked in the mirror and decided to compromise. I loosened a curl, rolled back my shirtsleeves, unbuttoned one more button at the neck, and knotted a small ribbon over the elastic band that held my hair. By 7:30 I was out the door.

For more than a week I had all but forgotten Samuel Ryder and Abe Mitchell. But following the Rover's accident and an eerie dream I'd had about it, I longed for Mayor Ryder's reassurance. In the dream I had watched the Rover move away again, swinging rhythmically back and forth from a hook, while letters flowed from its front suspension forming words to a silly tune:

"We laughed, we cried,
We lived, we died.

We laughed, we cried,
We lived, we died..."

As it disappeared from my dream, its unearthly chant melted into quiet laughter.

~

I HAD TO FIND ANOTHER STONE ARCH and the only one that came to mind was at Gorhambury. It belonged to the Earl of Verulam and I hoped he wouldn't mind if I used it. I wheeled my dark green Raleigh bicycle—made in England, brought from America—down the driveway. Just as I reached the road I saw our mailman, on *his* dark green Raleigh, turn into the close. He raced toward me holding up a letter, rolled to a stop, and handed it to me. I had already read the morning mail—it had been lying in the vestibule below the mail slot when we came down for breakfast. Her Majesty's postman explained that he had found my letter in his pouch when he returned to the post office. Must have missed it somehow, he said, and since it was from America he thought it might be important. I was incredulous.

"Out for your morning exercise, then?" he asked me. "You will want to mind the traffic at this hour."

The letter was from my college, soliciting funds. As I slipped the envelope into my pants pocket, I mentioned to him casually that on the route I planned to take I had to negotiate a roundabout and I had never done it on a bicycle.

"Which roundabout will that be then miss?"

I told him it was the one at Verulam Road and Batchwood Drive—that I wanted to go straight on, toward the Verulamium Museum.

"On my way," he responded enthusiastically. "If you will allow me, I'll ride with you and show you where to cross."

It was comforting to be looked after by one's mailman, I decided, as we proceeded toward Batchwood Drive in tandem. Although he looked young in his uniform shorts, his fashionable sideburns were flecked with gray. He glanced back at me now and then like a mother hen, but he needn't have worried—English drivers, I had observed, were courteous and considerate of bikers, other drivers, and pedestrians, all of which they were themselves at one time or another. They easily understood the Golden Rule as it applied to vehicular traffic, a principle of the road that never made it to the Continent. Not that all was well on British streets—there were the bent figures of the women on mopeds who maneuvered darkly through traffic on market days, challenging the very heart of the system.

When we arrived at the roundabout, my civil servant, with his quadriceps and hamstrings working admirably about his knees, escorted me across the A5. I chose this moment to mention to him that sometime I'd like to ride up the hill to Gorhambury. "Do you know a way inside when the main gate is closed?" I asked.

He said, "It might be wise to wait until the main gate is open."

"Yes," I responded, ignoring his evasion.

"Well, there might be space enough for you and your bicycle between the gate and turnstile." I thanked him for his kindness and he said there was no need. He had a cousin lived in America.

I found the way onto the Earl's property as the postman had described it. For several hundred yards Gorhambury Drive coincided precisely with the part of Watling Street that had run smack dab through the center of Verulamium. I rode past digs of the oldest parts of the city, through a triumphal arch no longer there, alongside the Roman theater partially restored. Imagine owning a Roman theater and part of Watling Street, I thought. In the 1930s, some of Verulamium had been carefully excavated, dated, photographed, and then gently covered over. Successive owners of Gorhambury must have found it a burden to have a Roman junkyard on the premises. But now that Britain had become the overseas destination for the tourists of the world, a site such as Verulamium would soon become financially rewarding. On the negative side, according to Tony, it brought into focus a moral dilemma faced by estate and road builders who lived in fear that the odd bulldozer would inadvertently unearth a Roman villa or some other ancient marvel and shut down construction, permanently perhaps.

I shifted down as I started up the long hill and wondered if I could make it to the top without stopping. No one would claim golf, my only exercise, was aerobic or strengthening. When I felt fire in my thighs I gave in easily, planted my feet in the dry grass at the side of the road and looked across the fields below toward the A5. I saw the River Ver—an ever-flowing witness to history, tortured into conformity and silence, its natural twists and turns all but obliterated by man's never-ending quest to improve upon nature. I tried to imagine the marshy valley three thousand years ago and the ethnic groups that had lived there before the Romans came. Then I pondered what it had to do with me and decided it had everything to do with me.

Before I turned away from the valley I thought about what lay ahead over the rise. I wondered about the things that had happened since I met Mr. Ryder for the first time—how Abe had appeared at the archway, the Vicar's timely arrival, my small wishes fulfilled at whatever cost, our strange meandering journey through the countryside in a Rover that could have killed us if we had not turned back in the nick of time, even Tony's mesmerizing performance as the mayor. And now, this morning, the postman. In light of Mr. Ryder's proprietary attitude toward my well-being, my reservations about what lay ahead seemed to be idle and inappropriate speculation. In any case, since my thoughts were seldom my own these days, I was sure that whatever it was between us was out of my hands. And, truth to tell, although I hadn't a clue what it was all about, I was a willing player.

I crested the hill and rode toward the ruins of Nicholas Bacon's Gorhambury. The new Gorhambury, the color of Devonshire cream, was on my left. It was the stately residence of the present Earl of Verulam, a nice young man who had sold me a fine box of matches one Sunday afternoon when he opened his home for public view—something, I supposed, he never would have done if he had not needed the money to pay his taxes. On that same afternoon I had walked around my present destination, the remains of the sixteenth-century Tudor Gorhambury with an archway still intact. It was more or less hidden in the trees further on.

Mr. Ryder was standing in the road ahead, opposite the ruins. I waved my hand and in that instant he sent me a telepathic greeting I could have done without. I received a physical *whump* right in my solar plexus that took my breath away and brought tears to my eyes. I rode up to him, slowed to a stop and set my foot down. He frowned with concern, as if to say, "What have I done to her now?"

He placed his hands on the handlebars of my bicycle. I felt the excessive feeling leave my breast as if he had taken it from me. Then he drew a clean handkerchief from his pocket and said, "I misjudged the distance. You were closer than I thought." I took the soft lisle from him and touched my eyes.

We walked my bicycle a little way toward old Gorhambury and he laid it in the long grass beneath a blackthorn tree. We stood side by side and surveyed the ruins rising from the weeds. Attempts had been made to shore up the remains with brick but virtually the whole manor had fallen except for a marble archway with two wide steps leading to it.

"Nicholas Bacon, Lord Chancellor to Queen Elizabeth, built it 400 years ago," Mr. Ryder pronounced as if it were a lesson. "His second son, Francis, a man whose name is synonymous with Western thought, became lord of the manor after his father died. He cherished this countryside. It was a haven where he could dig in the soil and forget the political intrigues of the Jacobean court. It was here he pondered the nature of mankind and wrote his essays and books that shaped a Western philosophy toward science that persists to this day, and is one of the principal reasons why the civilised Westerner doesn't get the point of human existence. He saw every truth but one—the possibility of his own evolution. He had only begun to fulfill his potential. To this day Western thought does not recognize what people are for. One day, science will demonstrate that man can change the quality of his energy and it is this transformed energy that is immortal. Then the study of mankind can begin again. But until that happens, a man's best hope for immortality is to play golf so that he can at least see how little he knows about himself. Are you familiar with Francis Bacon?"

"Only that he said money was like manure—'not good unless it be spread.' My father told me that. I read his *Essays* in college and believed, along with my classmates, that he was Shakespeare until someone pointed out to us that Bacon would never have committed the errors found in Shakespeare's writing. I suppose you know the truth of that by now?"

"Yes, I do."

"And?"

"Let's say I'm surprised." He sat on the threshold and leaned against the arch while I stepped back with my hands in my pants pockets and examined the ruins.

"Here, sit on the step and I'll tell you about the Bacons. The father Nicholas entertained Queen Elizabeth here four times. She teased him about the small size of his house, so he enlarged it and that is probably when this arch was built. The first King James, whose mother Mary Queen of Scots played golf on the fields of Seton on the day she had her husband murdered, gave Nicholas Bacon's son Francis the title Baron Verulam of Verulam. For a time Gorhambury was the site of political extravaganzas, but it was also a quiet place in which to record his advice on how to run the world. Near the end of his life Lord Verulam, as he was known, met with a series of misfortunes, the result of bribes of convenience in judicial matters. When his enemies at court caught him up, even his friend King James could not look the other way and sent him to the Tower, although he was released in two day's time. In any case, as I say, Lord Verulam cared deeply for Gorhambury and found his inspiration here—but I doubt if he found it here beneath your arch."

"My arch? Didn't you guide me here?"

"Yes, well, but you knew how to find this one. You see..." Then he feigned a sigh and said, "Never mind. I just wanted to point out to you that this arch is not at all like the one on our golf course. Our Verulam arch, and another further along Cottonmill Lane, belonged to New Barnes Hall, now Sopwell Manor. The arches were erected sometime after Edward Strong bought it. Strong, the chief master stonemason to Wren's St. Paul's Cathedral and Blenheim Palace, was a man who understood the simple laws of the universe. Well, sometime you will want to ponder how the masons became the master builders of the great cathedrals of Western Europe without the science of Pythagoras." Mr. Ryder shifted his position and looked at me. "But enough of that. You are a sea of questions. Where shall you begin?"

I looked into his intelligent eyes and tried to decide which question I dared ask first. Then there it was. He had picked it for me—the one farthest from my heart.

"Did you mean it when you said we are merely a sea of

pulsing charges?"

"Ah! I don't think I said 'merely.' Perhaps 'charges' is too specific for you but if I were to tell you precisely about how the universe works, you would say I was talking rubbish. It is the weakness of language that even the smallest difference between speaker and listener will cause misunderstanding and misinterpretation. And believe me, there is a world of difference between us. Therefore, while I explain something to you, I try to keep you focused on the whole of it and not let you stray off into associative thinking."

With that he sat straighter and rested one hand on each knee. I assumed a similar pose thinking it would help me listen and understand.

"Let me begin this way: If you had asked me, 'What is the universe?' I would have answered, 'The universe is energy—first and last, it is energy.' Then if you were to ask me, 'What is energy?' I would say, 'Energy is activity.' The universe is in a state of perpetual, interdependent activity or movement, correcting 'too much of this' and 'too little of that.' Everything is the result of something else. We are the result of something and something is the result of us. We play an interactive role in the universe and we cannot disregard it.

"But how does it work? What happens?"

"I think of it as the law of This, That, and the Other Thing. *This* seed lies in *that* soil, but until the *other thing* is added nothing happens. Add water and something new is created—a flower. 'This' is active, 'That' is passive, and the 'Other Thing' is conscious interference. Interference of this sort is how the universe runs and how we ourselves evolve.

"At the present time human activity degrades energy at an ever increasing rate. Some scientists say that since humanity is doing such a good job of disorganising the planet as fast as possible, it must be what people are for. But it is not so. The purpose of human life is to transform energy required for the 'reciprocal maintenance' of the universe—in utter violation, I might add, of the second law of thermodynamics."

"What do you mean by 'conscious interference'?"

I could see he was pleased by my question. "Well, the Laws of Nature, for example, are analogous to 'conscious interference.' Consider the point of view that it is Nature's job to keep biological life going on earth because biological life has its limited energy role to play in the universe. Humanity is the *only* life form capable of 'conscious interference' on its own behalf. Yet this ability, when misused, causes madness, or so it would seem; otherwise people would not kill their own kind—not that Mother Nature minds this, as long it keeps her Garden of Eden fertilized. Nature manipulates our fates according to her natural laws, keeping us from our higher purpose while she fulfills her own. 'Conscious interference' results in 'doing' and it is the only way to escape nature's relentless design."

"Why are you telling me what I can't possibly understand?"

"Because," he said as he slapped his knee and rose to his feet, "it has to do with golf and why golf is the only game God is interested in."

"We must be in pretty bad shape if the only thing that can save us is golf. Isn't it time you told me what it is you want me to do?"

"That's just it. The way you are now you cannot *do* anything. But if, by your own efforts, a finer energy comes within your experience, it will change your perception. You will begin to understand, to see what others cannot see. It is all there for you to grasp and once you grasp it, you will know what to do and how to do it."

"Is this open for discussion?" I asked.

"No, I don't think so."

"I'm not surprised. I heard your mayor's speech last night."

"Yes? And what did you think of the mayor?" he asked,

helping me to my feet.

I laughed, relieved we were on a subject I understood. "You were a master of sarcasm," I said as we started walking toward my bicycle. "What happened to your proposals? Did you get away with your insults?"

"I was without pity, wasn't I? You can be sure I didn't win any popularity contest with the older members of the Council. But I expected more from our elected officials. Unfortunately, I was an ineffective mayor, sick throughout the year. The whole family was sick, in fact, especially little Joan. The only reason the Councillors put up with me was they thought I might die at any moment."

"Did the Council adopt your ward system?"

"No. They voted it down the following April. It was seven more years before it passed. There was nothing new in my speech, you know—wards had been proposed before. There was one line that was mine, however. I said I had gone into the homes of poor people and they were much better people than we thought they were. I swear there was not one person in the room that understood I meant poor people should not stand low and be ignored. The English, you see, have persuaded themselves that it comforts the poor to know where they stand—surely an absurd idea in universal terms, but assumed by the English to be a helpful concept at all levels of society. I was very young when I decided that any man that thought he knew where he stood in relation to another man had better think again or he would go straight to hell. God knows no such concept. But even our sweet-natured golf writer Bernard Darwin was guilty. He wrote in 1927, 'There is a good deal to be said in this life for having our sphere definitely marked out for us, for knowing exactly where we stand.' Can you imagine an American knowing his station in life?"

The Invitation

Mr. Ryder retrieved my bicycle from the weeds beneath the tree and stood it up in front of me. As he picked a blade of grass off the chrome handlebars, it popped into my mind that I could stop by the music store in Holywell Hill on my way home and get a Brahms piano piece I had heard on BBC radio.

Mr. Ryder said, "Since you are going to the town centre, I suggest you continue along this track and look at a farmhouse not far from here, hundreds of years old, my favourite house in Hertfordshire. Ride about—no one will mind. Look at the house from the walled garden. When the light is right, and just now it is, it evokes a common response in all who see it. When you're done, ride on to the Hemel Hempstead road, turn left, and head for town.

"And whilst you're in Holywell Hill you might look at my office building. It's almost opposite the music store—the central post office it is now. Nellie laid the foundation stone in 1911 and it was, I don't hesitate to say, the finest office building in St. Albans. Twenty years later I built the adjoining floral hall that displayed blooms from Ryder seeds in a garden setting. We prepared the penny packets in the large building at the rear. During our busiest months, we employed more than 200 women to count and package the fragile seeds. Business flourished in their gentle and patient hands. I told them, and I meant it, that seeds, handled with loving care, will fulfill their promise. Seeds handled with indifference will perform in kind.

"They worked decent hours in hygienic, warm, cheerful surroundings. If illness beset them and kept them home, I paid them anyway. You can imagine how the town leaders exclaimed over that one. 'That's unheard of, Ryder!' and I thought to myself, more's the pity. Those that didn't laugh at me complained I set a bad example, said I would lose my profits. Well, they were wrong. I was never taken advantage of—not for a moment. In fact, whilst I was mayor it was a comfort to know that at least my employees liked me. I have a silver salver presented to me at the time with an illuminated address that said I was 'a generous, considerate, and kind employer.' And it was true. I was."

He told me that as mayor he thought he could legislate against the poverty, dirt, cold, and darkness that the rich, industrious nation had brought to its working classes. But he soon found that mayors had basically one overriding problem: what to do with all that shit, to use my word, he said. There was nothing more compelling than human waste when there was too much of it in the wrong place. It seemed to him that's what he did the whole time—address the efficiency and size of the sewage disposal arrangements, a local institution called the Sewage Farm. Then he laughed at a memory he chose not to share with me.

"I tried to use common sense in the way I gave away my money so I would not stifle the generous impulses of others. I didn't want anyone to say, 'Well, I was going to help the project but old Ryder stepped in and paid the lot.' Rather, it was my style to make up the deficit, or get things rolling and let others take over and receive the credit, or the blame.

"I would gladly have taken credit for everything I did, and more, but I knew someone was watching—and I don't mean God; I mean Nellie. It was very difficult to remember at times that a good deed was not good for the soul unless it was anonymous, so she was there to remind me. Thus it was announced in the newspaper, 'A golf enthusiast whose name has not been made public is ready to give a Challenge Cup for professional golfers, similar to the Walker Cup.' But I changed my mind about anonymity in this case because my purpose in giving the Cup was to lend the reputation of my name to professional golf.

"Nellie usually blessed my activities but she thought I'd lost my reason when I spent my time and money to help professional golfers. The Heath and Heather Tournament at Verulam in 1923, sponsored by my brother James and me, left her baffled. She couldn't understand what we wanted to accomplish. James, a retired schoolteacher, was managing director of our new herbal seed firm Heath and Heather, and he thought the tournament would advertise his fledgling business. He was right. It did advertise Heath and Heather but Heath and Heather, in turn, advertised professional golf, and that was my purpose. Whatever, it was a magnificent competition. Everyone came, and every one of the 48 players was assured £5 just for appearing—otherwise most of them could not have afforded to come. The rest of our £450 budget was prize money. It was a concept we thought would catch on, but it never did. There were no ready sponsors for unknown professionals.

"The Heath and Heather Tournament was a grand, almost festive, occasion. Nell and I followed the players, and she smiled at me when I cheered for my favourites. Finally, she said, 'Mr. Ryder, you're happy.' And I answered, 'By heaven,

Mrs. Ryder, I am. I never thought about it before, but yes, I am.' We made a film of it, you know, the first movie ever made of a golf tournament, and it's still around. Harry Vardon, Sandy Herd, Ted Ray, James Braid, J.H. Taylor, George Duncan, Abe Mitchell, the Whitcombes—they are in it and so are the Ryders. It was shown at the Odeon in St. Albans for a week. Verulam has it. Arthur Havers, who had just won the Open the week before, won it—£50, only £25 less than the Open prize.

"It wasn't our purpose to help the top professional golfers; they never worried me. They were respected and made a decent income, although they would have done much better in America. But they were retiring from competition and were as concerned as I was about the future of British professional golf. It was the 30 or so younger professional hopefuls, the ones who skulked about the fringes of the game looking like fugitives from justice, that we tried to encourage. All the elder statesmen of golf treated them kindly and tried to inspire in them a wish to improve their games.

"Where did it come from, your compulsion to help everybody?" I asked.

"My father. I've already sold you a bill of goods about what a modest, unassuming man I was. In fact, as a little boy, I thought I was such a fine person that I owed it to everyone to let them know. My symptoms were so manifest that my father brought me to God to pray for help. He said, 'You must spend your life helping yourself and God by helping others, and you must start by causing the least amount of trouble to your mother and sisters who love you.' It was a modest beginning.

"While I drew prizes at school, I taught children in our Sunday school, not much younger than I, about humility. Humph! I did not have a humble bone in my body, but I was genuinely blessed with the clear understanding that, just as I was the hero of my own life story, all men and women were heroes of theirs. And if I thought otherwise, I knew it was only because I had not walked in their shoes.

"My family and my fellow magistrates, even Abe, used to chide me for giving money away indiscriminately, when patently I had been lied to by a beggar or a thief. My critics would exhort, 'You don't believe his story, do you?' And I would answer, 'Goodness no. I wouldn't sleep if I thought any man carried such a burden on his shoulders.' But I saw what the beggar or the thief didn't tell me, and I knew I hadn't done enough.

"Abstract philanthropy I judged to be oftentimes harmful. I stepped in and helped only when I could see the consequences of my action. I left no charitable gifts in my will, believing that giving during my lifetime was the greater benefit. Except for the Ryder companies, only £28,000 remained in my estate. There would have been more, but I invested unwisely in some Canadian ventures.

"Abe said once that it did my soul no good to give my money away, since I enjoyed doing it. He said I was a hopeless case. 'You must suffer,' he laughed, 'as I would suffer if I gave away my money on purpose.'

"Thus, we chided each other in our friendship. We studied our natures unmercifully and discovered we were nothing alike. It was my nature, for example, to believe that life treated me unfairly at times. Accordingly, when my putt went into the hole and then popped out again, I felt it was unfair. On the golf course, as in life, I expected justice to prevail. Although I acknowledged that golf knew no equity, I didn't understand it. Of course, when my errant shots prospered, to my opponents' dismay, I somehow saw justice in it.

"This greatly amused Abe who never weighed one thing against another. Abe played each shot as he found it without expectations. He took his medicine, as they say, and enjoyed the next shot, never disturbing his harmony with the golf course nor confusing justice with his game. He once suggested that what I saw as injustice may have been, in fact, God's design, and that perhaps I had no right to interfere in another man's adversity. I told him that I didn't know he was assigned to judge my case.

"Well, as you can probably tell, we enjoyed our banter. Now, back to the task at hand. Before you go to the music store, visit my office. Someone at the post office will let you go upstairs. My desk faced the large bank of leaded-glass windows that looks out onto the street. The best architects and craftsmen—it was an expensive stage setting for a thriving business run by a man who didn't own the house he lived in. And the whole time God and Nell were looking on. How do we come to grips with our monumental insignificance? How did I come to grips with mine? Take in the monogram carved on the wooden mantelpiece. Is it RS or SR? Ryder and Son or Samuel Ryder? Or the domed glass ceiling beneath the rooftop designed to catch and reflect His holy light in the event my good intentions faltered. Nellie said I needed such moral reminders since I shared a supporting wall with the White Hart Inn next door, one of the best and oldest dispensers of warm whisky on a cold night in all of England. I like to think that if my building did nothing else, at least it prevented the White Hart from falling down Holywell Hill."

My thoughts had wandered because I remembered that within days my houseguests would descend upon me. How would I have time for Mr. Ryder?

"Ah, yes," he murmured. He pondered me for some moments, theatrically stroking his chin, and then he offered me a staggering invitation.

"What do you say to a round of golf on the Royal Ashdown Forest golf course on the Wednesday after your houseguests leave? We'll do it in a timeless fashion—you, Abe, and I."

The prospect of any golf game had always warmed my

insides, but this! When I found my voice I said a ridiculous thing. "I play golf with the Vicar of St. Botolph's on Wednesdays."

"That's when we will do it then. The Vicar will never know, although if he is a good man of the cloth, he might sense that something is adrift. During the play of the 4th hole, you will find yourself with us on Ashdown Forest. The thing is, you see, we will play our golf outside of time."

" 'Outside of time'?"

"Yes," he said, "we will play our game in my dimension where time conveniently does not apply. Inconveniently, your shoelaces will come untied, but that's of no consequence."

"How do I get there?"

"With my guidance, of course," he answered as if I should know these things.

"I might not sleep thinking about it."

"In that case I'll see that you don't think about it until just before it happens. But here, let me show you." He took my bicycle and set it against the blackthorn tree. "Now give me your hand. I know, but give it to me anyway." Which I did.

Instantly, with no sensation of change, I was in a garden which could only have been Mr. Ryder's practice hole at Marlborough House. A man in shirtsleeves with his collar unbuttoned and hanging by the stud at the back of his neck was chipping golf balls over a hedge while a small girl followed him about, reciting from a parchment that she held unrolled between her hands. I recognized the words from Captain John Rattray's 13 'laws at golf' penned in 1745. Mr. Ryder had told me this was how he taught his youngest daughter Joan to read cursive script, by pretending that she was helping him learn the rules of golf while he practiced. Her light brown curls danced on her shoulders and her bangs were precisely cut above eyes as large and dark as her father's.

"Law number 12," she read, "*He whose Ball lies farthest from the Hole is obliged to play first.* And here is the last one, Daddy. Law number 13, *Neither French, Ditch or Dyke, made for the preservation of the Links, nor the Scholar's Holes or the Soldiers Lines, Shall be accounted a Hazard, But the Ball is to be taken out, Teed and played with any Iron Club.*"

"What did you say, dear? French ditch? Look at it again, Joan. It's Trench, Ditch, or Dyke, isn't it?"

"Maybe it's a *French Trench*," she giggled.

"It must have been a way to drain the course. You know, I think I've heard the term '*French* drain', although it certainly isn't a horticultural term or I would know about it. But there *is* such a thing as a *Trench* drain. Hmm. I wonder if they are made in the same way: dig a narrow trench and fill it with rocks and rubble in order to drain off surface water. If they are the same, we may be on to something. I must look it up. If a French drain and a Trench drain are made in the same way, you may not be the only person to see Trench as French. In any case, it's a dry subject, isn't it?"

"You're funny."

"It would be especially telling, wouldn't it, if the term French drain was first used within a short time after John Rattray wrote his 'Laws and Articles?' The subject has not been mentioned in any golf rules since Rattray's day, but it is my guess that your French Ditch or Drain will surface again sometime, find its wrongful place in English usage and no one will ever know what a clever young lady you are. Now, where is your putter? Go get your putter and we'll have a contest."

While Joan fetched her putter, his oldest daughter Marjorie arrived at her father's side and whispered to him, "That awful Mr. Hurlock is here to see you."

"I hope you invited him in."

"I didn't. He finds fault with everything."

"Marjorie, dear, I have it on very good authority that Alderman Hurlock's wife feeds him solely on a diet of nuts.

Now what man can give of his best under such circumstances?" And he hurried inside.

And that was it. Mr. Ryder handed me my bicycle, saying I would not remember our golf date until the time came because I would only daydream about it. When I tried to return his lisle handkerchief he told me to keep it. He had plenty more.

I rode to the stone farmhouse. Mr. Ryder was right. It was strikingly old and beautiful—the home that my friends back in America imagined I lived in. After I circled the property on a small service road I set my bike aside in order to walk up several steps to a walled garden, a casual laboratory for flowering plants arranged around a perfect lawn. From there I looked over a low knapped-flint wall to the most agreeable arrangement of shapes I thought I had ever seen. Handmade tiles waved in fine unruly lines along steep, sunlit roofs, hipped at the ends to make a warm terra-cotta design. The whole was outlined by rounded finishing tiles, so that one roof flowed rythmically into another at various levels, describing a U-shaped house of one and two stories. I supposed it was this harmony of pattern, as evocative as a composer's theme, that Mr. Ryder wanted to share with me.

~

By the time I had examined the Seed Hall and Mr. Ryder's office it was nearly twelve o'clock so I hurried through the front door of the music store to get inside before the midday closing. This was no frivolous shop, I thought, as the clatter of my entrance echoed off the shelves. The interior was set in the sepia shades of an old photograph, relieved only here and there by a glimpse of Schirmer yellow. It was redolent of old classrooms, as well as of its musty neighbour, the St. Albans Cathedral, which loomed just doors away up a narrow lane.

The shop breathed such serious intentions that I almost turned around and walked out because the music I wanted to buy was an obscure and unimportant piece, in the key of C, and I didn't know the name of it. But I gathered my courage and proceeded down the center aisle to a counter at the back. Reluctantly I made my uninformed inquiry to a tall, wispy lady with lots on her mind.

"I think it was composed by Brahms," I said.

"Yes," she said without inflection, glancing at the clock.

"I can sing a few bars," I said bravely, and tentatively proceeded to do so.

"*da*-da-da, *da*...da, *da*-da-*da*, da..." My lady joined in at that point and we da-daed together for several measures before a young clerk chimed in from the front of the store. Thereupon, a black-suited gentleman, a stocky mismatch for his thin wife, drifted in from a back room and merged his voice with ours. The four of us finished off the passage in grand style and then we laughed. When we came to our senses, the proprietor said, "I believe it is one of his intermezzi."

Guests

For eight weeks a steady stream of friends and relatives arrived in St. Albans to stay with us. We hung the Stars and Stripes, last seen over the *boulevard*, by the front door. This startling display of chauvinism amused our English friends who kept their hand-sized Union Jacks tightly furled on pantry shelves. But a stranger to our close needed such a clue to find our house, sequestered as it was by the most purposefully unpaved street in town. Potholes and protruding rocks, exacerbated by the dry summer, effectively discouraged drivers from using the street as a shortcut and were probably the reason the Rover came to grief, although it did not occur to us at the time.

Our parade of guests began with Mother, whom we greeted at Southampton in a setting devoid of glamour. We stood behind portable metal barriers, those ubiquitous European devices that so effectively put people in their place. From there we spotted her in a long line that inched across a cavernous dockside shed—a humbling reception, to say the least. "Welcome to jolly olde England," I whispered to Steve. It seemed to me Cunard could have found a better way.

Mother waved to us. She was sandwiched between Dick Cavett and Alistair Cooke with whom she exchanged words now and again. When I recognized the television stars, I experienced spasms of pointing and making faces. Mother was cool as could be, perhaps because she didn't know who they were. At 77, she was saving television for her old age.

Once the coordinated visits had begun, Sam and Abe took leave, temporarily relieving me of what I saw as my twofold task: learn to be a perfect human being and write a book. Who would take an assignment of such proportions seriously? Yet I did, most of the time. On the morning Mother was to arrive, Mr. Ryder was in my kitchen when I came downstairs to prepare breakfast. He was examining my new electric kettle.

"You startled me."

"Come now, you expected I'd be here." It was true; I had expected him. What startled me was how good it felt to see him there.

"No more surprises, I promise. You will always have a 'premonition', as they say. I wanted a word with you before your guests arrive, and then I'll leave you until we play golf at Royal Ashdown."

"I had forgotten all about our date," I said, and as quickly as I remembered I forgot again.

"Meanwhile," he said, "there are two things I want you to do that will help you develop the objective eye you will need for the work ahead. I want you to make a serious attempt, first of all, to recognize your automatic negative responses. When you spot one, try to catch it in midair and change it to a positive response. Do it on the golf course where it is especially easy to detect psychological changes."

"For example?" I asked.

"A downhill lie. I always disliked a downhill lie."

"My choice is the 30-inch putt," I offered. "I hate 30-inch putts."

"What would happen, do you imagine, if you said to yourself, 'I love a 30-inch putt'?"

"I would sink it."

"Precisely. You work better and last longer in a positive atmosphere. You will actually have a longer life if you don't waste your energy on spurts of anger, dislike, and other useless negative emotions. Hate depletes energy, while love—the kind one feels for a cat or a dog—preserves it. One is evil and the other is good; it is the only morality in the universe."

"You make everything sound so simple. What else do you want me to do?"

"All right. When you feel tired, or anytime for that matter, you must sit by yourself in a chair or on the floor if you like; sit relaxed and straight with only one thought. Your one thought will be that you must have only one thought. That's it—no other thought is allowed. Twenty minutes—lock yourself in the bathroom if necessary. If you do it right it's almost as good as a night's sleep."

"I've heard of this but I understood that one must have no thought at all," I said.

"That is too difficult for you."

"I'll miss you, Samuel Ryder."

"I'll see that you don't." With that he shook his head in disbelief, it seemed to me, that I was the person for the job, and then he was gone.

~

OUR SECOND GUEST WAS BILL, our rich friend from Paris who worked for the *New York Times*. He was a person who gave much more than he took, and besides, he was apt to cuddle me from time to time for no reason and I liked that. He thought the only way to anywhere, short of walking, was by the slowest, cheapest possible means. "I didn't get rich giving it away," he liked to say to cloud the issue, whenever we asked him why he didn't fly. But I believed he had premonitions left over from his days as a Navy pilot. He told me once in a serious moment, that as a flyer he had fancied he owned a book of tickets that guaranteed a safe return, but after the war he lost the book without knowing how many tickets remained.

By metro, bus, and midnight ferry he traveled the short distance to England in 18 hours, carrying two suitcases, and a paper package of Muenster cheese tucked under his arm. From Dover by train to Charing Cross, by Underground to St. Pancras and by train again to St. Albans was another eight hours. At no time was Bill crowded by other passengers; they granted him room to stretch out his tall frame and sleep when he cared to. In some cases his fellow travelers even preferred to stand in the corridor rather than share the heady atmosphere with the cheese. We picked him up at the station at 5:00. "Opening time," Bill declared just as "The Jolly Sailor" came into view at the end of Sandpit Lane. We must stop in, he said. Up until Bill's visit, Steve and I had never stopped at a pub simply to have a beer.

Early the next morning Steve, Mother, and I, and Bill with his prehistoric Muenster drove to Stonehenge. In 1976 there was no prohibition against lolling about the sarsen stones in the warm sunshine and this we did for hours until Bill and Steve were satisfied they understood the solar and lunar complexities of the place. We returned to the car and tightened the strap on the Muenster skulking in the boot, which clearly was not airtight.

From the Wiltshire countryside we drove to Oxford, where we casually found space in the car park at Magdalen—Maudlin, Mother said—a parking impossibility, I've since been told. After we used their facilities, we crossed the street and followed the Thames—the Isis, Mother said—to a cricket ground where we lolled some more and watched a wonderfully soporific cricket match. Whenever there was detectable movement on the field, Bill explained it in unbelievable detail. He knew these things because his wife, my best friend, who had died not long before without our permission, had been captain of the cricket team at her boarding school in New England. At 4 P.M. we returned to the car where the Muenster's presence confronted us for the last time. We uncorked a bottle, unleashed the cheese and ate the entire thing on biscuits in the open air. Even then, its power remained until I found a trashcan for the wrapper—a dustbin would not have sufficed. Later, I asked Mr. Ryder how something so delicious could smell so bad and he said that it was a good example of the universal law of reconciliation.

~

MOTHER WAS THE EASIEST OF our guests. She had seen the British Isles by hired car and driver, not once, but twice. A real traveler, she thought, stayed in one place. Now her interests would be local, she said, and she put St. Albans Abbey at the top of her agenda. During my first nap after her arrival she walked the considerable distance to the abbey, explored it, bought a book, took tea in a nearby tearoom, and walked home. It became her routine and before long she had nodding acquaintances along the way. She assumed that I had been to the abbey many times, otherwise she would have invited me to go along. But I never went to the abbey and I don't know why. I wondered if Mr. Ryder had anything to do with it and then decided not. I was just not "religious." Only after Mother tried to share its history and architecture did I let her be my guide.

My father and I had tried very hard to be religious when we moved away from Clifton Springs to the university town that had a wide selection of Christian churches. To make a point, he took me to a different denominational service every

Sunday. Sometimes we veered off on another day to hear the cantor sing. In the end Steve's Presbyterian Church suited us as well as any. He sat with his parents in the third pew to the right of the right-hand aisle, just as he sat with them in the first three seats of the eighth row to the left of the center aisle in the movie theater. I asked Mr. Ryder why the professor did that and Mr. Ryder said, "He knew his place."

Mother explained that the abbey was an illustrated history of Western Europe. "It gives me a sense of how short a time we've been out of the caves. I don't mind so much that we are making a hash of it when I realize that we are just getting started. Look at the Magna Carta, for example. It was first addressed right here in St. Albans, in 1213. That was only 763 years ago. Why I've been alive more than one-tenth of that time."

"Mother," I said, "the Magna Carta was signed at Runnymede in 1215."

"But it started here two years earlier, in 1213, when the Archbishop of Canterbury forced King John—not a good man—to summon a representative council of men to St. Albans Abbey to discuss an old charter from Henry I's time which spoke of liberties for freemen. The old charter was amended and modified on subsequent occasions and finally submitted in its final form at Runnymede. It was the beginning of Parliament and the rule of law."

Next, she wanted me to hear about Alban's bones. This particularly interested Mother because she had been to a church in Odense in 1966 where she was told the bones of St. Alban were enshrined, having been stolen from the St. Albans Abbey in the tenth century when the Danes invaded the region. A pair of Benedictine monks from St. Albans tricked the Danes into returning the bones, but the Danes later said they knew what was going on and palmed off some fake bones. To add to the confusion, when it was rumored the Danes planned another raid on the St. Albans shrine, its Saxon Abbot asked the monks at Ely to hide Alban's bones. When the danger had passed, the Ely monks gave back some substituted bones, a ruse easily exposed, for the Saxon Abbot had secretly marked the bones before he gave them to Ely. Thus began a century-long lawsuit at the end of which Pope Adrian IV— an Englishman from nearby King's Langley, by the way—ordered Ely to own up.

"Mother, that can't be right."

"Wait, there's more. What no one knew was that our wise Saxon Abbot had distrusted the Ely monks in the first place and hidden the real bones in the abbey wall. Well, it makes one wonder, doesn't it? Do you remember Professor Morris Bishop of the History Department? He told me that when St. Thomas Aquinas fell ill and died while on a journey to the monastery of Fossanuova, the monks immediately decapitated him and boiled the body for its precious bones. And St. Romualdus of Ravenna escaped from France by feigning madness, since the people proposed to kill him in order to make certain of his relics. Professor Bishop told it much better than I do."

Mother also told me the abbey was haunted, a conclusion drawn by an air raid warden one moonlit night at Christmas—a 'bomber's moon'—in 1944. A bell had tolled in the empty Norman tower, and the organ echoed through the darkened nave. The 12 great bells had been wrapped and stored below for protection from the war and the untouched organ keys were seen to move in the light of a burning candle by the warden on his nightly rounds.

On her third Sunday with us, Tony invited Mother to be his partner at foursomes against Steve and me. I would have liked to have been Tony's partner, but that's the way it was with Mother. Such was her appeal that on the few occasions Steve and I were at domestic loggerheads, he told me firmly, "I'm going home to your mother." Everything about her was feminine except her brain, a magic combination that fostered friendships with men who were her colleagues, and most women. She'd had but one run-in with a woman in her life. Two days out of Singapore, aboard *SS President Polk*, a menopausal duplicate bridge player named Rosa Hammersmith had called her a hussy, in a voice so audible that it was heard by a room full of serious people, half of whom needed the word explained. Mother liked to tell the story.

Ann decided she wanted to join us at Verulam and carry Mother's golf clubs, a bag of ancient sticks—two no-name woods, inscribed "George Hall," three Patty Berg irons, and a fairly new Acushnet putter, won on the strength of her putting with her old putter. It would be Ann's first time on any golf course and we suggested that her opera slippers might not do. Tony was particularly excited to have Ann along, probably the reason he hooked his opening drive onto British Rail. For this he took an unmerciful ribbing from Ann, who naturally had no comprehension of what constituted detestable behavior on the links. Mother had quiet words with her to the effect that laughter of derision on a golf course, other than at oneself, packed a wallop out of all proportion and was why golf was referred to as a gentleman's game. The game would not have survived otherwise. The raw edges of exposed emotions were vulnerable to even imagined laughter, so one had to be especially careful in one's comments, lest offense be taken.

Ann gracefully covered her mouth in contrition and, after that, observed us carefully and quietly. Halfway down the 6th fairway she came to me holding Mother's 5-iron.

"Is this right?" she asked arranging her fingers around the handle. I showed her how to grip the club and she strode off to the side. Now and then I would catch a glimpse of her behind a grassy knoll swinging the 5-iron. I was relieved and impressed that she hadn't the least tendency to lose her footing. That's half the battle right there, I thought. At the 12th hole I handed her my new 7-wood and a red plastic tee and told her to stick it in the ground and try to hit it. Off she went but in moments she was back again.

"I can't do it."

I showed her how to stand and told her to pretend she was launching a stick for Berry to chase. She ran off again like a gazelle. Then I heard a grunt of satisfaction and saw her move forward. She swung time after time, hardly setting herself, only pausing to stick the peg in the ground. At the green she breathlessly apologized to everyone for forsaking her duties. Her excitement was contagious. At least it was for me.

While the boys were driving off at the 13th, I told Ann and Mother that this was the hole where Abe Mitchell used to drive the green with a towering fade. Then, naturally, I had to tell them who Abe Mitchell was. I mentioned to Ann that a nice young man from Welwyn Garden City, with whom I played recently, tried the Mitchell shot and had lost his ball in the woods to the left. The next thing I knew Ann was poking about in the left-hand trees with my 7-wood. Suddenly she came bounding from the woods, her eyes wide with surprise as if she'd found a plum in a bin of brussel sprouts.

"I've found a ball!" she said.

"Jolly good," Tony said and got on with his game, ignoring her obvious expectations to be invited to play, now that she was equipped. She put the ball in her pocket and held the flagstick for us with exaggerated politeness. It was painful to watch.

As we approached the 17th hole to tee-off over the cars, Ann caught up to me and whispered, "Don't worry about it. I understand—really I do."

I had thought of Mother the first time I played the 17th, and now, here she was assessing what club to use, or so I thought. Actually, she was deciding firmly not to play the hole at all.

"It's lunacy," she declared. "What person in his right mind would do such a thing? It's what's wrong with the human race."

We each gave advice.

"We'll tell you when no cars are coming."

"It's easy."

"Just relax and pop it on the green."

"Oh, all right," she said before we had a chance to say more, which we were fully prepared to do. She loaded up, waited for the all clear, and fired with a 3-wood. The ball sailed to the back of the green and trickled back down the slope. Then, from the public footpath a voice cried out, "It almost went in!" Mother picked up her tee, gave her 3-wood to Ann and led the way down the dirt path through the trees and across Cottonmill Lane as if she owned the place.

Over drinks in the lounge after our game, I asked Ann if she would care to come to the practice range with me. She knocked back her drink and stood up, ready to go help me practice. She and I would drive home while the rest could go in Steve's car, she ordered. We went to the golf shop to get range balls from Denis. As usual, he asked me how I played. Good and bad, I told him, and introduced Ann.

"Mrs. Winchester here," Denis confided to Ann, "is one of the best deep bunker players at Verulam." To me he said, "Saw Nick last week. He sends you his regards. He's been on a winning streak, you know. Plans to play in the Open next summer and hopes to make the Ryder Cup team.

Once we were out the door, Ann whispered, "I say, *he's* a good-looking chap."

With my golf bag on her shoulder, Ann led the way to the range.

Rain

Our splendid summer weather ended abruptly two weeks after Bill's departure. By train, boat, bus, and metro he had made his way safely back to Paris. We would see him again in March — Chamonix. Bill didn't play golf but he liked to ski. In my sulfur water drinking days I never mastered the rope tow so why did I think I could ski in the Alps? I knew why. Mr. Ryder's admonition to like my dislikes had left me with an acutely optimistic disposition. This positive attitude permeated the entire fabric of my life.

Take, for example, the traffic ticket stuck to my windscreen after I had parked briefly in front of the bake shop in the High Street and fetched Florentines for my dinner guests. Was I upset, put out, any of those things? Not I. A gift from heaven, I thought, a chance to queue up and pay my fine at the police station. How many Americans had the opportunity to stand in a line of law-abiding citizens, oddly cheerful about paying their fines, as if it indicated to them there was a system and it was working? Kim Philby might sell State secrets and parliamentarians might sleep with spies, but they would never sneak ahead in an English queue.

The high point of my queuing life was with Dorothy, the retiring doctor whose squatters still held fiercely to her Suffolk home. The queue was on a cold, wintry February morning at Burlington House for the Pompeii Exhibit, a show I wasn't tall enough to see from behind the broad shoulders of the other voyeurs. Fortunately, Mother had been to the real Pompeii with her camera some years before, so I had seen everything—as in "Now I've seen everything." However, I did learn one or two relevant things standing in line. Amidst occasional flakes of snow, our line snaked back and forth at a snail's pace along metal fences so that at each section we passed between several Oxonians on one side and several Cantabrigians on the other. The two groups, although strangers to each other, had quickly found their common ground and were swapping stories across our line to pass the time. They moved in one direction, while we moved in the other, and thus we met up at regular intervals four or five times. They debated and joked—too witty 'by half,' as I learned to say that morning—across the queuers that divided them. But each time Dorothy and I came in sight, we were greeted warmly and included in their wonderfully pointless discussions. When we finally entered the glorious warmth of Burlington House, a charming Cambridge man, who had backpedaled several times to remain beside me as our positions diverged, broke away from his group to tell me emphatically that I was a delightful and intelligent young woman.

~

I SELDOM MADE LISTS, for what was the point when my life had been prearranged by an outside agency? But if I'd had a list of important things to do, teaching Ann to play golf would have been foremost. She longed to play—I could see it plain enough, and besides, she dropped hints. But there wasn't time. As Mother's departure neared, we experienced a spate of activities that included an unscheduled trip to Paris, precipitated by a remark Mother had made as we paused to view a poster of the Eiffel Tower in Thomas Cook's window on High Street. "I've never been to Paris," she had said wistfully. "On a ship one never sees the insides of countries."

In November the crowds at my house and on the golf course had thinned so I could attend to Ann. Dorothy, the golf lesson expert, suggested we take Ann to Batchwood on a rainy day. Temperatures in late autumn ranged from 48° to 58° Fahrenheit but that wasn't why players were scarce. The mud put them off—a thin layer of new grass, after the drought, did little to protect golfers from the wet clay that grabbed their shoes.

It had been Dorothy's idea to have Ann walk along and swing a club at the ball occasionally. She still had "Faldo's" ball so I put her to work with my 7-wood just off the fairway. She was soon swinging with the same abandon she had used against the plastic tee at Verulam. My only contribution to the miracle that unfolded in the cold drizzle was to use my best form for her to imitate.

On the 3rd hole her ball sailed off the clubface and flew 20 yards further than I had ever hit a ball in my life. As she smacked her open hand against her chest, I walked toward her wide, blue, almond-shaped eyes and we fell into a tumble of arms. It was an emotional thing to be in attendance when golf takes possession. Ann was excited but she didn't realize, as I did, that her life had changed. She didn't hear "the drums go bang and the cymbals clang." She was just pleased to have pleased me so much.

We had a grand day. Dorothy left us after nine holes for the tearoom in Batchwood Hall. Ann bought a nine-hole ticket, three Penfold golf balls and a glove, and with Dorothy's clubs, we set off again. I observed that Ann had become adept at making a whiff look like a practice swing, until I realized it was her practice swing, executed with the all-out determination of a real stroke. She raced after her errant shots, always returning in nothing flat, with the ball in her hand. At the 12th hole she began to lose heart and said, "Won't I ever hit another good one?" Maybe it was time I spoke up, I decided. I asked her if she remembered what her swing felt like when she nailed it.

"Yep," trying to cheer me with some American mimicry because she thought her game was depressing me. It wasn't, but I could feel my energy flowing in her direction.

"Well, feel it again!"

She stood over the ball, her stance narrower and more ladylike than I would have liked. She stuck out her behind, keeping the line of her back straight as a ruler. Then she relaxed her muscles, her head lifted, her neck stretched out, and finally her shoulders circled and fell in a smooth motion rather like an ostrich. I wondered if she had got that from me or thought of it herself.

She hit the sweet spot. *Wow*, I thought, with envy. Aloud, I said, "A hit like that can come untethered."

"Sorry?" which was English for "I don't understand."

"Oh, nothing—just a joke. It's something someone said to me once. If we get up there and can't find your ball, we'll know it got away, found a Kalusa-Klein tower of nongravitational forces and zipped off to God knows where."

I noted what was right about her stroke so I could feed it back to her in time of need. She had taken the club back high and at the top of her swing the clubhead pointed straight toward the flagstick. When she finished her swing the club was wrapped around her ear. What happened in between, I had no idea. But she looked right—relaxed, balanced. As we moved from hole to hole she gained consistency and, as so often happens, she parred the most difficult hole on the course. Naturally, she nearly whiffed her next stroke in a spray of mud.

"Damn!" said she, and I knew we had ourselves a golfer. *I didn't even have to wish for it*, I thought carelessly. Then I realized how wrong I was, as I remembered Mr. Ryder fleetingly with an anticipation I hadn't felt since my guests arrived.

~

THE VICAR AND I, BUNDLED against the cold, walked through the majestic larch trees at the back of the 3rd green toward our favorite view of St. Albans huddled on the horizon above the 4th fairway. Basil shouldered our bags. Nigel was in school these cool autumn days and his older brother had inherited the job. Nothing about golf impressed Basil. The weight of our bags was not as heavy as the stoicism that bore upon his narrow frame. I missed Nigel who had liked golf and seemed to root for me in moments of intense competition. I asked the Vicar, after one embarrassing display of partisanship, if he minded. He replied, somewhat cryptically I thought, that it only proved the validity of his profession, for what man would need religion if he were without weakness.

"I aim for the cathedral," the Vicar announced as usual, as he faced the view. He teed his ball, stood behind it, positioned his clubhead and stepped into his stance. He waggled, swooped, and cracked the ball gently. I watched it climb toward the abbey.

"What must it have been like for Samuel Ryder—a Nonconformist in a cathedral town?" I asked.

He looked at me carefully as if to measure the extent of his answer. "Well, we didn't burn our heretics in Sam's day, if that is what you are getting at. But we did our best to make Nonconformists feel uncomfortable—they were not much better than Catholics and Jews in the eyes of a good Anglican. And, I can tell you, it was no easy job telling one of them from us, since all white people look alike."

I laughed. "I like that. May I quote you?"

"If you like. Best wait a few years. But to answer your question, Sam's oldest daughter Marjorie—lives in Harpenden—Marjorie has told me there was a hard line drawn between church and chapel in those days. They shopped denominationally, going to Mr. Watson, the Congregationalist, for draperies rather than to Mr. Green, the churchwarden of the abbey. That sort of thing. When Sam became mayor in 1905, tradition demanded he escort the town corporation to his church, Trinity Congregational Church, the first Sunday he was in office. Councillors, aldermen, and officers clearly disliked their task, but after the service they had to admit they had been impressed. Even Alderman Hurlock was surprised it had been so Christian.

"I always believed Sam and his family enjoyed the religious dissent of their Quaker and Wesleyan ancestors. They were, after all, dissenting against men, not God. Sam had a deeper well of determination and commitment for all that, I think. He said Anglicans never did enough for the poor, especially the children. He grumbled about it all the time, and, to be truthful, I believe the structure of the Church of England prevented it from doing the kind of thing Sam had in mind. So Sam rolled up his sleeves and did what he could himself, ran an excellent Sunday school system, and proceeded to do everything he could through politics, his chapel, and his own pocket. I might add, he did it in full partnership with his wife and daughters."

The Vicar broke off when we arrived at my tee, located some 30 yards forward but 10 feet below his tee. The distance advantage was clearly negated by the drop in elevation. Furthermore, it had been built at the left side of a left-sloping

fairway so that to reach my landing area I had to drive somewhat diagonally upward into the hill. If I had aimed straight toward the cathedral tower as the Vicar had done, my ball would have come to rest in the left rough. "Nothing is as straightforward for women as it is for men, is it?" I sighed aloud.

"Sorry, my dear?" he said, uncomprehending. "Oh, well done," he added after my drive rolled to a stop just short of his.

As we walked forward, I said, "I heard somewhere that Sam Ryder and his brother James acted together in helping professional golfers. I wonder if the "Ryder" in Ryder Cup doesn't represent both men," I ventured.

"Oh, I don't think so. As I recall, the words engraved on the Cup are:

PRESENTED BY SAMUEL RYDER ESQ JP. OF ST. ALBANS
TO THE PROFESSIONAL GOLFERS' ASSOCIATION
OF GREAT BRITAIN MAY 1927

The Vicar speculated that the brothers broke off their partnership as joint patrons of golf in early 1926 because they were not of the same philosophical mind: James was in it for the advertising and Sam was in it out of compassion. The original 1923 Heath and Heather Tournament, the one that was filmed, brought good advertising for the firm, but some of the lesser Heath and Heather challenges of '24 and '25 did not, perhaps to the disenchantment of James's wife Alice, an excellent businesswoman.

"We know that Abe moved to St. Albans in late 1925 to work for Sam," he said. "It's not generally known, however, that *both* brothers together approached Abe with their offer of employment in the autumn of 1925. Dora Mitchell, Abe's wife, told me so. But then something happened a short time later, probably during the initial planning stages for the Ryder Cup, and James withdrew. James may have wanted a trophy to be called the Heath and Heather Cup, or something of the sort. Well, Sam wasn't about to be a part of anything that smacked of commercialism, when his purpose was to convince English amateur golfers that their professional counterparts belonged in the highest ranks of golf. The English amateur, you see, believed he owned golf, and those who made money off the game were no better than his servants. This had a most stultifying effect on aspiring professionals. By comparison, professionals in America flourished in an egalitarian climate that had encouraged Walter Hagen and his fellow Americans to assault our shores and carry off our Open trophy. We British watched, dismayed, as our famous professionals grew old with no one to replace them, except Abe Mitchell and George Duncan. When the Heath and Heather competitions failed to improve the image and status of professionals, Sam, prodded by Hagen, through Mitchell and Duncan, and various news publications, decided to support an international match for professionals, like the Walker Cup. It would challenge young pros to qualify for the team and, at the same time, expose them to some American self-respect, particularly when they travelled to your country. But the important thing for Sam was that, if he donated a trophy, it must not be construed as an advertising tool. It must be a privately donated trophy, just as amateur trophies were donated privately. Prize money for the contestants would also be counterproductive to his purpose.

"Now that I've burdened you with all that history," the Vicar continued. "here is some apocrypha for you. There has long been a rumour that the present lid of the Ryder Cup is not the original one, that it was replaced at one time or another. When and for what reason no one seems to know. It's not important, I suppose, but I'm curious as a cat about things like that. Sometimes the answers to such questions reveal more than one imagines.

"Back to Marjorie—she has wonderful tales to tell. Especially interesting to me is one about Sam and his close friend Arthur Faulkner who, like Sam, was a wealthy Nonconformist, mayor, and all that. But, unlike Sam, Faulkner was obsessively opposed to drink. One story goes that when they served on the bench together, Sam particularly infuriated Arthur by his leniency toward a gipsy woman found intoxicated and singing on St. Peter's Street. Perhaps it was just such instances of tolerance that influenced Faulkner because here's the thing: he was treasurer to Thomas Cook, a like-minded teetotaler who inaugurated temperance outings called 'Band of Hope.' That's how Cook made his start in the travel business. I have often wondered if Sam, through Arthur, didn't introduce tolerance into the business, making Thomas Cook's the most successful travel firmmmmm..." The Vicar's voice began to fade. As I lost the thread of what he was saying, I recalled the purpose of the morning and what was supposed to happen on the 4th hole. Before I had time to perish from excitement, I quietly joined my companions on the 1st tee of the Royal Ashdown Forest golf course. As it happened, they were too busy talking to notice my arrival.

The Game

ABE CALMLY POLISHED THE head of his driver as he listened to what Mr. Ryder was saying. A single bag of clubs lay on the ground between the two men, who were unmindful of my presence. "Lord Derby knows this Jack Nicklaus personally, so Nicklaus is our man. Don't you agree?" Mr. Ryder asked me, as if I'd been there the whole time.

"Agree to what?"

"We are choosing another Instrument of Fate, my dear, but we'll discuss it another time. Now it's time to play! We'll play a threesome—our ball against Abe's. How does that sound?"

"I like it, Mr. Ryder!" I said, trying to match his high spirits.

"If we're going to be partners you must call me Sam. I told Abe to call me Sam but he would never do it."

"I like your red coat, Sam."

"Yes. I wore it for you. On the sandy wastes of Scotland the red coat signified there were golfers approaching, a warning to strollers, picnickers, archers, and others to watch their heads."

I gazed across the landscape. The moorlike setting, almost devoid of trees, was obscured here and there by a stationary cloud pinioned to a hilltop. Remnants of mist blanketed the low ground, waiting for the sun to do its work. The heather's purple flower, faded and dried, and fern in its wintry bracken hues, guarded the narrow fairways side to side. An untamed stream, awaiting the unarmed golfer, worked its way through the lowest elevations, and gorse waited dangerously at the verge.

Abe moved behind me and stood at my shoulder. He raised his arm and swept the horizon with his hand. "Welcome to Royal Ashdown Forest. I read somewhere the reason I drove the ball so far was that I felled the trees. Well, I can't take the credit. There *were* no trees on Ashdown Forest to speak of, not for centuries. Over there," he pointed, "lies the Royal Ashdown Ladies Course, only the second such in England when it was built.

"Now let me warn you—I know this place like the back of my hand, so you and the boss will need—how many strokes would you say?" he asked Sam. "Ten bisques sound right?"

"Nine will do," I shot back at him in fun. My heart surged with pleasure at this strange camaraderie.

"You'll get no run here, mind you, but then again, you won't have to contend with bunkers either. Bunkers not allowed by order of the Royal Conservators, although I have seen a few come and go in my time."

He lifted a wooden-shafted brassie from our common golf bag. "Here, I want you to try this. I suggest you use it off the tee *and* the fairway." I took the leather grip in my hands and swung the club a few times. The head was larger than I was used to, yet it was not heavy. In fact, it was so well balanced it seemed to swing itself.

"Did you make this?" I asked.

"I did. I made it for you. For myself I make a driving club with a shaft like a weaver's beam, the head weighing 15 ounces even with a little lead taken out. But for you, something light and supple."

"Thank you, Abe. Um, what's a bisque?"

"It's a handicap scheme," Sam broke in. "At threesomes—our ball against Abe's—Abe will give us strokes, called bisques in this case, according to our handicaps. Now, let's see—bogey at Royal Ashdown is 75 and par is 67. Abe would be expected to card a 62. Right, Abe?" Abe nodded. "You, perhaps an 81, and I am at bogey. That would give our team 16 handicap strokes. However, we have the advantage of calling in our bisques whenever we choose, even after a hole is over. In these generous circumstances we will take only 8 bisques off Abe."

"What's it mean, 'bogey is 75?'" I asked. Tony had often referred to "bogey" in a puzzling way and I had yet to understand his explanations. To me, "bogey" meant only one thing: one over par.

Sam was patently intent on starting our game and not wasting time otherwise. "Bogey," he began resignedly, "is a score that a *very good golfer*, playing flawless golf, would be expected to make at a hole. 'Par,' on the other hand, is a mechanical measurement based on driving distance of a scratch golfer, a formula that doesn't measure the difficulty of a hole. On some holes bogey is the same as par, but generally, an overall bogey score will add up to from five to ten strokes higher than par. As you can see, this overall ratio of bogey to par actually describes the difficulty of a golf course and therefore golf courses can be statistically compared.

"Now this should please you," he elaborated despite his eagerness to play. "Before the turn of the century someone of your fair sex, Issette Pearson, captain of the Ladies' Golf Union, used this—let's call it 'bogey rating'—to set forth a reliable handicapping and rating scheme among LGU member clubs, an achievement in uniformity that the men failed to do until many years later."

With that, he thrust a ball in my hand. "You start us off, then."

I looked ahead for a women's teeing ground before I remembered there would be no such thing. For some reason this did a great deal for my attitude and I hit the ball a ton, square and long and slightly left with the club Abe had made for me. Then it was Abe's turn. *Thwack!* Henry Longhurst, among others, had said he would know the sound of Abe striking a golf ball anywhere.

Sam and I walked the narrow pathways that meandered through the heather to look for our ball that had dribbled out of sight. We found it in a tangle of dried blossoms. Unplayable, we decided. Sam found some short grass on a line that extended from the flagstick through our unplayable ball. He picked up the ball and dropped it in a good lie for a stroke penalty. He played a superb mid-iron to the edge of the green, posed on his follow-through, and raised his brows in mock surprise, a gesture I had come to recognize.

"I missed you, Sam—once in a while."

"That's allowable, I guess. But you mustn't daydream, remember."

I was impressed by his swing. He was obviously a born athlete. It looked to me as if the power and accuracy of his stroke was built on the simple, rhythmic weight shift and arm movement of a pitch shot, gradually lengthened in practice to a full swing.

Abe meanwhile had a short pitch to the green and was in for four to our five. My partner and I agreed to collect a handicap stroke—bisque—for a half. And so we worked our way around the outward nine of Royal Ashdown, conspiring against Abe who simply amazed us. There was no hiding it from each other: we both wanted Abe to win—but not to the extent he was doing.

At the short 6th hole, Sam pulled his mashie across the island green into the creek. I dropped behind the water into coarse grass growing against my stroke where my angle of approach left no green to work with. I took a death grip on my niblick, swayed, looked up and chunked the ball back into the stream. It was then that I received some silent advice from Abe, "Move *within* yourself." Sam immediately claimed the hole.

"Hold on," Abe objected. "The *Rules of Golf* do not contemplate *telepathic* advice."

"You may be right," Sam conceded. "In any case, since the advice is good we will withdraw the claim." I laughed appreciatively at the sobriety of the exchange.

Abe had a tale to tell at every hole, delaying our progress to show us a pile of stones where a house once stood or an old marking deep within the bracken where a small private railroad, one-half mile long, once crossed the course from the Broadstone estate. At the 7th hole he walked us to a ditch. It was from this ditch, he said, that the Reverend Williams had foozled his ball directly into the fundament of a grazing outside agency with a full udder; once the startled animal recovered from her surprise, Abe's aunt Polly Mitchell retrieved, cleaned, and returned the ball to the Reverend Williams and, by doing so, enhanced her reputation as one of Royal Ashdown's best caddies.

At the 8th hole I learned that Horace Hutchinson, the versatile authority on all aspects of golf during the game's initial surge to popularity before and after the turn of century, and the first Englishman to captain the R&A, lived just across the valley at Coleman's Hatch. It was Horace Hutchinson, Abe said, who recruited him three times, first in 1910, to play for England in the amateur international team match against Scotland, an experience that had so impressed Abe that its effect extended to the founding of the Ryder Cup. I learned that A. A. Milne lived somewhere at the edge of Ashdown Forest, and it was hereabouts that Christopher Robin and Pooh organized their "expotitions" and Eeyore lost his tail.

As we approached the 13th tee Abe was visibly anticipating something ahead. He smoothed his mustache as he peered toward the distant green. Suddenly, behind us, there was a great thrashing of breaking sticks and growling dogs. I wheeled around and there on the hill behind the 12th green loomed an ageless madman in a top hat and flowing overcoat, menacing us with a long staff, while his agitated animals milled about his legs.

"You've no right!" he bellowed at us as he staggered precariously among his noisy dogs. "You've no right!"

"It's old Grievous," Abe told us. "George Heasman. He lives in a caravan and finds golf balls to sell. He never worked in an accepted way other than to go to war. There are others like Grievous who, as we say, control their destiny—living deep within the Forest, lifting a turnip now and then from a farmer's field for a rabbit stew, buying only sugar, tea, and a bit of drink to ease the joints."

"George, it's me. It's Abe! Abe Mitchell!" George fell silent then, as if reassured. Abe, his voice level, called to him, "Go home, Grievous, go home."

When Grievous turned away, Abe once more directed his vigilance toward the 13th green. "This hole is called the 'Apollyon,' so watch yourselves." His excitement was contagious.

"What is it?" I whispered to Sam.

"Abe was born over there across this small valley—he likes to show off in front of his relatives. You'll see."

While Abe teed his ball, several heads peered over the rise 355 yards beyond. Then more heads came into view as he took his stance. He hit a spectacular drive over the creek, over the first landing area and into the uphill slope of the second fairway.

"Even when I see it," said Sam, "I can't believe it. It's simply not possible to fly a ball that far. I was at Royal Lytham when he hit the very best shot of his life. At least he said it was, and so it must have been, because we never found it." Sam looked at me. "We supposed it had come untethered and escaped into the lap of God."

Abe's gallery saw some pitiful golf from Sam and me as our partnership went into decline. We took three strokes to reach Abe's ball and after he pitched to within inches of the cup, we wisely conceded the hole. Abe picked up our bag and the three of us walked up the hill together toward the small crowd of men, women, and children. His demeanor expressed nothing of a hero to the gathering. Sam told me that they once greeted Abe with a brass band at the railway station in Forest Row after he had won yet another famous challenge.

A lad of seven or eight escaped from restraining hands and ran toward us.

"'Lo there, George," Abe said, man to man. To us he said, "This is my sister Mabel's lad. George, this is Mrs. Winchester and Mr. Ryder." We got a quick nod. "He'll make a fine golfer one day. Won't you, George?"

"Uncle Abe, you hit nearest my mark! I won the bets!"

"Leave them be, George, 'til they've done," someone called.

"We've done, Sophe," Abe called back. "That's my sister Sophe Seymour, one of the best golfers that ever was, man or woman. She was on Fred Robson's professional staff at Cooden Beach. After the war Fred, Sophe, our brother Mark Seymour and I took great pleasure in playing the Kentish courses together. Mark won the amateur Gold Vase in 1921, 11 years after I did. He went on to make a fine reputation in Scotland—Scottish professional champion three times. And there's 'Twine'—could have been a pro but his health never recovered from the war."

The gallery closed in on Abe, while Sam and I wandered off toward the 14th tee, through a settlement of crofts with a cow or two, a few hens, geese, and pigs mucking about the gardens. He showed me George Mitchell's house where the infant Abe

lived before his mother married Mark Seymour, Sr. Abe had been born at his Aunt Emily's house in East Grinstead. He showed me a small dam Abe had built as handyman at Broadstone, where his stepfather Mark Seymour, Sr. had been bailiff, before he kept the green at Royal Ashdown.

Abe and his followers were waiting for us on the tee of the 14th hole, a 215-yard downhill par-3 hole that was intimately understood by those who lived nearby. They watched Abe hit a high fade to within five feet of the hole. Sam had a decent drive but short. It would not be good enough for a half unless I pitched it close. The gallery descended to my ball as one and watched me closely while I executed my favorite shot. I laid back the face of my niblick and flipped the ball gracefully off a fluffy lie. It landed softly and rolled to a stop directly between Abe's ball and the hole. Well, you would have thought I had invented the wheel, such were the oohs and aahs of appreciation.

"'Ello. What's all this, then?" Abe declared when he saw what I had done. "Laid me a stymie, 'as she?" The Foresters laughed and Abe marched up and down assessing his options. Finally he selected his niblick, opened the blade and snicked the ball over mine to within two inches of the hole. Sam, now stymied, drew his forehead into a frown and gave our ball a gentle tap into the back of Abe's ball, holing both balls, a successful negotiation since, knowing full well the foolishness of leftovers should the match end abruptly, we spent our last bisque for a half.

On the 15th tee Abe was only two up as he addressed the ball. He was about to initiate the backswing when he stopped and beckoned me to stand where I could clearly see the flight of his ball. Then he concentrated again and struck the ball. It soared. Just as it reached its zenith it slowly tended toward a white cottage sitting cozily at the boundary of the course. As we watched, someone said, "No." Another groaned. There was a palpable sense of the inevitable in the crowd as the ball flew through a small window to the sound of breaking glass.

"George, you run ahead. See that no one's hurt. That was Kit Heasman's kitchen window that took my ball," Abe explained to me, "and Kit is not an easy woman. She's kind but she's not easy. Everyone needs a Kit Heasman in his life. It's good for the soul."

"Heasman?" I said.

"A good Sussex name," Abe responded.

"She'll castrate ya for this one, Abe," someone called as we moved toward the small white cottage. Sure enough, the nice lady coming at us, carrying a large bowl and brandishing a wooden spoon, looked as if she had it in mind.

"Abe Mitchell, you bastard!" she yelled at him, and everybody laughed because it was true. "Look what you've done. Spoiled the pudding, haven't you? What did you say?"

"I didn't say anything, Missus. I'll have the window fixed in no time."

"What about my pudding?" she nagged. "How am I to mix my Sunday pud with glass and golf balls in. What! Your mum would be ashamed of you."

Abe hung his head and stuttered a few words of apology but it did no good and he moved quickly away from her persistent whine in a most cowardly and unmanly fashion, at least in the eyes of young George, who thought his uncle should have shown a modicum of self-defense.

"I suppose I'll have to fix the window myself as if I hadn't enough to do. You hear me, Abe Mitchell?" she shouted at his back as he melted into the crowd that had come to see the show.

Sam and I won that hole since Abe hadn't played another ball and Kit's pudding was out-of-bounds.

When we arrived at the 16th teeing ground nothing would do but that Sam and I meet the Cantelupe Golf Club in a reception line of sorts that had materialized for the occasion of our visit. Abe ushered us over and introduced us in timeless disorder. Alf Padgham whose name I knew—Open Champion and Ryder Cup player—was standing by his widely admired nephew Hector Padgham, professional at Royal Ashdown. Hector informed me that he was taught to play golf by the two ladies next to him, his mother and sister, prominent members of the Harebells, the feminine wing of the Cantelupe. Next to them, another Harebell, Mrs. Slow, who was quick to point out that she was the *wife* of Mr. Slow. Jack Smith stood by her side, an incredibly big, handsome man, winner of the World's Longest Driving title at the 1922 and 1924 Open Championships with a driver made for him by Abe. Jack, Abe informed me, was denied the opportunity of competing as an amateur because he breached a rule of amateur status when he carried clubs for profit at the age of 14. Next to him was Harry Underwood, young George's father, a man of some unreliability but admired for his game all the same. And there was Kit Heasman, smiling and sweet. They told me her strange wheedling sounds hid a generous heart. There were more Mitchells and Seymours than I could sort out except for the Mark Seymours, father and son, and Abe's mum Polly Mitchell Seymour at the end of the line.

Abe introduced us to his stepfather Mark Seymour, explaining it was this man who had negotiated the founding of the Cantelupe. He turned a potential threat into a bloody miracle, when the toffs, without a clear right to do so, set down their golf course on protected land, a fact that Grievous and his frightful dogs had challenged near the 12th green.

Sam said to him, for my benefit I think, "Mr. Seymour, sir, I blame you for the existence of the Ryder Cup." Then, while Sam was talking, I slipped away from the scene without any warning whatsoever. *Not another power failure*, I thought, as I fought to hang on just a little longer.

"Such a serious expression, my dear. It's only a game."

It was the Vicar, and we were on the 4th hole at Verulam. I could have cried with frustration. My heart was pounding in my chest and all my switches were on high. I was breathless.

"Would you mind ringing Mrs. Claisen?" I asked the Vicar. "Tell her who I am and that I would like to talk to her about her father. Then, if she wouldn't mind, I'll call her, and invite her to tea or something. Do you know, I've never made a real cup of tea in my life? I have a tea service. I brought it from the States. Art Nouveau. It's Mother's—she thought I should have a tea service in England. What sort of tea, do you think? What's a good time? I've heard that the English don't use lemon. And the scones, or is it crumpets? Where do I get them?"

I was very near tears for no reason. The Vicar searched my face and urgently interrupted. "Since we are near the club-house, why don't we leave off our golf game and go in? I have a feeling it is the right thing to do."

Captain Mitchell

BEFORE THE DAY WAS OUT I WAS in the care of Tony's family doctor, a man, Tony assured me, of some reliability on the golf course and therefore in life. I was hospitalized and the staff was set to bustling on my behalf. After two days of observation and tests they were still puzzled. Machines that gauged my functions printed out gibberish. I could have told them about my electrical system but I didn't bother. Steve and I were the least distressed of the players moving steadily in and out of the pale green hospital corridors, despite the whispered consultations. I asked Sam if he knew what was wrong, and he said he did.

Sam and Abe had appeared beside my bed four days into my week-long stay, just when my bravery level was getting low. I knew they were coming. I had been given my premonition. To prepare for them I combed my hair, smoothed the bedcovers, and watered a plant on my bedside table. Steve had brought it—a cyclamen with shy white blossoms that gracefully nodded in quiet contemplation. It was meant to calm me, according to a small card slipped between the leaves, written by Adele, Steve's indispensable secretary.

Abe was looking particularly intrepid, I thought, as he smiled at me by way of greeting. Sam had given the whiskers of his mustache a one-sided twirl that looked smart, indeed. He explained that my unplanned departure from Ashdown Forest had been caused by an energy that I had not been exposed to before.

"Will I recover?"

"I don't see why not. You may even benefit from it. Your active participation in our recent adventure required a different energy but now that it has been introduced into your system, it will be easier the next time.

"A golf game, you see,"—Sam, like Steve, had a compulsion to explain things—"is an external experience in space, for a length of time. In order for you to take part in our complex episode, we used a refinement of your mentation not unlike imagination and memory, two inner processes that have no space-time restrictions. Since we are 'merely'—your word—a sea of rippling charges organized at various levels of energy, it may have confused your circuitry. In any case we will stay in your dimension for the time being."

"Mentation? I've heard you use that word before. What does it mean?" I asked.

"It's his favourite subject," Abe informed me.

"I suppose it is," Sam agreed. "Mentation means 'minding,' a verbal noun: the process of minding. It is an integrated system of minds that controls a single living organism. It operates on the simple principle of impulse and response, action and reaction. Mankind, unlike other life forms, has a *thinking* mind as a part of his mentation, which, when tuned to the other minds of his system—movement, instinct, emotion—opens doors to all his human possibilities. Harmonious integration of the thinking mind within the process of mentation can occur only with effort of a kind you know nothing about."

"Why does it take so much effort?"

19: *Captain Mitchell*

"*Because*," he emphasized in a whisper, "unless you work to become aware of your automatic reactive system, you will remain at the mercy of it. You must work to understand your mentation so that you can act independently of it.

"Man's mentation, as I said, includes a mind that thinks. He assumes, therefore, that because he can 'think,' he has control over himself and his situation, that he can avoid reacting and responding. But it simply is not true. Man is not conscious enough to see that his behavior and so-called 'thinking' is nothing more than the action-reaction response he was born with. Human mentation that proceeds without consciousness is the cause of 'inhuman' behavior."

"You should mention also," Abe added, "that whether you are conscious or not, it makes no difference to Mother Nature. She gets to use your bones in any case. But it does make a difference to God because God gets to use the energy of your consciousness to maintain the universe."

"I think I'm beginning to understand."

"Well, the Lord be thankful," Sam said and laughed at himself.

Abe turned away and walked to the window. He stood there for a time looking out, his hands clasped behind his back. "I was in this hospital. Late May, early June in 1927. I was supposed to be in Massachusetts playing on the first Ryder Cup team to travel to America, but instead, the 'Mighty Captain' was having his appendix removed. Appendix, for God's sake!" His eyes narrowed as he stared at the horizon beyond the abbey tower. Then he faced Sam and made a self-deprecating sound. "I could have willed that sickness away, you know. I have always thought so, and I was never reconciled that I was unable to do it. Oh, I know. I heard your words: 'We accomplished what we set out to do, Abe,' you said. 'It makes no difference whether we win or lose, it's the doing that counts, with or without us.' That is what you said.

I knew your disappointment was not for yourself, but for me."

"Abe." Sam stopped him. The moment was so heavy that I surmised the words had never been said between them. Sam stared at his hands, then he added quietly, "My friend, there wasn't one of us who didn't understand and feel your anguish. Except me." It was an admission.

After another pause, Sam addressed me briskly, "One thing is certain: no one over here gave a tinker's damn that we lost that Ryder Cup at Worcester, because by then we knew Abe was out of danger."

"When did you actually know it was appendicitis?" I asked Abe.

"You know, I was in such a fog that I can't remember. But I had been plagued by pain long before departure. I wasn't right during the *Daily Mail* tournament two weeks before."

"Which he won, by the way," Sam interjected.

"The last I was able to play was at Verulam the following week—Duncan and I lost to the Whitcombe brothers. During the afternoon match, I could not keep down what little I had eaten at lunch. Dora made me see our doctor. X-rays suggested kidney trouble—nothing new for me. I'd been playing through kidney problems since 1921. I attended to affairs as best I could, but my spells became more frequent and Dora thought I had a fever. Certainly, I was not getting better. I told Duncan how sick I was, knowing he should be captain if I could not, but he said he wouldn't have the heart for it if I wasn't there. Ted Ray, pipe clenched in his teeth, then consented to lead the team.

"Three days before the ship sailed for America, May 18th, I think it was, I stood around and watched our team play in a 36-hole send-off competition at Verulam. Afterward, at a luncheon ceremony for the players and guests, Mrs. Ryder opened a large box from Mappin and Webb. She removed the tissues one by one, then lifted the trophy from the box. She

said a few formal words about giving ownership of the Cup to the Professional Golfers' Association of Great Britain and handed it to George Gadd, saying she was presenting the Ryder Cup on behalf of her husband. After the applause and some polite cheers, everyone was curious to see the Cup and it was passed amongst the guests; some rose from their chairs and gathered in groups. Words of praise and other soft-spoken phrases I didn't understand drifted by me. 'Will you look at that?' 'Upon my word, it's Abe.' 'By heaven, it is.' Then my old friend Fred Robson had it in his hand. He brought it 'round the table for me to see. I hadn't seen it for a year and didn't remember it was so beautiful. Maybe I cried. Some say I did—I can't imagine it. I don't know. Fred whispered, 'It's you, Abe. You see?' I didn't understand and looked across the table at the chief. He had been smiling at me, pleased, I guess, that the Ryder Cup was now official. That's the last I remembered until I awoke in my bed at home. I've seen a photograph to commemorate the occasion where I'm seated next to the boss, holding the Cup in my lap, but I had no memory of it being taken. Dora told me I had appendicitis and must have an operation. I said it would have to wait until the boys sailed."

Sam took up the story. "I was there beside his bed when he said it. Dora looked to me for help but, instead of helping, I suggested we play it by ear. He might regain his strength with a good night's rest and staying in bed. Abe was powerless to disagree.

"On Sunday morning Dora and Abe took a taxi to the St. Albans station. I met them there. It was one of the few sensible things I did—not insist on driving to the ship. The long, rough motorcar ride surely would have killed him. On the train he and Dora sat quietly in a compartment. Team members, in ones and twos, visited Abe briefly on the pretext of seeking advice, in order to wish their 'captain' a quick recovery. Fred Robson was particularly shaken by Abe's condition and came to me about it. I assured him I was equally concerned and everything possible would be done for Abe. I remember he looked at me hard and long—deciding, I suppose, that I had lost my reason and it would do no good to argue.

"It wasn't a long train ride and we were soon aboard the *Aquitania*, but anyone could see that Abe should not have been there. He was an apparition, drawn and wasted inside his long overcoat. He stood in front of a crowd, gathered to give the team a warm farewell but by the look in his eye I sensed he was elsewhere in his mind."

Sam described how Duncan spoke poignantly about how much they valued Abe who would be with them in spirit at

Worcester, lining up their putts and seeing them dead in the hole. Sam said that George Philpot, the team manager and editor of *Golf Illustrated*, carried the Ryder Cup in his arms, Abe's small gold figure cradled in the palm of his hand. George promised to bring it back. "After all," he had said, "we are much the same team that vanquished the Americans a year ago at Wentworth." John Henry Taylor, speaking for Harry Vardon and James Braid, the men who had selected Captain Mitchell and his team, assured the team that Ted Ray would captain them to victory.

"Then we left them to their departure celebrations. George Duncan helped us get Abe aboard the return train where, mercifully, he collapsed in Dora's arms. As steam rolled past the windows and obscured my last view of the ship, I looked at Abe and Dora and wondered at the shocking tableau before me. Slowly my mind cleared of sentimental nonsense and I saw what I had done to my friend. Where had I been? What senseless aim had so possessed me that I was blind to his mortal danger? He was going to die.

"I sat stunned across from Dora in the railway carriage and watched her tears and wished that I could cry. Tears came easily to me. At Stratford I always cried when the stage curtain fell on the death of yet another tragic hero. But when the hero dies before the play begins, what was one to do? Dora must have read my utter despair for she set Abe's head on a pillow and moved beside me. She took my hand and said, 'You mustn't blame yourself. You could not have changed his mind.'"

With that, Sam ended his story and he looked at me in silence. Satisfied with my response, he handed me his ever-ready lisle handkerchief to blot the glisten in my eyes.

"The British team lost badly, didn't it?" I said, subdued.

"9½ to 2½, and for the strangest reason," Sam answered. "A *New York Times* headline read 'Poor Putting Lost for British.'

The news story went on to describe how the British were consistently on the greens closer to the hole than the Americans but then they would three-putt from incredibly short distances, leaving the ball short again and again. Can you imagine why? Well, Ted Ray explained it to me shortly after they returned home.

"'It started,' Ted said, 'on the fourth day at sea when Fred Robson, no drunker than the rest of us, reminded the team of George Duncan's departure speech, about how Abe would be with us in spirit, lining up our putts and seeing them dead in the hole. Fred had got it in his head, you see, that if our putts started to drop, it would mean Abe had died and his spirit was guiding our putts into the hole. Duncan insisted he meant no such thing, but to humour Fred we solemnly allowed that his theory might be true all the same. Then, as reasonable men, we dismissed it. But, do you know, that little suggestion worked its way into our heads, slowly taking dead aim on the purpose of our putting strokes. Here,' Ted said, 'I brought you a clipping from the *New York Times* by William D. Richardson,' and he read it to me:

> It was no uncommon sight to see one of the visitors take three putts from within thirty, nay twenty, feet of the pin... The putting malady that seemed to affect the visitors was the worst form of such an affliction, namely, that of being forever on the short side of the hole. Most of their putting mistakes came in not giving the ball a chance, or even half a chance, to get up to the hole. That, of course, is fatal since the hole itself is stationary.

" 'But that was just it, wasn't it?' Ted concluded."

The Haig

Abe filled the water glass on my bedside table and handed it to me. "You played on other Ryder Cup teams," I said to him, "so why weren't you captain another time?"

Sam answered. "We never asked him."

"Dora told them not to ask me again," Abe said. "I was in a coma after the operation and Dora watched over me day after day. They said she held me, told me stories and sang little songs. She believed it was her singing that brought me back to life. One day while she was humming an old Sussex hymn, I opened my eyes and told her to stop. I asked for a cigarette and promised not to die if she would not sing to me any more."

"Don't you believe it," Sam laughed. "But Dora did tell us Abe would rather die than make a speech in public and perhaps we shouldn't press him to be captain."

"What do captains do?" I asked.

Abe put on a face. "They talk," he said. But then he explained that they assign partners at foursomes and determine in what order the players go out. The two captains work separately setting pairings and the playing order, making it an educated guessing game using logic and wiliness.

"You knew Hagen better than anyone," Sam said to Abe, "so it was a pity you were never captain." He turned to me and added, "Walter Hagen was the American Ryder Cup captain for more than a decade. Essentially, he was a one-man committee—choosing his teams, making arrangements, buying their smart wardrobes with his own money—for six Ryder Cups. I wondered at times whether America was taking our Cup seriously. While Walter worked to make the international match a success he also jeopardised it with his adolescent diplomacy. He nearly destroyed efforts toward our first Ryder Cup Match in America."

To illustrate his point Sam said that in 1926 when Bobby Jones won the Open and American players nearly swept the first 10 places—Al Watrous was second and Hagen third—Walter announced to the British press, "I don't believe American golfers will come back for a few years. What's the use of coming over here to play among ourselves? We can do that at home."

"For the life of me," Sam added, "I could not see what he was trying to achieve by such a statement. But, do you know, I always believed his words angered the R&A, who administered the Open. Walter's remarks had followed closely upon a most congenial meeting between the R&A and the USGA at which the two governing bodies of golf agreed to act as one. For the good of the game they would take no unilateral action that would affect the other association, such as setting dates for their national Open Championships. Then Walter said those words. The next thing we knew, the R&A, without consultation, set June 22nd through 24th for its 1927 Open. That did not sit well with the USGA, which promptly set its Open date for June 23rd through the 25th, effectively destroying any chance of a British team travelling to Massachusetts for a

Ryder Cup Match in 1927. Fortunately, the rift was resolved within a reasonable time."

Abe observed that Walter was apt to make unfortunate remarks after a few drinks. Not many people knew that Walter didn't drink or smoke until he was over 25 years old, after he married Margaret Johnson and moved to Detroit. And despite appearances, Abe assured me the martini at the 1st tee box was a hoax, and if Walter stayed up all night it was usually to another purpose.

"I liked Walter," Abe concluded, "if only because he was able to curl up and sleep like a baby, anywhere, anytime. He changed my life for the better several times, and even though he was a devil with his gamesmanship, I enjoyed our matches. With one exception."

"Enough!" Sam said. "He's the only man I chose not to understand simply because I thought it would upset me if I did. He put two and two together and took them apart better than anyone I knew."

"He never broke or bent the *Rules of Golf*," Abe argued, "and no one knew them better. But if it wasn't written down somewhere, watch out. I told Ted Ray this when he took my place as captain. He said he'd played against Hagen for many years and had no reservations. But with all Ted's experience, something went wrong at that first Ryder Cup in America. According to newspaper reports Captain Hagen had trouble making up his mind. Sam handed me a clipping from the *New York Times*, June 6, 1927.

> [Hagen's] initial lineup failed to satisfy the members of the team and it was changed. He then arranged matters so Mehlhorn, instead of Diegel, played the tee shots to the short holes. He also was slow to make up his mind as to the lineups, which did not please the majority of the publicists.

Abe surmised that, in the circumstances, Ted may have revealed his order-of-play prematurely, making it possible for Captain Hagen to place his men to best advantage. If Walter already knew Ted's order before he made his own list, it took away some of the guesswork.

Abe picked up a small folding chair, flipped it open beside my bed, straddled the seat, folded his arms over the backrest, and told me that he had been to Rochester. It was after he and Hagen had both failed to win the Western New York Open Championship at Orchard Park in Buffalo. "Who gives a hoot?" Hagen had said to Abe, and told him to hop in the car and they'd go see where Hagen was born. They drove 90 miles, top down, to Corbett's Glen on the edge of Rochester. Just up the hill from this scenic glen was the Country Club of Rochester where Walter had progressed from caddie to club pro before he was 25. His exposure to the gentlemanly ways of the toffs was much like Abe's, except that Walter was an employee and had never played amateur golf. Abe and Walter often examined their similarities, comparing themselves to Francis Ouimet, the consummate amateur—the 20-year-old store clerk in Brookline who walked across the road from his middle-class house to win the 1913 U.S. Open at The Country Club. Hagen could never figure out why Ouimet never turned pro, while Abe wistfully watched Ouimet's amateur career.

"Francis Ouimet remained an amateur all his life," Abe said. "He put an 'artisan' face on amateur golf in your country, playing on the first eight Walker Cup teams, twice as captain, and even becoming the first American captain of the Royal and Ancient Golf Club at St. Andrews." Saying this, Abe looked at Sam and rolled his eyes comically. "*If only* I hadn't turned professional. If only I had a *second chance*. As an amateur I would have led our British Walker Cup team to victory after victory, beating Francis Ouimet and Bobby Jones at their best. They would have invited me to be Captain of the R&A and..."

"And there never would have been a Ryder Cup," I said and was pleased that I made them laugh. "How did you get to know Walter so well?"

"My career and Walter's," Abe responded, "intersected to the extent that after he won the U.S. Open Championship in Chicago in 1914, Rodman Wanamaker, the Philadelphia department store magnate, invited Walter to help form a professional golfers' association. Walter was one of 35 men who met in New York City in January 1916 to found the PGA of America, with a championship patterned after our British professional championship—a 36-hole elimination match called the *News of the World* PGA Match Play Championship —which I won in 1919, 1920, and 1924."

"Whoa," I said. "You're saying that the *News of the World* is really the PGA of Great Britain Championship?"

"That's what I'm saying. I was invited to America because I was our PGA Champion. When Walter Hagen came to England for the first time for the Open in 1920, he discovered George Duncan, who won that Open that year, and me and arranged a U.S. tour for us through Mr. Wanamaker.

"George and I were fascinated by Hagen. He was a new kind of professional, a rich itinerant pro, an independent businessman. When he arrived at Deal he was a free man with his own publicity writer, H. B. Martin, in tow. It was not an easy concept for British pros to grasp. Very few got the picture when Hagen, with his pal Jim Barnes, drove up in a chauffeured Austin-Daimler and parked outside the front entrance to Royal Cinque Ports clubhouse, a building off-limits to professionals. The limousine was their locker room where they could tidy up and change their shoes.

"The British were not amused," Abe said, noting that J. H. Taylor, for all his fame and income, still thought of himself as Horace Hutchinson's houseboy and caddie at Westward Ho!. Taylor thought Hagen was an impertinence that had no place in golf. "He'd get sacked if he worked for me," J.H. had said. But that was the point, Abe stressed. No one could fire Walter Hagen.

The Haig, the showman, now had a new nickname. The British press called him "Sir Walter." But that wasn't the side that Abe saw. Hagen had eased Abe's defeat at Deal by looking at it another way. "Abraham," Hagen had said, "anyone who can lose so flamingly should be exhibited." That's when Abe decided to like him.

So, George Duncan and Abe Mitchell went to America for three months at a time, doing exhibitions in 1921, 1922, and November of 1924 through March of 1925. They were treated like royalty, especially in Canada where they were sometimes assigned the Royal Suite. They were immensely popular, drew sizable galleries who thought the Englishman charming and the Scotsman hilarious. And they won challenge matches wherever they went and made a lot of money. After they defeated Sarazen and Hagen in a 36-hole match in Florida in December 1924, a *New York Times* sports commentary read:

> Although the prowess of Duncan and Mitchell, Britain's famous golf pair now touring in America, is well known on this side, their defeat of Hagen and Sarazen came as quite a surprise. They won with apparent ease, judging by the score. Further than that Mitchell, on the day before the match, captured the chief prize in the Miami Open.
>
> It is doubtful if there has ever been a pair of golfers who teamed better than do Duncan and Mitchell. When they were here the last time [they] made a record that excelled any previous record made by any pair of tourists and a record that may never be equaled. Few golf professionals are able to go back over beaten paths time and again and remain as big an attraction as

> ever. Mitchell is quiet and unassuming and [has] the ability to knock a golf ball farther [and straight] than almost any other man living.

Abe explained, "Hagen's tour and ours were different but whenever our paths crossed, life improved. One of those times was Buffalo. I remember the Haig was making headlines because he chose to play in Buffalo against Duncan and me rather than defend his PGA Championship title at Oakmont. It was 1922."

"Okay. What *were* you doing in Buffalo?"

"Well, the publisher of the *Buffalo Evening News*, Ganson Depew, had just founded the Western New York Golf Association. And, incidentally, he founded the Women's Golf Association of Western New York at the same time."

"I'm a member! Founded by a man?"

"Mr. Depew staged a 72-hole open championship for his new association, August 17-18, 1922. Using Duncan and me, the British champions, and a healthy purse for two days' work, Hagen was lured away from defending his PGA title, scheduled for August 12-18. Ultimately Hagen won the Wanamaker Cup six times, but he could easily have won more if he had bothered to defend his title. Hagen also chose to play with us the following week at the Shenecossett Links in New London, Connecticut, rather than defend his Western Championship title in Detroit.

"The Western considered its championship almost as important as the U.S. Open, so you can imagine how upset they were to lose their main attraction. Hagen and his road managers Robert E. Harlow and H. B. Martin were viciously attacked. Walter and the newspapers loved it. The Detroit paper wanted Harlow 'out of golf!' Naturally, the *Buffalo Evening News* responded. 'Al Wallace, wealthy Detroit friend of Hagen in high favor, was detailed by the Western to secure

Hagen's appearance in the Western open at whatever cost.' When Wallace approached him in New York with an offer of $1,500 if Hagen would come to Detroit and defend his title, Walter said, 'Too late, I must keep faith with the people with whom I have made contracts.' That is, Hagen passed up an offer that would have paid him much better to have accepted than to have carried out his arrangements with the eastern club, who had meanwhile booked him.

"All this attention generated the desired publicity and gossip which James Harnett of *Golf Illustrated*, Harlow, Martin, Hagen, Duncan, and I reviewed nightly in the bar. We would sit around 'shootin' the breeze,' they called it, and our topics usually included starting an international team competition for pros, such as the amateurs had for themselves in the Walker Cup. We actually played such a match at James Braid's new Gleneagles course the previous summer when the Americans were over for the £2000 Match Play Championship at St. Andrews. Jim Harnett had asked for and received a small amount of money from the PGA of America to help the idea along. We won 9-3. It's interesting that even then, in '21, there was a residence requirement imposed upon the American team members, to prevent the recent influx of Scottish emigrants from using the PGA of America for a free ride back home to see their families."

"Question—before we leave the subject," I said holding up my hand. "Who won the Western New York Open Championship?"

"Duncan won it and for the rest of his life he had to explain where in the world Western New York was. Hagen was second and always blamed his Uncle Henry for it. Uncle Henry Hagen had come over to Orchard Park from his nearby farm to see his nephew play golf, a game about which Uncle Henry knew nothing. He caught up to us near the end of the contest on the 17th hole, as we were looking over our putts.

"'Is that you, Nephew?' Uncle Henry called out as Walter prepared to stroke his putt.

"'What the deuce,' Hagen said, 'it's Uncle Henry,' and his face broke into a big grin. They hugged and patted in the center of the green, Uncle Henry tromping on our lines with his big boots. 'This is my Uncle Henry Hagen, my dad's brother.'

"'Holy cow, you fellas look like them Bloomer girls over there to Newark,' Uncle Henry shouted, looking to the silent spectators to support his opinion of plus fours.

"'Caught your picture in the papers and come right over.' And then to satisfy his puzzled gallery wrapped around the green, he boomed, 'I got a farm over to Ellicott,' and he pointed south.

"To our lasting pleasure the Hagens took about 10 minutes to catch up on their news. Finally, Walter asked his uncle to step aside for a moment and proceeded to three-putt. Since Duncan won the title by five strokes, we were on Uncle Henry's side when he said it wasn't his fault his nephew didn't win."

"I don't believe you, Abe Mitchell."

"God's truth. It was written up in the *Buffalo Evening News* the next day. Now back to the Ryder Cup. It was like the Walker Cup except for its eligibility requirements."

"You keep talking about the Walker Cup. Who was Walker?" I asked.

Sam had been leaning against the wall at the foot of my bed smiling at Abe's story. He pushed himself away and addressed my question.

"Walker was George Herbert Walker, president of the United States Golf Association. He had attended matches between the U.S. and Canada in 1919 and 1920, and been inspired to propose a worldwide annual Challenge Cup. In 1920, the USGA invited all countries to send teams to America to compete in 1921, but so soon after the war no country could afford to accept. Out of sheer enthusiasm, however, William

Fownes, the 1910 U.S. Amateur Champion, rounded up an American team and sailed for England in early spring, 1921, to play at Hoylake for a cup that George Walker had donated. The Americans won 9 to 3. When invitations were issued the following year, Great Britain and Ireland accepted. Again the Americans won. For the first three years the Walker Cup, as it came to be known, was an annual event, but for practical reasons went to a biennial schedule after 1924."

"This put ideas in our heads, especially Walter's," Abe said. "We wanted a professional counterpart to the Walker Cup. I knew from experience that our pros would benefit from playing overseas where class barriers were defined not by occupation, but by nationality. I had no idea I was such a fine fellow until I played in North America where English is the best nationality to be. The Ryders' Heath and Heather exhibitions might improve our games but, to my way of thinking at the time, we should look to competition with America to improve our self-esteem. With this in mind, we persuaded Walter to talk to Mr. Ryder."

In the end it was Walter who convinced Sam Ryder that if something in the spirit of the Walker Cup was going to happen for professionals in Britain, it fell to Sam to do it. Walter told Sam that in England, and to a lesser extent in America, golf professionals were mired in an unfortunate tradition and only Sam could save them. There was a reason, Walter said, why Opens were stroke play championships, while other championships were match play. Open championships were usually conducted by amateur associations—the R&A and the USGA, for example—and "open" to professionals. They were *stroke* play tournaments because amateurs believed that the economic and social disparity between amateurs and professionals made the inherently personal nature of *match* play untenable.

Hagen also pointed out to Sam that the Great Triumvirate,

Vardon, Taylor, and Braid, never shed their servant-class mentality even when they lived like middle-class gentlemen. Vardon, so revered at Ganton and South Herts, never entered the clubhouse by the front door unless he was invited to do so by a member. And Abe as well, for all his honorary memberships. It wasn't the men, it was their occupation that put them, and held them, in place.

In making plans for an international match they discussed remuneration for the winning side. Walter, they discovered, viewed the proposed match less as a sporting event than an exhibition with himself as ringmaster. And he assumed a worthy prize for the winning side. How else to spark interest, he had asked. Abe and Sam countered that in order to emulate the spirit of the Walker Cup, the game should be its own reward, whereupon Walter changed his tune, saying that he, for one, would refuse to play for money. "Money," he said, "would blur the meaning and dull the motivation of such an international rivalry designed to bring our two great countries together in friendship."

"It wasn't until 1926 that we got a chance to implement our plans. The R&A..."

I had closed my eyes, the better to listen, but it worked the other way and everything they said became a muddle. Their voices faded until the last I heard was Sam saying, "I knew that if we kept at it long enough we would put her to sleep." I felt a small tuck at the bed covers and that was it. The nurses said I slept 14 hours without moving a muscle.

Tea

One of the first things I did once I regained my health was visit Marjorie Claisen, nee Lucy Margaret Ryder, Sam's oldest daughter. I rode the few miles to Harpenden on my green Raleigh bicycle. Women on green bicycles, I reasoned, were more credible than women in cars, in case she was uneasy about my visit. The Vicar had arranged it. He had explained that I wanted to inquire about Sam and, bless him, he wangled an invitation to tea for me.

When she opened her door, I could see that my precaution had been unnecessary. We liked each other instantly. There was a direct look in her eye that made me comfortable. Once we were settled among a bewildering assortment of pots, cups and saucers, strawberries, little cakes and scones, I asked myself why I feared this process that seemed like second nature to everyone else. The reason, I decided, was that no one had taught me tea—it was as simple as that. Yet I didn't fear the lake water before I learned to swim, or bicycles, or sex.

"What was your father like, Mrs. Claisen?" I asked, dispensing with the small talk to the point of impropriety.

"Please call me Marjorie." She set her teacup on the table and regarded me. "But tell me first, what has given you this great curiosity about Father?"

"Yes, of course. Forgive me. I should have explained myself, although I'm not at all sure I can. I play golf at Verulam, you see, and I am also a portrait artist. I frequently sit and look at your father's portrait in the dining..."

"Say no more." There was something of Sam in her wry smile. "That painting hung on the wall behind you, right there, and I know what you are going to say. You talk to it, don't you? Well, I did too, and it's one of the reasons I gave it to Verulam. I thought I was losing my moorings."

I confessed to a few words with the portrait and an unaccountable urge to know more about her father. I told her that it had even occurred to me to write about his life.

"Oh?" she said. "Are you a writer?"

"No," and, again, Sam was there in her sidelong glance.

"Well, I'll tell you all I know," she said. There was no hiding her enthusiasm as she launched into what was obviously her favorite subject. "The older I get—I'm 82, mind you—the more convinced I am that Father was the nearest to a saint I have ever found in a long and varied life. I do not mean that he was pious. He was not—his good humour made that impossible. He liked to warn us, in fact, against the man who walked about with a Bible tucked under his arm: 'If he has got a hymnbook as well,' he would say, 'and he has strapped the two together like a schoolboy, he needs watching.'

Father was a compassionate man. But, I must say, if he took a dislike to someone there was no talking him out of it. Usually, however, he had an open mind for everyone, perhaps because, as a boy in Manchester, he helped his mother take food to hungry families during the cotton slump. He saw poverty and hunger but he also saw that the victims were ashamed. His youthful mind contrived that if hunger and poverty were fashionable, there would be no shame and enough food to go 'round. He found it unacceptable that people were valued by the arbitrary standards of British society, and it was this he tried to redress through Sunday schools, politics, the court, and even professional golf. He used to say over the many years he was a county justice that it was his job to *justify*—square up the margins so everyone had a fair shake. The Ryder Cup was just such an attempt at squaring things up. It is God's good joke that Father is remembered for the accomplishment that caused him the least sacrifice and gave him the most happiness."

He loved sports, she recalled, especially cricket. And cars, he loved cars, and a knock of Johnnie Walker whisky before he retired at night. He drove, or had a driver, everywhere he went, except when he took them to the Savoy in a hansom cab for an evening of Gilbert and Sullivan. He played the piano, though not well, but he loved music. Her mother was a pianist, organist, violinist, singer. They had their own in-house quintet: Marjorie played the cello, her mother the violin, Joan helped her father at the piano, and her sister Kit sang. Kit had inherited their mother's voice and, after training, was accepted into the finest choral societies in and around London. She lived in a special world that touched all their lives.

"Kitten wrote a small memoir. If you would care to read it sometime I would gladly lend it to you. She married Roy Barrett. She suffered from harsh asthmatic attacks—died some time ago..." Marjorie's voice trailed off.

"And the theatre. He loved the theatre. He liked to tell us that he and his two younger brothers saved their pennies to see a Saturday matinee in which Editha foiled the burglar who tried to steal her dead mother's candlesticks. It made him cry, he told us proudly. Years later at the Shakespeare festivals, he, like so many others, had script in hand. Shakespeare's characters were his companions, so much so that it broke his heart to see old Falstaff snubbed by the young king. He actually left his seat until the scene was over. He disliked modern plays with one exception. Can you guess which one?" She paused and said, "It was *Charlie's Aunt*. He knew all the jokes—we all did. No one dared mention Brazil nuts.

"I found it curious that his compassion was for rich and poor alike. I asked him once why he did not discriminate amongst the people he helped. 'They are all going to die, you see,' he had answered."

She said it puzzled him that other people were puzzled by his generosity, but he never for a moment let on that he thought others should follow suit. He was a born teacher, she added, who taught his lessons obliquely and by example. If he wanted to make something clear to her, he would explain it to Joan or Kitten in her presence so that she could listen without the need to cloud the issue with a response.

"He simply would not join in if we spoke critically or unkindly of someone. He was a master at putting the foibles of others in perspective by telling us tales that fostered our understanding of human behavior. When our sisterly quarreling became insufferable, he would say some such words as, 'I am destined to die of an overdose of women in my life. You are beyond salvation,' and out he would go, closing the door firmly behind him.

"But we never doubted his love. He had a great depth of feeling for his girls. When Mother sang her sweet, sad Edwardian songs to us at bedtime, I would see him standing in the hallway listening in his special way."

Marjorie said he enjoyed reading aloud to them—Sherlock Holmes, Dickens—stories that he liked, saying he was doing it for himself. *Pilgrim's Progress* was her personal favorite and his, too. She remembered protesting that it wasn't fair that Christian had armor only in the front with no protection on his back when he fought Apollyon. Her father agreed with her but said, "Christian will be all right as long as he *faces* his problems." When she insisted that it was not fair, he answered, "Life is often like that. We will never be disappointed if we don't expect life to be fair, just as we will surely be pleasantly surprised when it is—something I learned on the golf course."

She had observed that he had a curious self-awareness on public occasions that made him incurably theatrical when he played "The Mayor," "The Benefactor," "The Boss," sometimes parodying his role by humourous scowls and uneasy gestures—embarrassed, she supposed, by his own self-pride.

"He went to great pains to share, even give, credit for his work and ideas. A good example is the match at Wentworth in 1926. I've seen it written dozens of times that Major J. H. Hinds and George Duncan promoted it and that 'Sam Ryder *happened* to be in the crowd.' Well, of course he was. He was running the show!

"When Abe Mitchell came into his life in the 1920s, Father retired from most of his public commitments to embrace the cause of professional golf 'with his might,' as he liked to say. Abe became a large factor in all our lives because Father was forever carting us off to watch Abe walk silently about the fairways, 'playing,' as Father put it, 'the finest golf the world had ever seen.' Abe was a perfect gentleman and grand company as he went quietly about his business. He and Father hit it off. They genuinely liked each other—you could see it.

"During the winter months they planned Abe's schedule—Father offering his services as friend and agent. Sometimes the Mitchells came to tea or dinner but the men soon excused themselves to discuss yet another golf project. Suddenly, however, in April of 1926, only three months after Abe started working for Father, we found ourselves in the midst of conducting an international match with America. Frankly, I thought we had all lost our minds, and I said so. His response was, 'It's all right, my dear. We are doing His work. Golf is the only game God is interested in.' And he said it time and again. In 1931, when the Ryder Cup was played in the United States the second time, in Ohio, I think it was—can't think of the name of the golf course—he broadcast a message to the teams by radio." Marjorie got up and took a picture off the wall.

"Scioto! That's the name. Here's his picture at the microphone and the text of what he said." She straightened up and spoke solemnly:

> I look upon the Royal and Ancient game as being a powerful moral force that influences the best things in humanity. I trust the effect of these matches will be to influence a cordial, friendly, and peaceful feeling throughout the whole world.

"I always thought it was asking a bit much of the poor old game, myself," she added.

When Marjorie became engaged to Leslie Claisen, her father saw to it he learned golf. Abe Mitchell taught him with amazing success, she said. It was because Leslie became so keen on golf that there was, in fact, another Ryder Cup. When they were married in 1929, her father bought them a farm in Rhodesia—a source for new seeds and a warm place for her father to visit in the wintertime to escape his respiratory problems. Rhodesia had been her mother's idea since she had gone to Sunday school with Cecil Rhodes in Bishops Stortford. After they settled near Umtali, her new husband made a small golf course on the adjoining veldt. He did it for her, he said. "Well," Marjorie remarked, "I liked golf but I wasn't mentally handicapped by it the way he was. Now, where was I?"

"The other Ryder Cup."

"Yes. In the early '30s, I asked Father to sponsor a Ryder Cup competition for the Manicaland farmers of Rhodesia.

Soon a silver cup arrived with his name inscribed. It became a much anticipated national event until the war, when it was shelved at Umtali's Hillside Golf Club. But in the 1960s it was revived for the farmers. It was so successful that, with my permission, African Distillers took over sponsorship in 1972. I provided Ryder Shooting Sticks to the winners, symbolic of a shooting stick presented to Father at an early international match. This year the 'Ryder Cup' is on the 25th and 26th of September. I know because I just posted a cheque for the shooting sticks."

"What format is used?"

"The two Ryder Cups are nothing alike—they are opposite, in fact. Ours is for amateurs, both men and women, stroke play, for good and bad players. There is even a prize for 'Most Golf'—for the highest score. Prime Minister Ian Smith presented the prizes last year. Wouldn't Father have been pleased to know?!"

"Maybe he does," I said in the manner of small talk.

"I'm sure he does," she said. "Golf changed Father radically, you know. He was truly grateful for the happiness and perspective it brought him. Another thing he said in that radio talk to Scioto Country Club was, 'I hope I have done several things in my life for the benefit of my fellow men, but I am certain I have never done a happier thing than this.'

"He had a clear idea that if each man watched out for the welfare of his wife and children, parents, brothers and sisters, and at least one other person besides, that pretty much everyone in the world would grow and thrive like flowers in a well-tended garden. Yet, the sad truth of it is, isn't it, that a man's relatives are usually the ones that he can least abide because they remind him of his responsibilities."

"Do you remember when your father was mayor?"

"Yes, but I would rather not. We were sick the whole time, especially little Joan. It's more fun to remember how he got to be mayor. He was a dyed-in-the-wool Liberal at the turn of the century and joined a movement to unseat Sir Hildred Carlisle, an entrenched St. Albans Tory, and replace him with Liberal Bamford Slack. Father assisted 'The Liberal Choir,' a group of farmers, lorry drivers, cattle drovers, anyone with a loud voice. They sang in parades and at political rallies. Whenever the Tories got the upper hand, the Liberal Choir would burst into song with words of praise for Slack, put to familiar tunes. I asked Father how such a choir was formed in a Tory town and he said, 'Bribery and corruption, my dear. St. Albans is noted for it. Besides, anyone would sing anywhere for a few bob.' Slack won and Father found himself in politics. I wish you could have heard his feisty mayor's speech."

"I did. I mean, I read it."

"He claimed," Marjorie said, "he had a distaste for public life, yet he pursued it for a time. He declined several opportunities to stand for parliament. But he shared platforms and rotten Tory fruit with David Lloyd George and Winston Churchill, in Churchill's Liberal days. 'That young Churchill will go far,' he liked to say."

"I find it odd that your father, or any of your family, never attended a Ryder Cup Match in the United States," I commented.

"I, for one, was never invited. But I'm not sure just why Father never went, except that first time when Abe Mitchell was so sick. I moved away in 1929. Joan will know. She's never missed a Match in this country and gets royal treatment. She is the one who should be invited. But in America, where the Ryder Cup has so little importance, they must think she just wouldn't want to bother. No one knows her contributions to Father's crusade for professional golfers. She was his business manager, friend to all the teams and their wives—the more so as years went on. She was never recognized for her participation. I don't suppose she wanted to be really, but she was in on the whole thing, making decisions, doing much of the work. And, of course, when Father died, in 1936, she took over the reins of Ryder and Son and later, Heath and Heather, jobs for which he had prepared her.

"I was Father's Girl Friday for a time. Mother had no interest in seeds or flowers, although she was in on the start of the penny packet business 100% and an active member of the Board until she died. It was my good fortune to accompany Father on his travels, visiting seed farms and horticultural experts in this country, on the Continent and in South Africa, searching for new plants to introduce into this country. We wandered over an amazing variety of gardens, trial grounds, and experimental plots. Arctotis, Dimorphothenkas, Gazanias, and Ursinias were rarities ordered by Father from the Kirstenboche botanical garden on the slopes of Table Mountain in South Africa. When I see them growing in our English gardens I feel very pleased."

When I asked about her mother, Marjorie went to her desk. "I have something that might help you know them both. It's a letter of proposal of marriage. Sit here, we'll read it together—you can help me with the words—his handwriting was slapdash. You don't think he would mind, do you?" I was tempted, but I didn't say anything.

"He wrote it to Helen Mary Barnard of Bishops Stortford from Stowey, his home in Broad Road, Sale, southeast of Manchester. He was 29 years old and my mother was 23. As a girl she assisted a blind organist of the Congregational Church, and as a result of this, she became a fine organist herself. I always surmised it was their chapel and music that brought them together.

September 1, 1887

Dear Miss Nelly,

Long before you left us I resolved to write you on a

> matter concerning my happiness. Since I have known you I have esteemed and admired you more than anyone I have ever known. I love you, as I never thought I could love anyone. So I write, I fear, abruptly to ask if you can love me in return and if you will be my wife.

"He gets right down to it, doesn't he?" I remarked.

> I find in you the rest every true man looks for and you understand me as no other woman ever did or will. I believe I understand you too. You will find in me the strength of unchanging love you must have from your husband. If I were not sure of this I would never speak to you of love.
>
> My affection has not suddenly sprung into existence as a result of our pleasant times together, for I have loved you longer than you can imagine. But for reasons I shall explain, if I ever have a chance, I have felt honourably bound to give you no idea of my feeling.

I interrupted again. " 'Honorably bound'? What's that about?"

Marjorie thought a moment. "I had assumed he or she may have been involved with someone else at the time, but now that I think about it, I'm not so sure. The two families were associated through Nonconformist causes, and Mother was especially fond of Auntie Marie, one of Father's five sisters. I rather think it was a family matter of some sort, a promise made and kept. But let's go on. This is my favourite part."

> I should like you to know why I love you. Although I do admire you for your endowments and attainment and their sweet influence on me, it is not for them I love you. It is for the beauty of your own self because

> you are in character what I know you to be. This is clumsy and would not recommend me, I fancy, to an ordinary woman, but I cannot find the words. I know this, however—I love you for what I know you would wish me to love you for. And, because I cannot help it.

"Just what a woman wants hear, don't you think?"

"I'd marry him on the spot," I said.

"He goes on to tell her about his religious feelings and hopes."

> I want to do well the work which seems to be mine, and that I may do it well, I want you in my life. As far as human thought can judge, I have the power to make you happy.

"He assures her that she will have the unrestricted affection of all his relatives and that he has written to her mother."

> If you consent I should like to come at once. I shall be in London for a day or two and could easily come down for a few hours—before going to Henley. I shall pray for the right answer. I am Ever Yours, Sam Ryder

We both sighed like schoolgirls. Marjorie said, "There's another letter upstairs, but perhaps another time—something to lure you back because it gives me such pleasure to talk about him. The other letter was written on New Year's Eve 1887 and there are some words I can't make out at all. Without question, he was having a lonely celebration at his writing desk because the letter becomes less and less legible as the evening wears on, and it was a long letter. Well, you'll see. Meanwhile, you should talk with Dora Mitchell. I'll ring her in the next few days and tell her about you."

Dora

WINTER WAS NEARLY OVER, daylight had returned to England, and those who were depressed by darkness could breathe again. Large sunlit daffodils, growing tightly against the brick, greeted me as I bounced up to the front door of Abe Mitchell's house on Cunningham Avenue. Mrs. Mitchell opened it just as I was about to flick a finger at the doorbell. My enthusiasm was running high for so late in the day.

"I saw you drive up," she said. "You parked in Mr. Ryder's space. There weren't many cars in those days. I'm very happy you've come. Not many people remember who Abe was anymore. Well, he's gone now these 30 years, isn't he? Do come in. There's a nip in the air."

"So many memories you have of him," I said, looking around her comfortable sitting room at the plaques and pictures, and a large cabinet of medals, cups, and salvers. I walked directly to the trophy that Abe had described to me, one of several sitting outside the trophy case. I held it up.

"The Tooting Bec Cup, a replica with the PGA engraved medal," Mrs. Mitchell said warmly. "It was the comfort of his old age, not that he had an old age. He was only 60 when he died. He won it when he was 46 for the lowest single round score, 68, by a home player in the Open. That was 1933, at St. Andrews. Andra Kirkaldy, who succeeded Old Tom Morris in 1910, was still there then. It was his custom to sit in an armchair by the 18th green. When Abe arrived, Andra ceremoniously rose from his chair, walked to the flagstick and removed it as a mark of his respect. It was discussed in the press whether Andra might not have cost Abe strokes in the circumstances because Abe's ball was outside the 20 yards rule and he had a right to use the stick to stop his ball. Abe said, "Rubbish," when he read it. Andra died soon after that. After three rounds Abe shared the lead but that was that."

"And this?" I asked because it had an American flag on it.

"He won that in Miami in December 1924. He wasn't home for Christmas that year. And this in 1922—the Southern States Championship—southern United States, that is. He and George Duncan were there from June to October in 1922—sailed home on the *Homeric* on October 21, shortly after they trounced Hagen—Open champion—and Jim Barnes—U.S. Open champion—in a charity event for the Pelham Summer Home for Cardiac Children. Enormously popular, they were—offered several important professional posts. Abe asked me once if I would mind living in the States, and I told him I *would* mind. He wasn't terribly keen on it himself. He thought your water disagreed with him. You see, during his first tour, in 1921, he developed a kidney disorder and since the problem recurred each time he toured there, he blamed America. He had to withdraw from two of your Opens and was dismal in the others he played in. Fatigue did it, I think. Despite that, I'm certain, but for Mr. Ryder's generous proposition, we would have gone to America."

"There never would have been a Ryder Cup, in that case," I said. "A Hagen Cup, perhaps, but not a Ryder Cup." When

Dora made a face, I added. "Yes, I've heard a few dubious things about Sir Walter lately."

"Walter was very good to Abe—you must understand that, no matter what you have heard." Then she told me the story I had heard so many times about the 1920 Open when George Duncan picked up 13 strokes on Abe in 18 holes to win the Claret Jug. Then she added, "After the Open, Walter made friends with George and Abe and persuaded them to enter the French Open at La Boulie at Versailles the following week, something they would not otherwise have done. Their accommodations were in a fly-infested, smelly stable, so Walter, with Abe and George in tow, marched to the clubhouse, to confront *Monsieur le President* Pierre Deschamps with his options: either Monsieur Deschamps allowed them freedom of the La Boulie clubhouse or they—Monsieur Duncan the British Open Champion, Monsieur Mitchell the British PGA Champion, and himself, the American Open Champion—would withdraw. So while the rest of the field used the stable, our boys had the run of the clubhouse, although I was told Abe needed a push through the front door each time they entered."

Dora, as she spoke to me, exuded good cheer. She bubbled even as she told me of the hardships of a touring professional and his family. She described her life without Abe when he toured and how fatigued he was when he returned. Championships took their toll, she said, and cited English golfer Joyce Wethered, who went to bed for days after an important match. "Bobby Jones thought, and Abe agreed, that Miss Wethered was the world's most consistent golfer. In Mr. Jones's Grand Slam year, 1930, he played the Old Course with Miss Wethered. He said, 'We played from the very back, the championship tees. I had never played golf with anyone, man or woman, amateur or professional, who made me feel so utterly outclassed.' Her concentration was a lesson to all, but no one was quite sure what she was concentrating on. Abe said she knew better than anyone how to guide physical movement *indirectly* with her mind—whatever he meant, I don't know—but he said it gave her the ability to duplicate shots without error one after another."

"They say she played in a trance," I remarked.

"Did you know that Abe and Mr. Ryder used to study that sort of thing together? Spent hours working it out. Abe sometimes lost his concentration in front of large galleries, and Mr. Ryder tried to help him with it. Mr. Darwin wrote that it looked to him as if Abe would rather be playing a peaceful game with a friend away from the shouting and the tumult. To use his words, 'That may have been the reason so truly magnificent a hitter of the ball had not won the Open.'

"To recover from a long tour, we would take a honeymoon suite at the Granville Hotel for a month, or go to Harrogate for its miraculous sulphur water. He was sure it was the chalybeate sulphur waters that restored him. My town of Tunbridge Wells had such waters. When Abe was courting me we often strolled its covered walks to drink from the springs in Bath Square. He said he picked me because the springs had made me special."

I wanted to tell her that he picked me for the same reason.

"Shall we have tea before we look at other things?"

There were small sandwiches, scones, thick cream and a jam, cakes—different from Marjorie's table, yet frightening all the same. "My town had sulfur springs and covered walks," I said as we drank our tea, and Abe was forgotten for a time while we lost ourselves in childhood memories.

"Was he good-looking—Abe?" I asked it because I couldn't decide. There were times I could not get past the slick hairstyle of the day that did nothing to conceal his ears. I wanted to erase the lines between his eyes, make him smile and, more than anything, I wanted to remove the ever-present cigarette jammed between the knuckles.

Mrs. Mitchell answered me without hesitation, "Oh, he was very handsome, indeed. But 'manly' describes him best. The ladies flocked to see him at Madame Tussaud's Museum in London," she laughed. "Montmorency painted his portrait, commissioned by Mr. Ryder. It was exhibited at the Royal Academy and then given to the Professional Golfing Association. I believe they sold it for £100, and it is now owned by Mrs. Scarfe, Mr. Ryder's youngest daughter.

"But it was his natural reserve and honourable style that people noticed. Women found him to be a delightful partner at golf. He coached Miss Horsfield of Verulam and they won the Bystander Trophy three times. Of all the national championships he played in, he enjoyed that one the most. There are the medals: 1927 (before his illness), 1929, and 1930. He had a quiet dignity that was as much a part of him as his large, strong hands. I asked him once how a bumpkin like himself could be so courteous of others and he said there was no reason not to be.

"I must confess, however, he was not always genial to our son Leonard, who could be exasperating. It wasn't Abe's way to sit on the floor to play with his son, although they had a fine relationship once Len was older. Len, you know, is the golf professional at Crewes Hills in Enfield—has been for almost 30 years. He's a bachelor, lives here and takes care of his old mum—not that I need it, mind you. There were times Leonard and I felt neglected. I recall that I was provoked to write a 'Dear Abraham' letter. He was touring sunny South Africa, enjoying the hospitality of his millionaire patron of his early years, Sir Abe Bailey, whilst I had to get the boy to boarding school in an unheated taxi. We got stuck in snow during a raging blizzard. By the time I returned home late at night, nearly frozen to death, I was not reasonable. I let him have it in the letter, signed it 'your unwilling servant.' Just then, the radio announced he'd won an important tournament in South

Africa. Well, what was I to do? I tore up my letter and wrote another telling him how proud I was to be Abe Mitchell's wife and it was true.

"I had always been proud to be his wife. 'That's Mrs. Abe Mitchell,' I'd hear people say. I was singled out as 'Abe's choice.' Imagine me, Dora Deagh, a school teacher. I taught at the Murray School for Girls in Tunbridge Wells. He liked to tell his friends he had no idea how little he knew until he married me. If I explained too much or nattered on about my day, his eyes would fasten on my nose. Without changing my voice, I'd say, 'Where are you, Abe?' A part of him would hear me and he'd set his thoughts aside and come to me. Words were not his preferred means of communication.

"He was a busy-quiet man, smoked incessantly—just to keep his hands busy, I say. He was known for bringing his shoes to a perfect shine, but I think he polished them excessively to keep his hands in motion. Making a new golf club brought him contentment, selecting the best hickory to suit the purpose of the club, testing strength and flexibility, and finally shaping for torsion—putting his spell on it, he called it. He worked with great concentration and purpose, and just enough patience. If something unimportant went wrong, I'd hear, 'Dash!' But if his labor was spoilt by his own hand, he became ever so calm. Then I would bake an apple tart and take it to him.

"I gave his favourite brassie to Verulam after he died. Not long ago a nice young man, Richard his name was, called me to say that he'd used Abe's brassie in a Drive In ceremony at Verulam and wanted me to know what a genuine surprise it had been. He'd used an easy stroke for the sake of the old wooden shaft and had as good a result as he had ever had with his new, expensive clubs. Many good golfers in the 1930s who went to the steel shaft were amazed that Abe would try it, then revert to hickory, again and again. Henry Cotton said

Abe could not make himself play just one stroke, that he liked to fade the ball up to the flag and found the steel shaft let him down when he attempted to play a controlled fade or any special stroke. He missed the torsion of the hickory shaft. He was too much of an artist to enjoy steel, Henry said."

"What is a 'drive in' ceremony?"

"When a new captain takes office, whether it's Verulam or the R&A, there is a ceremony designed to inebriate responsible men, especially the new captain. The way Abe explained it to me, there is a brief drinks party for the captain's guests and ex-captains. Then the new captain changes into his golf clothes and goes to the first tee with the club professional, with the jolly party in tow. The professional tees the ball and pours the captain a dram of whisky. The captain knocks it back and attempts to drive. This is repeated two more times amidst guffaws—well, you can imagine it's not always a pretty sight—and then it's back to the clubhouse for the meal and speeches and more quick drams."

"I see Abe was 'Captain of the PGA of Great Britain, 1934." I had stood up and was reading the plaques on the wall. "And this is for his war relief exhibitions with Henry Cotton and Pam Barton. Who was she?"

"She was British Ladies' champion and an officer in WAAF. I believe she won your Women's Amateur Championship as well, in 1936. We were deeply affected when she was killed in 1943. Only 26 years old she was."

"You must look at this one," Dora continued. "It is the most important medal Abe ever won. At least, I think so. He won almost every tournament he entered right after the war. But this is the 1919 Open, won jointly with George Duncan. It was played at St. Andrews and called the 'Victory' Championship. Although it was unofficial, there was a play-off over the Eden course the next day. Abe won and was given the medal but his victory was never celebrated. In light of golf history, many regret it, but the R&A's decision was reasonable. They felt some men were not prepared to play so soon after the war, but most professionals agreed it was the Open championship in all but name.

"In 1920, Lord Northcliffe, the newspaper magnate, persuaded Abe to run the golf club at North Foreland and be his private professional at the same time. So, after our marriage we lived at the edge of the golf course overlooking the North Sea, by the lighthouse. On Fridays, when Lord Northcliffe arrived from London for the weekend, Abe had dinner at his home. Their golf always included a dictating machine to carry on 'the Lord's business,' as Abe put it. Walter Hagen joined them on one occasion after the 1920 Open. His Lordship and Walter were acquainted because Lord Northcliffe had played at the Country Club of Rochester when Walter was an assistant there."

"I come from Rochester."

"Now, isn't that a coincidence! I sent a studio photograph of Leonard and me to Abe in 1922 and he received it in Buffalo where he was playing in a tournament with Walter. When Walter saw that photograph—it's there on the table beside you—he took Abe to Rochester to meet *his* son and see his childhood home in a glen. I think Walter had divorced his first wife by that time."

"I know the glen very well," I said. "Corbett's Glen. I'm sure he wanted Abe to see the railroad bridge. Never was so much engineering expended to span so small a problem—except in England. There are small waterfalls at the bridge, upstream and downstream, and hardly anyone knows it's there—the glen, I mean."

Dora said, "Walter told Abe the bridge and glen of his childhood represented his philosophy of life: it proved that if you put enough structure around a problem, people will forget what the problem is. Walter was always complicating matters, making room for himself to manoeuvre, it seemed to me."

"Living by the North Foreland lighthouse—how beautiful it must have been, looking out over the North Sea, watching the ships enter and leave the Thames estuary. You must have been sorry to move away."

"It *was* beautiful—constantly changing. Abe's contract at North Foreland was up in 1925, however, and since Lord Northcliffe died in 1922, we had no reason to stay. Mr. Ryder and his brother James asked Abe to consider working for them at the Ryder companies in order to expedite an international challenge cup they had talked about so long. The offer surprised Abe and he was noncommittal, so the Ryders invited us to come to St. Albans to get acquainted with the community. We stayed at *The Peahen* for three days. At dinner the third night Abe agreed to Samuel Ryder's generous offer—£500 annually plus £250 for expenses. He announced Abe's new position following a professional match at Verulam, in October 1925. I found it amusing that everyone knew the exact sum Abe was to be paid but it had been part of the plan that the public should know about it. People still say to me, 'I wonder what that would be worth today?' Well, it's hard to reckon it, when £100 was considered a healthy annual income. It was George Duncan's pay at Wentworth."

"Did you like Mr. Ryder, Mrs. Mitchell?"

"Dora—please. I think I did. Of course I did. If I hesitate, it is only because Abe almost died when he was captain of the Ryder Cup team in 1927 and, in my heart, I blamed Mr. Ryder. He *could* have changed Abe's mind, you see. He *could* have made him go to the hospital. If I said otherwise to Mr. Ryder at the time, it was only to comfort him. Never mind. I did like him. Mr. Ryder used to say to me he had liked Abe from the day he met him. Well, I did too, so I liked Mr. Ryder for that. I watched their friendship grow step by step and I was never less rich for it."

Dora went to her desk, opened a drawer and took out a heavy wooden box from which she extracted an envelope. "This says something, I think. It was written to me in early June 1927, when I needed it most."

> I have learned to most highly esteem Abe, and the longer I know him, the more do I admire his play and his character. I trust for years we will be together. The match for my cup will be played on Friday and Saturday next. Let us hope our team will win—but it is the play without the Prince of Denmark. —Sam Ryder

"Was Abe like a son to Mr. Ryder, would you say?" I asked.

"No, not really. How does one judge those things? I believe Mr. Ryder and Abe knew each other in a way that most men don't, but nevertheless, Abe always thought of Mr. Ryder as his boss. He never called him Sam to me or anyone else. Mr. Ryder was such a rich man, the word 'patron' easily comes to mind, but that is not the way it was, either. Mr. Ryder never patronised anyone. He and Abe enjoyed each other's company, being together, solving problems, laughing at the same things—more than once, I might add. For all his youth compared to Mr. Ryder, Abe still enjoyed the old stories best. Nothing sustained them more than jokes that sailed right over the listener's head. My favourite is one about the Gruyère cheese. One evening the Ryders were entertaining a large crowd at the Royal Hotel at Weymouth—friends from the Gloucester Street Congregational Church and golfers from an exhibition at Came Down. Abe and Mr. Ryder approached the church minister who was expounding on his latest concern: unemployment. Mr. Ryder said to him, 'I understand there are jobs out there, if a man is willing to do them. I met a worker just the other day who'd got a good job cutting holes in Swiss cheese. And Abe said, 'Is that so? I always thought it was done by machine.' And the minister said, 'Really! I had no idea.'"

Dora said that Abe appeared to be the more sophisticated of the two men. Once when she accused him of putting on airs, he looked down his nose at her and said, "Have *you* ever played quoits with Prime Minister and Mrs. Chamberlain?" Then they had a good laugh. He must have crossed the Atlantic a dozen times, each time enjoying the attention of important passengers, who were sociable and friendly on the outward journey, but retreated behind their social barriers as the ship neared England's shores.

Mr. Ryder aboard ship, on the other hand, could be found among the traveling cricket team, or with the loneliest passenger. Mrs. Claisen had told Dora that on a Union Castle steamer to Rhodesia her father befriended old, sick Horatio Bottomly, shunned by passengers because he was just out of prison. They played cards every day until a bad storm stopped the games. When calm resumed, Mr. Ryder said, "Thank God!" And Bottomly said, "I've done with God and He's done with me," to which her father responded, "We may be done with God, old friend, but He's never done with us." At Cape Town, Bottomly said, "I shall remember what you said to me, Ryder. Thank you."

Then Dora wanted me to know that among his many honors, Abe had had a flower named after him. She explained that one evening Mr. Ryder arrived at their door carrying a huge bunch of sweet peas. She put them in water and set them in a corner. Thereupon, he picked them up and put them in the center of the room. At intervals during the evening, he inspected them, asked what they thought of the colors, the stems, the leaves, and so forth. When he finally got them to admit the sweet peas were the finest sweet peas they had ever seen, Mr. Ryder brought forward his latest seed catalogue and showed them the listing: "Abe Mitchell Sweet Pea, scarlet; Mrs. Abe Mitchell Sweet Pea, pink."

Dora beckoned me to the window. "There they are along the fence, starting to sprout their leaves. The gardener watches over them as if his life depends upon it. I've read, by the way, that Abe was a gardener and that is why he and Mr. Ryder got on so well. Although he may have dug in a garden as a handyman around Forest Row, I can testify Abe was not a gardener and neither was Mr. Ryder, as far as I know. Selling seeds is one thing, putting them into the ground is another. I wonder where these stories come from. I've heard Abe was a lumberjack in Canada, a sickly boy in Scandinavia, and my favourite, a plumber who squeezed putty until his were the strongest hands in all of England."

Dora returned the wooden box and pulled down a scrapbook from a shelf above the desk. "I have many of these books but I keep this one out because it contains my favourite photograph of Abe. It was taken at the international match at Wentworth in 1926, right after he'd won his singles match against Jim Barnes to secure the first win for the Cup. Below his picture is the *Times* write-up."

> [Saturday, June 5] Mitchell's play stood as a thing apart. He went round in 68 with the utmost ease and without having to do anything on the green except tap the ball dead from a few yards away. He constantly putted for 3's at par 4 holes, and if he had had anything in the nature of a 'day out' on the green, Heaven knows what he might have done. Luckily, Nature does not waste her gifts and seldom allows the putts to go in on the day when all the iron shots perch round the holes.
>
> He missed one or two short ones and bombarded an oak tree, and the rest was remorseless accuracy. He himself said that not for months had he played the shot up to the pin so well, and Barnes said that his adversary had been kind to him. What description could be more

> eloquent? He made Barnes look commonplace and yet Barnes was round in 71 and playing a conspicuously courageous and resourceful game.

"Were you there?"

She said she was, along with many thousand others on both days. The first day was foursomes and the second day was singles matches. Wentworth is at Virginia Water, the most beautiful and aristocratic setting in the countryside near London, and for two days, Friday and Saturday, June 4th and 5th, the weather was mild and windless with a watery sun that hardly cast a shadow. Conditions were ideal.

"On Friday, most of the spectators were drawn to the foursomes match of Abe and George Duncan versus Walter Hagen and Jim Barnes. Jim was the reigning Open champion and Walter Hagen was already twice Open champion. The world's best golfers were there. The American Walker Cup team—Bobby Jones, Francis Ouimet and others who had just trounced the British at St. Andrews—felt right at home in the gallery. There was little of 'this side' versus 'that side'."

"Tell me everything," I said, suddenly caught up in her story about an important event of which I knew nothing.

"What I remember best is Walter Hagen's clothes. His ensemble in shades of white and tan was, indeed, picturesque; he was dressed to win this international match that was as much his idea as Mr. Ryder's.

"One incident in particular remains with me. It happened at the 18th green in the morning round on Friday. Depending upon your point of view, it was hilarious. Abe and George were three up when George put their third shot in a greenside bunker. Meanwhile, Jim and Walter were comfortably on the green in two, leaving Walter with a short putt for a birdie. Jim, thinking the hole would be conceded, was on his way to lunch when Abe blasted out of the bunker into the hole for a four.

Hagen then missed his putt, Barnes had to be called back, he missed his putt as well, and they lost the hole entirely.

"Abe told me once," Dora added, "legend to the contrary, that Walter did not forget a bad shot. I believe that scene at the 18th was equivalent to a bad shot for Walter. While no one snickered, the groans were on the playful side, if you take my meaning. Over the years I've wondered if that episode didn't harden Walter's determination to prevail—somehow. It's all speculation. In any case, George and Abe prevailed that day, 9 and 8, the first point ever made, at least to our way of thinking.

"Britain took all five matches that day, so for the Americans to win they would have to take eight of the ten singles matches the second day. Abe and Jim Barnes were the third match out. As you saw, the *Times* was effusive about Abe's play. He won 8 and 7. Here is the clipping with the result of the singles matches. George Duncan won over Walter 6 and 5, Aubrey Boomer beat Tommy Armour 2 and 1, Bill Mehlhorn won over Archie Compston 1 up, George Gadd downed Joe Kirkwood 8 and 7, Ted Ray won over Al Watrous 7 and 5, Fred Robson took Cyril Walker 5 and 4, Arthur Havers beat Fred McLeod 10 and 9, Ernest Whitcombe halved with Emmet French, and Herb Jolly beat Joe Stein 3 and 2.

"Your Bill Mehlhorn was the only American player with an outright win over the whole two days. Archie Compston deserved to lose for his tedious delays on the putting greens. When Emmet French halved with Ernest Whitcombe, the final score was 13½ to 1½."

Dora excused herself to fetch something she wanted me to see. While she was gone I saw another clipping on the page opposite. It had been clipped from the *New York Times*, written by Anthony Spalding.

> London, June 5, 1926.—The lead of five points which the British professional golfers yesterday established

over the American team in the international match for the *Ryder Cup* on the Wentworth links was translated into a victory when ten singles were played. Britain won a total of thirteen matches, lost one and halved one.

I read it again.

Two for Tea

In 1977, calling Paris was not for the uncommitted, but I had to talk to Bill. I couldn't believe what I had read in Dora's clipping from the *New York Times*. I thought that Bill, because of his job, could verify it for me, even enlarge upon it. Steve and I took turns trying to get through to Paris and then, by accident surely, I heard Bill's voice momentarily and asked him to call me in the morning. He dutifully rang me the next day.

Without so much as a friendly greeting, I shouted to his French telephone, "I want all the news stories leading up to, and including, an international golf match between teams of American and British professional golfers at Wentworth, June 4 and 5, 1926."

"1926!"

"You heard me. Let me finish. The key names to search for are Walter Hagen, Abe Mitchell, George Duncan, and Samuel Ryder," and I spelled them out. In an unusually gentle voice he said he would do as I directed as quickly as possible. Was that okay? I learned later that after I had hung up he called

Steve at work to alert him to my unstable condition. "She's not herself," he said.

Within days a manila envelope arrived from Paris, delivered well before sunrise by my muscular postman in winter garb. Steve handed the package to me as he prepared to leave for work. "What's this?" he asked, ever the master of the unanswerable question.

"Dunno. Tell you after I've read it."

I worked about the house, washing up, sorting magazines, polishing brass knobs, always circling back to see if the envelope had moved. I even stepped outside to check the primroses beneath the front window, but then I quickly returned, too weak to wait any longer to open the mail. I always saved the best for last—meat from a lobster's tail, removed and set aside, the smallest present on Christmas morning, the icing on the cake. I snuggled into a comfortable chair by the picture window, close to my winter companion the radiator, and unwound the string on the sturdy manila envelope, carefully tracing figure eights in the air. By the time the sun was well along its daily roll across the treetops on the southern horizon I had read the newspaper clippings, found the prize I was looking for and more besides. After my excitement settled I sat for a very long time and stared out the window, pondering why I gave a hoot about any of it. I was just factoring in Sam and Abe when the telephone sounded its insistent double ring.

A pleasant voice introduced herself as a Mrs. Moore, Mrs. Mary Moore, Mrs. Claisen's daughter.

"Is your mother all right?" I asked.

"Oh, yes. My Aunt Jo is coming to visit next week and Mother wants you to come for tea." I took the bull by the horns and invited them, including Mrs. Moore, to my house. I blamed my lack of caution on the *New York Times* and the excitement of discovery. Well, it was about time I learned a crumpet from a scone.

"Just a moment, I'll ask her. Yes, that will be fine." The answer came back so quickly that I surmised Marjorie had it in mind all along. Mrs. Moore turned me down, however. She was only visiting her mother for the day. We set a time and I said, "Give my best to your mother."

"I will."

"She's all right, you say?"

"Oh, yes."

I considered my short exchange and recognized that, like me, Marjorie Claisen would drive 50 miles to make an inquiry rather than pick up a telephone.

To prepare for the Ryder sisters, I invited Ann over to instruct me in tea. She arrived in a little black dress, buttoned to the neck, and a white voile apron that matched the cuffs of her long sleeves. Across her forehead, just above her eyebrows, sat a smart, frilly cap. It was the costume of the afternoon maid, given to her by her grandmother on her tenth birthday for playing dress-up.

"Blimey," I said as she curtsied her way into my parlor.

Ann showed me how to arrange my mother's silver tea service. She taught me to cut thin, thin slices of bread that could be rolled. She brought me her own hand-embroidered linens and a small folding table called a cakestand with three tiers on which to put cucumber sandwiches and my home-made cakes (should I make the effort). She promised to contribute mouthful balls of rich sponge, each sitting in its paper cup. "Where shall I put the scones?" I wanted to know.

"Scones?" Ann said. "I don't know anything about scones."

~

"We've put you to a great deal of bother," Marjorie exclaimed after she had introduced me to her sister Joan and looked at my extensive preparations for afternoon tea. Everything had been done to English prescription, except for small bowls of salted nuts and crispy corn chips. These, and the amusing size of my American teaspoons, did more than anything to ease our way.

The hour proceeded as if choreographed by an outside agency, which it probably was. Joan and Marjorie reminisced, telling stories about their father that left me with more questions than answers. They spoke of the breakdown in his health shortly after he became mayor, but they could not recall the exact nature of the collapse that nearly killed him. The road outside Marlborough House had been laid with straw to hush the sound of wagon wheels and horses' hooves. But they did remember the frequent visits of their monocled family doctor, attired, it seemed to them, for the Royal Enclosure at Ascot. He made his housecalls in "a smart dogcart, with high, yellow wheels, driven by a groom, with two beautiful Dalmatian dogs trotting behind."

It was for health reasons, they decided, that their father never attended a Ryder Cup Match in the United States, something he dearly wanted to do. Illness kept him from many things, including his banquet for the victorious British Ryder Cup team in 1929 at the Shakespeare Hotel in Stratford-on-Avon. Yet they thought of their father as a muscularly trim, healthy man.

"It was just his lungs were bad, you see, and if he caught cold there was danger of pneumonia," Marjorie explained. "Our Rhodesian climate did him a world of good."

"But what specifically was wrong with his lungs?" I wanted to know.

Marjorie said, "Why don't you ask him?"

"What..." Joan laughed.

"Well, she talks to the portrait, the one I gave to Verulam," Marjorie confided to Joan, smiling broadly, "same as I used to do."

Joan addressed me kindly, in the manner of advice. "I have the stunning portrait of Father painted late in his life, also by Frank Salisbury. I would never part with it; it comforts me, but I don't believe I'd speak to it. But it is true, Mardi, isn't it, about his health, I mean, once you think about it? There was always something. Do you remember how ill he was in 1933? Well, of course you don't; you were in Rhodesia. But he insisted we go to Royal Lytham. Even the Prince of Wales commented on it when he awarded the Cup to the British side. After he credited Father with starting one of the most important international sporting events in the world, he added, 'We are pleased he could be here, as he has been very sick.' We helped him," Joan continued, "to a few strategic positions about the course to watch the play, especially the 9 and 8 drubbing Abe Mitchell handed Olin Dutra in the singles. Abe never used anything but an iron club that day. How I loved to watch him play. I never looked away, as I'd seen others do when they were afraid for him. He was my hero, you know. I always thought Abe played better when Father and I were in his sights. I hoped it was so."

As I refilled our cups Marjorie asked me dryly, "Have you chatted with Father recently?"

To play the game I told her what I learned about Arthur Faulkner from the Vicar as if the words had come from Sam. I asked her if she thought her father's liberal views on drinking had affected Thomas Cook's travel business.

"It's possible," Marjorie said. "Certainly Faulkner and Father liked each other, despite their opposing views on Temperance. They were a philanthropic team in many ways, working for the Congregational Church and the city government, without perquisites and compensation. No one, however, abhorred Faulkner's political dinners more than Father, who thought that banquet food should never be served without a good glass of something. At one affair his table companion,

Councillor Hodding, suggested they leave the banquet entirely when he saw lime juice approaching their empty glasses, but just then, the head waiter, a familiar figure at Council dinners, appeared with a disguised bottle of whisky and filled their glasses. After the banquet everyone but Father, Mr. Hodding, *and* the headwaiter was taken ill.

"You should write down some of our family stories, Mardi. Mary would like them, I'm sure. And Rosalind is always begging me to tell her more about her grandfather and what our life was like back then. It's odd, isn't it, that Father has had only female descendants." Joan turned to me and explained, "I have Rosalind and Marjorie has Mary and that's it. Kit had no children."

"Perhaps I *should* write my recollections," Marjorie responded, "write about Edwardian times when even the simplest household had a helper. I don't know if I miss it or not, although I do like a gardener. In the early days of Father's business, when we were not at all well off, we had a cook, a housemaid, and nanny. I believe they shared an attic room. I sometimes think it's easier to do for oneself than order others around, don't you?"

To a degree, I mused, thinking of my English dinner parties. I would have welcomed a servant or two on those occasions that used every dish, utensil, and glass in my considerable inventory. Steve and I, laboring under a "when in Rome" mentality, learned to serve, clear, and pour seven courses without detectably rising from our dining room chairs. Invariably, when we washed up at three in the morning we wondered at our friends, all without automatic dishwashers and servants, who clung so fiercely to the spirit of "Upstairs, Downstairs" after the structure had collapsed.

"I remember," Joan said, "that we had a chauffeur, gardeners, dogs, cats, a parrot, and always visitors. We were especially fond of one elderly clergyman. When he came to stay we had family prayers before breakfast, something we didn't otherwise do. One morning, we had just begun the Lord's Prayer when the telephone rang. Our parrot yelled, 'I'll go, I'll go,' and began to sing *Onward Christian Soldiers* on and on until Mother covered the cage. When she apologised our clergyman said, 'Not at all, not at all, I like the animals to take part.' Strange what one remembers."

Marjorie, taking her turn, told me about her favorite aunt, Jeannie Wadsworth, a "disconcerting suffragette." Her father would say, "That disconcerting suffragette is coming to stay," knowing that they understood he loved his sister dearly and liked her views. Her interest in the women's vote began when she learned through her husband, a physician who supported her ideas to the detriment of his practice, that women had no legal say in the medical treatment of their children, often with tragic consequences. Aunt Jeannie, a gentle soul, assured them she was not a jailbird, however. "I am never militant, Samuel," she had responded when their father teased her about having a role in the latest headlines, especially when the suffragettes called attention to their issues by destroying mail from the letter boxes in St. Andrews village during the 1913 British Amateur championship. They also threatened to damage the putting greens and make play impossible. The *Times* reported that the entire Old Course had to be guarded day and night. Abe Mitchell was there. It was the last amateur tournament he played in.

Joan looked at her watch. "My ride will be here in 10 minutes, I'm afraid. I have a board meeting to attend and they're sending a driver to collect me. But we've had a jolly time remembering, haven't we?"

This was my moment. "Were you both at Wentworth for the first Ryder Cup in 1926?" I asked casually, not knowing how they would respond.

"Indeed, we were," Joan answered with enthusiasm. "It was

a culmination of months and months of musical chairs, changing plans and arrangements. Walter Hagen, Bob Harlow his manager, George Duncan, Major Hinds, Abe, Father—they were trying to sort out something that would work but no one was really in charge, you see. In March, Walter Hagen announced to the American press that the British PGA had asked him to select a team of American professionals to play an international match. The PGA of America gave him $1,000 to pay himself and three other pros $250 each to do it. In April, Mr. Hagen announced he was bringing a team, not of four, but of 12, all of whom would sign a waiver agreeing to split whatever money there was. He would send Bob Harlow ahead on the *Aquitania* on May 5, and the American professionals would follow on May 26.

"So, first it was four men, then 12—with a threat of more—then eight and eventually 10. And they would play either before, or after, the Open in late June, maybe at Gleneagles, or perhaps St. George's Hill one day and Wentworth another, or Wentworth for two days which, of course, was what they eventually did. The Match was played Friday and Saturday, June 4 and 5, a few days after the American players arrived on the *Aquitania*.

"For two perfect days a distinguished gallery moved like gathering waves across the new fairways of Wentworth. On Saturday, most spectators were caught up in Abe's match with Jim Barnes and Duncan's match with Hagen. Both Abe and Jim played superb golf but Abe was in another realm. We were standing near Bobby Jones when Abe drove the ball to the edge of the green on the 341 yard 10th hole. Mr. Jones looked at Father and smiled his approval. He had just played on a victorious American Walker Cup team at St. Andrews, and he would win our Open at Royal Lytham and St. Annes in three weeks' time."

Joan shifted in her chair before she continued. "After the

British side won 13½ to 1½, we invited all the players for champagne and chicken sandwiches so that the chaps would mix up together—get to know each other. Father gave the winning side £5 each and George Duncan, speaking for everyone there, thanked him and added, 'Mr. Ryder, you ought to make this an event. You give a cup. We'll call it the Ryder Cup.'"

Marjorie sighed and frowned at her sister. "Why do you persist with that silly story, Jo?"

"What would you have me say?"

Marjorie looked self-consciously down at her hands and changed the subject. "Father was fond of giving cups, cups for good behavior, incentive cups, that sort of thing. My favourite is the Wangler Cup. You have it, don't you, Joan? Yes. Well, it was a cup for the postal worker who could wangle Friday afternoon off from work in order to play golf with Father at Verulam. It was great fun for them at the post office. The winner not only had his round of golf with Father but got to keep the cup at his work station at least until the following Friday. Who else but Father would have thought of such a thing for the post office employees who were so much a part of his catalogue business?"

The doorbell rang just then and in a flurry of activity Joan left us. "No, no more tea, thank you," Marjorie said when we were seated again amidst the untidy mess we had made of my fancy tea. We returned to the subject of Sam. "I'm sure you can see we loved him. I suppose that is why it is so easy to fall into hyperbole when we speak of his virtues. But I would like you to grasp that he was different from most men."

She said that the "greatest good" for him started with a single person. The single person started with himself in that he did what his father told him to do: help himself and God by helping others. He did not willingly think of society as a whole; it was the single man he had in mind to help, who with a penny and his own hand could make a plant grow. When he made all that money, "seed money," he called it, he used it to get things started, make things grow. Starting with those closest to him and working outward, he dragged his beneficiaries into his enterprises. Then she gave me examples: he put his father's name to the penny seed packet—S. Ryder and Son; he put his retired brother James in charge of Heath and Heather, a Ryder subsidiary. James had been a schoolteacher for 40 years in the London slums and retired on a meagre pension. Together they ran the Heath and Heather golf tournaments.

"He prepared Joan to run the business after his death, which she did, and he bought me a Rhodesian plantation to facilitate his search for seed varieties, and give him respite from the cold damp winter when his lungs acted up. He was involving each of us to our benefit under the guise of helping him. He had Mother laying cornerstones, giving out golf prizes—charming Britain's most famous golfers.

"I can tell you more about his feelings for Mother. One morning at breakfast Father announced that as a young man he had promised himself that one day, when he could afford it, he would treat himself to three benefits—a good diamond ring for Mother, a Bechstein piano, and a journey to the Holy Land. He said, 'I have given your mother the ring. We have a lovely piano, and now, here are tickets for our journey to the Holy Land.' The three benefits for himself, you see, were the things he wanted to give her."

But there was another side to him, and Marjorie thought it was probably the reason he was as saintly as he was. She believed he had wrestled with enormous self-pride that manifested itself in swings from self-confidence to insecurity. He was kind and loving and easily hurt without reason, in shades of paranoia. "So," she said, "you had better not let on to his portrait that you read his letter of proposal."

"You don't think he would really mind, do you?"

"I suppose not, but it's an example of what I'm saying. He

misread people's intentions toward him at times, yet he never backed away. He was the first to tell you to do what is right, opinion be damned. He truly believed he was the most unpopular mayor St. Albans ever had, and he would announce it before anyone else had a chance. But it wasn't true at all. The only one who didn't like Father was Alderman Hurlock, and everyone knew that Alderman Hurlock didn't like anyone.

"This self-pride might have been the reason he never did anything until he was fully prepared, whether it was starting a penny packet seed company or playing golf. He was a thorough man, thought matters through to the other side."

I took this opportunity to look at Marjorie questioningly. When I hesitated, she said, "Yes? Out with it. What is on your mind?"

"Why did Joan say that nonsense about champagne and chicken sandwiches after the Wentworth match and what a good idea it would be for your father to donate a cup?"

"Ah, that. I wish she wouldn't do it. Actually, you caught her off guard for a moment and she told you the straight story—up to the ending. She usually pretends that Father said, 'I know what I'll do, if they agree. We'll have a competition, and I'll give a prize—a fiver for everyone on the team that wins.' It was pure sarcasm. It was Joan's way of protesting Father's decision to proclaim that first overwhelming British victory to be unofficial. When she first started saying it everyone knew it was a bitter joke. But as time went on, most people forgot what really happened and began to believe her. Now, how do you know it isn't true?"

"I've read the newspapers. The *New York Times* called the 1926 match at Wentworth 'The Ryder Cup' *before*, *during*, but seldom *after* it was played. It was even in the headlines, 'Hagen and Barnes Lose to Mitchell and Duncan in *Ryder Cup* Foursomes, 9 and 8.' But something made the press back off from calling it the *Ryder Cup*. Within a year the professionals from America were called a 'pick-up team,' not used to match play and British golf courses, which was poppycock. Tommy Armour, Jim Barnes, Walter Hagen, Emmet French were hardly a pick-up team. Bill Mehlhorn maybe, but he was the only one to win a point.

"And, I *know* there was a ceremony after the Match with speeches and that Ambassador Alanson Houghton awarded medals to the players. That's not exactly champagne and chicken sandwiches."

"But, does it really matter?" Marjorie asked as if she were tired of the whole thing. She reminded me of her father.

The Twist

The sleepy-eyed orthopedic surgeon in Chamonix, who was about to set my Colles' fracture, asked me, in heavily accented English, if I had ever skied before. I looked at the nurse for a clue to the intent of his question and she explained that it was the doctor's polite way of inquiring whether I was a sportswoman. I caught on immediately and answered that I *had* skied before and I was a golf champion. It was a lie but I wasn't born yesterday. My brother was a surgeon in sports medicine and I had learned there was a way for fixing sports and another way for fixing regular people.

It had been a simple accident, the result of another wish, I found out later. "I wish I was a better golfer," I had said to Bill and Steve while dipping into my fondue on our third evening in *Haute-Savoie*. And *voila!* I broke my left wrist in an icy field beneath a chairlift filled with bored French skiers. My guardians, Abe and Sam, confessed they had conferred and concurred that I would be a better golfer if I remembered to swing the club with a loose grip. And what better way was there to remember to swing with a loose grip than if it hurt not to do so. Abe said that a light grip on the club would give me the free wrist action needed to release the clubhead at the ball instead of several feet behind it. Apparently I spent most of my clubhead speed prematurely. They weren't the least contrite that their remedy caused me pain.

Bill and Steve continued to ski the rest of the week while I reclined on my sunny deck and watched the immutable peaks change their points of view with each passing cloud. I was not bored: I had clippings to read from American newspapers and magazines that Bill had brought from Paris. The latest batch of *New York Times* stories covered the weeks following the International Match at Wentworth, which I now thought of as the Ryder Cup, a term that rarely appeared in print after the first day's report. Occasionally, I found reference to an existing Cup, but then it was only a hint by the use of a single word such as "defend" or "capture": "the British will *defend* the Ryder Cup at Worcester," or "the Americans will try to *capture* the Ryder Cup at Worcester." Bernard Darwin, my favorite keen observer, bravely mentioned the Cup in *Vanity Fair* in an autumn issue in 1926, "...Mr. Ryder, a gentleman who gave the cup played for this year in the International match between the American and British professionals."

Most of the clippings were about Walter's gamesmanship on June 19, 1926, which, even for him, was extreme. Every time he tried to explain away what he had done, it only made matters worse. Each excuse was different from the one that preceded it. By the time he was ready to go home to America, he was so fed up with the British that he blasted them in a press interview at Waterloo Station. Of all the reports, my favorite was dated July 8, 1926, from London and printed in the *New York Times*. I read it aloud to the boys after they came in from skiing, had a snooze, and made drinks. In it, a British interviewer professed to defend Hagen against the accusation by a New York paper that Sir Walter was a "loud-mouthed braggart."

"The Modesty of Mr. Hagen"

I must defend him against such an unfounded accusation. Anyone privileged as I was to see him in his well-cut *yellow* and *white* shoes, discreetly colored pullover *and quiet check plus fours, in which no color was unduly favored*, might easily have mistaken him for an Old World gentleman of property. The very tones of his voice convey that impression. Mr. Hagen thinks deeply and sincerely on golf and does not come to hasty conclusions. In measured, judicial language, without a trace of passion, he told me our golfers 'were too gosh darned lazy."

"A man," he said in modulated, unhasty tones, "to win a championship must work like hell at golf and cut out the nerve stuff."

With eyes shadowed in sadness, he lamented, "You haven't a golfer with pep enough to win a championship."

And, with almost tears on his sun-burnished cheeks, Hagen added, "There is nobody in the world like an Englishman for kidding himself what a whale of a fellow he is when he's licked, what a hell of a sportsman he is."

To his lasting credit, Walter later denied he said "gosh."

Dora, I realized, had referred to the June 19 incident that started all Hagen's troubles. During my visit to her home we had been talking about Abe's even temperament when suddenly she said, "Not always," and led me to his workshop. Fastened to the wall over his worktable were two pieces of a broken wooden club, the jagged ends separated by several inches. She said it was one of Abe's best clubs and he broke it on June 19, 1926 after they returned from his match against Walter Hagen at St. George's Hill. It had been an exciting and exhausting fight for both men. Dora said, "I had no idea he was angry about it—he had been that calm and pleasant in the car coming home. When I saw what he had done to his favourite club, I said to him he ought not be upset—Walter Hagen was his friend. He said he wasn't angry at Walter, he was angry at himself. 'Walter is a fine chap; he just doesn't mean well. No one knows it better than I. Usually I know what he is up to and we enjoy our games because he knows I know. But this time...I don't want to talk about it.'"

~

THE BOYS RETIRED EARLY WITH visions of skiing the fall line and carving turns another day in Chamonix. They were bagged. I tidied up our small chalet and then went to bed myself; my naps on the sundeck had made me sleepy.

"Hey, babe, wake up. What is it? You were groaning and saying 'yeah.' Does your wrist hurt?" I opened my eyes and rolled into Steve's arms. It was a dream! Thank goodness! How could I get so upset by a dream? But was it a dream? All day long I had been frustrated by unanswered questions, in particular, why had the 1926 Ryder Cup Match at Wentworth been declared unofficial. I crawled into bed still thinking about it and as I drifted off to sleep I determined to find those guys when I got home and get at the truth. In fact, I'd go right now, and out I went to find Sam. But it was Abe I found, seated comfortably in the front seat of my car. We drove toward a small hotel just ahead, a sinister-looking Tudor inn, the sort inhabited by smugglers on the Cornish coast. We parked and Abe quickly ushered me inside.

Through a breathtaking miasma of tobacco smoke I detected Sam sitting at the head of a long table, his black dog at his side. He was pulling the flame of a match into the bowl of his pipe and didn't notice me. With his eyes locked on Walter Hagen he flicked the flame and flipped the match toward the hearth in one easy motion. Walter was dressed in a white shirt and tie, *plus fours made from a quiet check material in which no color was unduly favored*, and two-tone shoes in yellow and white. He was pacing about like a predator in a spotlight, so vividly did he stand out among the dark figures of Sam, George Duncan, and another man I did not know.

Abe pulled out a chair and seated me at the table. Hagen saw me, paused in his tracks, and said, "Hi, there, honey." Sam did not acknowledge me.

Walter looked back at Sam. "I have to hand it to you. You, George, and Abe did a bang-up job."

"As did you and Emmet," Sam responded, nodding to the man I didn't know.

"Who's that?" I whispered to Abe.

"Emmet French, born in Philadelphia. He was captain for your side when we first played this kind of international match at Gleneagles in 1921."

Hagen continued, "Yep. Today was almost perfect except you won all five foursomes matches."

"There's always tomorrow," Emmet said.

Walter laughed. "It's a good thing *we* didn't win all the matches today instead of you. The press would have said we couldn't have done it without the British-born players on our American team." Walter raised a serious eyebrow at Sam while Sam looked back at him expressionless. "It's sort of a no-win situation for us, if you see what I mean."

A log fire crackled loudly while we stared in silence, embarrassed for the beautiful trophy sitting in the center of the table. The gold cup with its simple ornamental lid was alive with reflections, but it did not gleam as brightly in my eyes as Walter Hagen.

"Your team," Walter said, "played inspired golf, sir, but that's the way it is when you play for your country. Isn't that so, Abe?" Walter continued to stare at Sam as he addressed Abe. "You've done it. You know. It gets confusing, though, for a chappie like Jim Barnes, doesn't it? Fresh from his native Cornwall, he doesn't know whose side he's on."

Emmet French chimed in, "Now hold on there, Walter. That's hardly fair. You were the one who looked as if you were playing for the other side today." Everyone laughed, including me, and Walter comically lifted an arm to ward off his critics. He and Jim Barnes had lost 6 and 5 to Mitchell and Duncan in the first day foursomes.

"It's true, however," Emmet went on, "we vary from the Walker Cup in this matter. Their players are required to be born in the countries they represent. I wonder if, by not doing the same, we are putting the very spirit of the Ryder Cup at risk."

"Your point is well taken, Emmet," Sam responded, but added that he was keenly aware of the eligibility difference between the Ryder Cup and the Walker Cup. "It is obviously not a problem for American amateurs to find excellent golfers among their native ranks. But your professionals are immigrants, by and large, who have come to richer pastures in America. In the circumstances the only possible requirement I could seek is that each player must be a member of his country's Professional Golfers' Association. Frankly, Emmet, I don't care where anyone was born or resides, as long as the Ryder Cup is a permanent means for professionals of both countries to enjoy a close association. It's vital to the spirit of the game that both amateurs and professionals feel united in their conduct. It is one game with many special interests, and unless it is played in friendship it will come apart. It is no less true of the countries of the world..."

"Don't start moralizing, Sam," I said loud enough to be heard.

Sam looked at Walter. "We discussed this already, Walter. Why are you bringing it up now? You are the one that said the United States could not field a homebred team that was competitive. Accordingly, I have not made it an eligibility requirement that players be native-born and I don't intend to."

Hagen placed his hands palms down on the table and said, "I understand the generosity inherent in your policy, but things have changed recently: I can count eight or nine American-born professionals of highest rank who would play if the Cup were held in America. There are Gene Sarazen, Leo Diegel, Johnny Farrell, to name a few. When I return to America I'm going to insist that our PGA *require* our players be American-born. What you do here, of course, is up to you. But wouldn't it eliminate several troublesome aspects if we inaugurate the Ryder Cup in the States in 1927, instead of this year as planned? That way, if the Cup finds it can't afford to be played annually, as you would like, it will begin a biennial schedule on the odd year to the Walker Cup's even year and your British players will be assured of playing in our 1927 Open. We want this friendly rivalry to be truly representative of our two nations. With all due respect, sir, I propose that this 1926 Ryder Cup at Wentworth be declared unofficial!"

George Duncan had been listening with grave attention, his fingers laid across his lips. At Walter's words his heavy black eyebrows shot right up to his hairline, and he dropped his hand at the wrist in astonishment. Sam, on the other hand, showed no sign and actually looked as if he thought there was value in Walter's remarks.

"You can't do that!" I shouted.

"What you say has merit, Walter," Sam said.

"Merit!" I yelled.

"Yes, it has merit," Emmet agreed," but surely there is no need to make this match unofficial, Mr. Ryder. Everybody knows we are playing for the Ryder Cup."

I sat there in disbelief while they thrashed it out. With his dark eyes beaming at us, Walter argued sportsmanship this way and that, redirecting his logic to suit his point. Then he expanded on his earlier remarks about the makeup of the teams. He said his team consisted of two Scots, Freddy McLeod and Tommy Armour, Cornish Jim Barnes and Lancastrian Cyril Walker, but he also could have had Jock Hutchison from St. Andrews, Willie Macfarlane from Aberdeen, Bobby Cruikshank from Edinburgh, Harry Cooper from London, and Macdonald Smith from Carnoustie. "There are more than enough British players for both Ryder Cup teams!" Hagen concluded.

When no one laughed he stressed that it was only because the Cup was so important to him that he was suggesting that the inaugural match be staged in America, in 1927. "It has got to be done right," he said soberly, "or not at all."

"Sam!" I screamed. Abe left the table.

George Duncan, a notoriously hot-tempered Scot, then asked Walter politely, why, in all his changes to the makeup of his team in the last six weeks, why in the world hadn't he thought this out before, and I called out, "Yeah!"

Steve nudged me awake.

SAM AND I STOOD AT THE DINING room windows and looked out at Verulam, as we had done so many times over the winter. A spring rain driving against the glass distorted our view of the golf course, dragging it into artful abstractions that washed away as quickly as we perceived them.

He had summoned me to this special meeting and I wasn't surprised. I was to show up at Verulam at two o'clock and bring the pencil sketch of the archway with me. I kept it in a silver frame beside my bed.

"May I say something?" I said.

He shook his head. "We're going to sit here and watch the rain."

That was the last thing I wanted to do. I had no room for anything but my urgent need to set the record straight about Wentworth, and I was determined to do it. But he was as determined as I, so I sat beside him and watched the lines of water shift and change, gather into one another and pour away. Gathering one into another, and then a third, again and again—gathering my attention until all the dreadfully important things on my mind fell away. Gradually I did not have better things to do than watch the rain. Sam, sitting quietly beside me, had not opened this strange door for me. I had done it myself. Nor did he intervene as he had done at our other meetings, to help me become part of the "real world," as he called it. "I'm giving you a head start," he once said.

After a long interval he said quietly, "Why do you keep the sketch beside your bed?"

I didn't know what to say. I looked down and mumbled something about how it reminded me of other, different worlds.

"I'll ask it again. 'Why do you keep the sketch beside your bed?'"

I tried to predict an answer that would please him but saw it wouldn't do. I answered as best I could. "It's mine and I'm proud of it."

With that, he calmly and deliberately reached into my handbag and lifted out the frame. He laid it face down on the table, opened the back, and extracted the drawing. He took a pencil from his pocket, placed the sketch in front of me, and told me to erase it. I did what I was told.

I held the corners of the paper down with my fingers and rubbed away the lines. When I hurried my pace to get it over with, Sam put his hand over my work and said, "Slow down." He did not want me to miss a nuance of self-pity as the eraser removed the stone shapes and trodden earth. A kaleidoscope of thoughts tumbled about my head including the possibility that this might mean the last of Sam and Abe. Only once in all the thoughts did I see what I was actually doing.

Sam, meanwhile, was unsympathetically concentrating on my progress, his elbow resting on the table and his chin propped lightly on his thumb. I worked with deliberate care until the last leaf and blade of grass had disappeared. Then I sat straight, shrugged, and glanced at him indifferently, to show I didn't care. He was smiling at me, his eyebrows raised expectantly, as if he were waiting for me to open a present. He kept looking, insisting, until I lowered my eyes and looked at the blank, white paper. Then, as if a knot had been untied, I felt free of a burden that I couldn't put a name to. I understood that there was nothing wrong with the picture, but there was something wrong with my attachment to it. Sam had told me once that if I disposed of all that possessed me, I would be free.

"You see how easy it is?" I had never seen a man so pleased with himself. "Did you know that you hum when you are upset?" He laughed.

"But now we must apply your new objectivity to other matters," he added. "I believe you want to challenge my judgment. You're going to say I let Walter Hagen talk me out of a Ryder Cup win. Well, it simply is not true."

"But I heard you say last January that if the *Americans* had won at Wentworth, you never in this world would have declared that Ryder Cup Match unofficial."

"No, I didn't say that. I said that Abe's figure would not be on the Cup if the Americans had won. But what you say is also true. If the Americans had won I would not have postponed the inaugural match until the following year. Winning or losing a match has no more meaning than the pencil marks that were on your paper, *if* it is a *good* match. But that match in 1926 was a travesty. The teams were so unbalanced there was no contest. It was no way to inaugurate an international trophy.

"But the world should know."

"Why?"

"Because—I don't know. For a dozen reasons. And what about that episode at St. George's Hill that Dora mentioned to me? Don't you think people should know about that? Tell me what happened and I'll tell the world. I think the angel in charge of golf wants the record set straight about June 1926."

He laughed at me. "I *am* the angel in charge of golf, as you put it, and I'm telling you that what happened 50 years ago doesn't matter any more. We must address the makeup of the teams now, in 1977. They are so unbalanced that a Ryder Cup Match played in America does not attract spectators. If something isn't done the British will take their Cup home and turn it into a *national* trophy which they have a right to do by my *Deed of Trust*, if they feel the Cup no longer serves a good purpose as an international trophy. Well, we don't want that to happen, do we? However, as long as the Ryder Cup remains the international competition described in the deed, it cannot be altered without my consent.

"Now, the matter of St. George's Hill: a story about the origins of the Ryder Cup will be incomplete without an account of that affair because it *is* the other reason Abe's figure is on the trophy."

Sam hitched his chair toward mine, crossed his legs, and, with obvious pleasure, he began his story.

"In 1926, Abe Mitchell and Walter Hagen were considered the two greatest professional golfers at match play in the world. They were both their national match-play champions. *Golf Illustrated* magazine offered £500 to the winner of a 72-hole match between them, scheduled to be played on June 18 and 19, after the Ryder Cup at Wentworth and before the Open. It would be the most prize money ever paid to a single golfer in England. The first 36 holes of the match were played at Wentworth on June 18. It was show business and the press did its best to dramatise it. American reporter Anthony Spalding wrote, '...behind [Walter Hagen's] ostensibly jovial manner there was cold hostility. Mitchell knew it and the crowd felt it.' Abe called that news story poppycock—Walter wasn't the hostile type and besides, they were good friends.

"In any case, both men played unremarkable golf. But at

the end of the first day at Wentworth Abe had a comfortable four hole lead, thanks to an undignified ending for Walter at the 36th hole: Abe had taken four strokes to reach the green while Walter's ball was over the green in two strokes but lodged in a waterlogged bunker. He waded in to the tops of his two-toned shoes, made several swipes at the ball, splashing sand and filth over his clothes. Walter lost the hole, six strokes to five. As Abe left the course he walked over to me and confided, 'He will pull something tomorrow—I know it. He can't help himself. This is too big a contest for him not to come up with an idea.'

"He'll probably be late," I offered.

"Well, if that's it I guess I can manage."

"That *was* it. Hagen was a master at arriving five to ten minutes late on the 1st tee. The match was to begin at 10:30. A good crowd had gathered from London, impatient to start. At 10:45, they were getting noisy and out of hand. Abe strode off toward the clubhouse carrying his driver. He found a quiet place to sit and began to unwind the lashing on the hosel. I approached him and said without thinking, 'Is that a good idea?' He nodded heavily and I left him alone. I sat in a lawn chair and lit my pipe. Another 10 minutes went by. Then, at 11:00, Walter drove in. He greeted Abe and me and disappeared into the clubhouse, talked with friends, changed, talked with friends, sauntered to the 1st tee and chatted some more. Several times an official reminded him his match was in progress.

"Abe lost four of the first six holes to bring the match all-square. Walter pulled off miracles while Abe missed his opportunities. Walter stymied himself at the 7th, glancing off Abe's ball only three inches from the hole. The gallery was pleased for Abe until Walter hopped the ball into the hole with his niblick for a half. Abe played the 9th hole in four perfect strokes while Walter had one stroke to the heather,

two strokes out of the heather, and one putt, or as he liked to say, 'three of them and one of those.'

"Walter took the lead at the 10th by holing a 70-foot downhill putt. They halved the next four holes and at the 525-yard 15th, Walter ploughed through the heather in one less than Abe to go two holes ahead. They halved the 16th hole, Abe won the 17th, the only hole he took all morning, and after halving the 18th, Walter was one up going to lunch.

"Abe and I and a few of my guests sat together under the marquee while Walter, God be praised, went off with a circle of friends whose laughter did nothing to ease the tension in our group. George Duncan, sitting next to Abe, chattered liked an idiot until Abe excused himself, walked to the drinks table and returned with a whisky in his hand which he placed in front of me. Then, before he sat down, he laid a strong hand on my shoulder, something he never did. It was an extreme measure from a man like Abe. Golf to me, you see, was seldom just a game and Abe often chided me for it. As I sipped my whisky I understood for the first time the full extent of my anger.

"The gallery size had almost doubled for the afternoon round, a condition known to inspire Walter and put Abe's game in disarray.

"Walter started the final round with a one-hole lead. Four holes and only four putts later he had a two hole lead. Abe won back a hole at the 6th. They halved for the next eight holes until Abe finally won the 15th to square the match. The hilly course and the competitive tension had taken their toll: both men were physically and mentally drained by then. Bernard Darwin was to write that it was the first time he had ever seen Hagen show strain, his lead squandered so near the end, all that work for naught.

"But then Hagen seemed to draw strength from the crowd that surged around the 16th tee. Abe topped his drive into a bunker and Walter pushed his onto a sandy road, and from there he won the hole. And the next. Hagen had won, two and one. After they shook hands warmly they helped each other off the green.

"Once it was over, I collected myself to some extent and could see that Walter had played an honest game with the heart of a warrior. Nonetheless, at 11:00 that morning, when I watched Hagen's car pull leisurely up to the front door, I made a determination, and I had no intention of changing my mind, no matter who won the match. I weighed Walter's outrageous disregard for all that was decent, against Abe's natural sportsmanship, and decided to indulge myself in some righteousness: I would return the Cup to Mappin and Webb and have a gold figure made for the top in the likeness of Abe. No one would know what I had done until the Cup was officially presented to the PGA of Great Britain, just before the team sailed the next year, in 1927. I could only hope that when Walter saw it in America, it would give him pause.

"Well, that's the story. Years later Hagen said in his autobiography, with specific reference to why he was 45 minutes late in teeing off at St. George's Hill, 'I never hurried, there was no use worrying—and I always took time to smell the flowers along the way.'"

"Now, who could have a bad opinion of such a man?" I said. Sam laughed.

"Abe was able to walk in Hagen's shoes, to understand him, accept him for what he was, appreciate his genius. I could not. I disliked the man and nothing he ever did gave me reason to change my mind.

"Moreover, my decision to make the 1926 Ryder Cup Match unofficial was influenced by Hagen only to the extent that he didn't turn down my offer to do so. If he had insisted, as Emmet French wanted him to, that our win was official I would have agreed. The decision to cancel, however, was primarily the result of our overwhelming victory. They won only one match in the whole two days. They didn't even put up a fight! What kind of Ryder Cup Match was that? It was a disaster. Your *New York Times* wrote, 'The American rout left Hagen's warriors strewn over greens so far distant from the clubhouse that it was with great difficulty they reassembled for the speechmaking ceremonies by Ambassador Alanson Houghton.' We awarded medals but decided not to award ourselves the Cup, thinking that, yes, it might be wiser to begin the following year. Maybe the Americans would play better at home, on familiar ground, when they weren't tired. Why *not* start in 1927, if it would make the Cup secure? I thought Joan would have a fit! She accused us of being three sheets to the wind in Virginia Water.

"Although Hagen must be recognised for his major role in founding this international competition, he brought a disturbing instability to the matches that the fledgling Cup could have done without. As one of your editorialists wrote, 'Walter Hagen is a complete master of the gentle art of making the English thoroughly dislike him.' His opinions were as inconsistent as his strokes on the golf course, but in both he knew how to strike home. There was the business at Waterloo Station after the 1926 Open, for example, when he was sore at the British for not accepting his excuses for being monumentally late for his match with Abe. And in early 1929, he reversed the very argument that he made about the makeup of the Ryder Cup teams in 1926, probably because he had learned, after the fact, that one of his team in 1927, Johnny Golden, was born in central Europe. The American Ryder Cup team, Walter declared in early 1929, need *not* be homebreds after all. Instead, the Haig would have naturalized citizens eligible for the team. The reason? I quote him word for word from Mr. P. C. Pulver's article in *The Professional Golfer of America*:

> 'There should be no discrimination in sport. There is no discrimination in time of war when the foreign-born citizens fight as quick as the native-born. We can stand being told in any foreign country that we have won with some of their men, if they persist in taking this view, far better than we can stand the thought that the boys who come over here and become citizens are not getting an even break.'

"What he said, if you can figure it out, was not important. It was relevant, however, that he added, 'The biggest objection to selected foreign-born professionals originates not in America but in Great Britain.' Of course, he knew that was tommyrot. We didn't care where their players were born or resided as long as they belonged to the PGA of America. To be more specific would infringe upon that association's rights. Therefore the subject of birth and residence was purposely omitted from the first *Deed of Trust*. America would attend to its eligibility regulations and we would attend to ours.

"The PGA of America strongly disagreed with Walter's liberal views in 1929. They wanted to retain strict eligibility requirements. Golden's name was never mentioned and he played in 1929 at Leeds. It wouldn't have mattered to us even if we had known, but to end the debate amongst the Americans, we drew up a new *Deed of Trust* specifying a strict, uniform birth and residence code for both sides after 1929, a move that weakened our team. Percy Alliss and Aubrey Boomer, two of our best players, members of the British PGA, resided outside the country. Boomer never played on our team again and Alliss missed the Cup until he made his home again in Britain.

"Golden was on a list to qualify for the Ryder Cup team in 1931 at Scioto but he didn't show up, probably because Hagen failed to plead his case successfully. There was always something to blur the edges and there always will be for as long as the Ryder Cup lasts, which it won't, because nothing does. But, right now, it is God's promotional device and we should preserve it as long as we can."

"Sam, what you did—put Abe on the Cup—it wasn't righteousness. It was out-and-out revenge. You wanted Walter to have his comeuppance.

"I avenged, perhaps. But I would not call mine an act of 'revenge.' Vengeance we leave to the Laws of the Universe. I thought my decision was inspired; harmful to no one, and satisfying to myself. During one of my many visits to the hospital when Abe was recovering from appendicitis, he asked me, 'Did I dream it, or am I really on the lid of the Ryder Cup?' I told him the Cup called for such an ornament and to me he was the perfect model. He embodied the ideal sportsman and golfer. I added that I didn't do it for him but for future generations who might wonder and take the trouble to ask, 'What about this gold man on the trophy? Who was he and what did he do?' I had hoped, you see, that Abe would become a legend to Ryder Cup teams, a very human reminder that it is the man that makes the game.

"After a time I saw that Abe's figure might be labelled a retaliation rather than a heritage. So what I did was never discuss the figure. No public word was uttered even at Verulam when Nellie presented the Cup to the PGA of Great Britain. Oh, the guests whispered amongst themselves—they were quite pleased, in fact—but otherwise they followed my lead. And within days, the boys sailed for Worcester, Massachusetts with the evidence. George Duncan told me, after he returned from America, that when the Cup was revealed to the American team, Hagen picked it up for a closer look. He humphed good-naturedly. Then his eyes searched the blank faces of the British players, and he said, 'Tell old Ryder I understand.' After that, the gold figure took on an air of anonymity.

"In defense of your position on the unofficial Ryder Cup Match at Wentworth, there are those who still count the 1927 match at Worcester as the second match, even the third if one includes Gleneagles in 1921. With such statistics Abe holds the best winning percentage record for a British player, 70%, of those who have played at least 10 matches."

"You don't have to sell Abe to me, Sam. I would put him on top of Nelson's column in Trafalgar Square. What I *do* seriously question is golf's ability to produce a real change in a person's understanding of himself. You were unique in your passion and your insight. You deserved God's gift to you, as you called it. Nowadays there's not one player in a million who deserves the game, who will use it as a tool to fulfill his evolutionary possibilities."

"Well, if that's the case, Abe and I have been wasting our time, haven't we?" and he laughed. "Fortunately, the universe seldom requires more than one or two people of special energy every thousand years or so to maintain itself."

The Robin

OUR SOJOURN IN ENGLAND STARTED to unravel soon after I erased my sketch of the archway. "An act of vandalism," Steve had called it when I explained why the drawing was missing from its frame. He even suggested that I forget about Sam Ryder before I did something really crazy. That was my old Steve talking and it was my first indication that the magic show might soon be over.

The next hint that our lives were returning to normal went unrecognized at first. The *Times* reported that British Foreign Secretary Tony Crosland and his wife had been sitting in their library reading by an evening fire. He turned to her and said, "Something happened." That's all he said. "Something happened," and then he died of a massive stroke. I read the news story thinking I would like to die with just that amount of awareness and speed, sitting by a warm fire in the library with Steve. It didn't occur to me that our landlord was Crosland's man in Pretoria, and that a new Secretary might prefer a man of his own. Sure enough, a letter soon arrived from South Africa asking us to vacate by the beginning of June.

And there were the rumblings from America. Our tenant

had barely survived a winter of record cold and snow. In early February she had remembered why it was she had moved away in the first place. She would soon leave Rochester, she wrote.

The list went on and on. Jim Nairn was confined to his bed, Dorothy would be leaving St. Albans now that a judge had ordered the "squatters" out of her house in Suffolk. Indeed, I feared for Tony and Ann, but I need not have. They, like the Vicar, went on as before.

My wrist had not mended for golf and Steve's corporate assignment was ending. A stupid Road Traffic Examiner flunked me for going hand-over-hand on the steering wheel and not applying the handbrake at a stoplight. Six months before I would cheerfully have accepted my failure and tried again. But now my happy nature had died with the Foreign Secretary.

Mrs. Graham Hill's cat ate our sweet little robin redbreast who once walked between my shoes where I was sitting in the garden. Mrs. Hill, recently widowed when Graham's plane crashed near St. Albans, had set a cherry pie to cool at an open window and my robin followed the waft of its fragrance to a cruel death.

When my morale flagged in the face of these misfortunes, Sam beckoned me to Bernard's Heath, a secret wilderness within sight of our house, a place of strange quiet and beauty, guarded by an equally strange, unkempt cottage called 'The Lodge,' so dark at the windows and overgrown at the doors that I thought no one lived there but ghosts. It struck me as droll, therefore, when Sam came out the front door, brushing cobwebs from his hair. "What a spooky house!" he said by way of greeting.

Sam held the branches out of my way as we entered the heath through a dark corridor of beech trees, our shoes stepping silently and soft on the bare earth beneath the smooth gray boughs. Satin leaves protected the darkness so that no grass grew where the roots rose like buttresses against the old

silver trunks. It had been my place to come and count my blessings in my cheerful days, but I could see now that it was receptive to all moods.

When we stopped walking, I sighed and kept my eyes averted from Sam as if I didn't want to hear what he had to say. He spoke, as I knew he would, without a trace of sympathy. "Why does death surprise? Why is death unexpected when it always comes?"

"Has my small robin's spirit flown off to be with Tony Crosland and Graham Hill?" I said, determined not to listen to reason.

"It isn't that way with birds and people. Moreover, I think you know that."

"What way is it, then?" I asked.

"I can't tell you."

"Try me."

"I did, but you were not prepared to understand and there was no way I could prepare you. You cannot even grasp the starting point. But if one day you find the truth, you will say, 'I knew it all along.' The truth is the snowflake. It is the symmetry that gives it away and when you see it, you see everything."

"Is this it, then?" I said, feeling like a little girl trying to act grown-up.

"In a manner of speaking, it is, yes. You may add me to your small list of beaus, if you like, but you mustn't daydream."

"No more free wishes?"

"No more free wishes. Your life will have no room for them once you erase your foolish preoccupations. Remember, however, you have wished for two things to come—a low handicap, and for the Ryder Cup Match to come to your town."

I asked him what his plans were for the Ryder Cup and he told me that Jack Nicklaus, when he came to the Open in July this year, will be *inspired* to approach Lord Derby, the President of the PGA of Great Britain, with a plan for a combined British and European Ryder Cup team. Lord Derby will be *inspired* to see the merits of the proposal, and Joan, representing the "Donor" in the *Deed of Trust*, will agree to it.

"And the book?"

"It is not your wish to write it, I know," Sam said. "So I will make the wish for you—now. It will work out, you'll see. When you return home, you will begin your work. You will learn every aspect of golf so that you can write about it with authority. Start with the rules. They are a metaphor for ethical living designed to give limits to the chaos that can occur during a serious game of golf, a chaos similar to man's fragile journey through life."

"How will I know when it's time to write the story?"

"The Ryder Cup will fall victim to controversy and abuse. When that happens, an incident will occur that so disturbs you, you will have an attack of righteous indignation, similar to my own, and you will sit down and begin to write what you know, not to be vengeful, mind you, but to give pause. You won't be able to stop yourself."

"Maybe someone in Great Britain will have written about the origins of the Ryder Cup by that time, pointing out an alternate way to count the wins and losses."

"That's just it, you see. The British would never suggest such a thing. If you are referring to Johnny Golden, in our country it is unsporting in match play to call a rule on an opponent if the opponent is ignorant of it."

"But the opponent can call the infraction upon himself when he learns about it, can't he?"

"Not if the results have already been posted." He laughed. "I believe, however, it is proper for an American to tell the story."

Abe appeared then, out of nowhere, as they say, and the two men stood shoulder to shoulder facing me. They were almost the same height, Sam an inch or two taller perhaps. For my benefit they were reenacting a photograph I had seen on Dora's wall and I dutifully etched it in my mind.

Abe stepped forward and held out his hand. My small hand in his palm all but disappeared as he closed his fingers firmly around it. "Mind you, drink your sulphur water," he said. After a moment he stepped back and went away.

I knew very well that the men had me reined in or I would have wept, for I'd had, in that quiet moment, a tender realization. I said to Sam, "You gave Abe a kind of immortality when you put his gold figure on the Cup. But Abe was never publicly identified as the model and he slipped into obscurity, inadvertently robbing the figure of its symbolic purpose—that Abe Mitchell exemplified the ideal professional golfer. Knowing what I know now, it's hard to imagine that this singular honor was never even mentioned in Abe's obituary. You are remembered, but he is not. And now you want me to rectify it by telling the story. That's the point, isn't it?"

"That's the point."

"Well, whether you like it or not, you'll not play second fiddle in any story I tell about the Ryder Cup."

"The mortal Sam Ryder and I are in no position to disagree with anything you say."

I shook my head, overwhelmed by him. "You're not going to make me forget you, are you, Sam?"

He studied me as if it were beyond his ability to make a choice. Finally, he handed me his lisle handkerchief, his eyes softened, and he said, "No."

Bibliography

Alliss, Peter with Michael Hobbs. *Who's Who of Golf.* Adelaide, Australia, 1983.

Ballesteros, Severiano with Dudley Doust. *Seve: The Young Champion.* London: Hodder & Stoughton, 1982.

Bishop, Morris. *A History of Cornell.* Ithaca, New York: Cornell University Press, 1962.

Fry, Peter. *Samuel Ryder, The Man Behind the Ryder Cup.* Dorset, UK: Wright Press, 2000.

Gee, John. *A Confident Century.* Worchester, UK: A Square One Publication, 1994.

Hagen, Walter with Margaret Heck. *The Walter Hagen Story.* New York: Simon and Schuster, 1956.

Leonard, Terri. *In the Women's Clubhouse.* Chicago: Contemporary Books, 2000.

Needleman, Jacob and Baker, George, Editors. *Gurdjieff.* New York: Continuum, 1996. Basarab Nicolescu: *Gurdjieff's Philosophy of Nature.*

Niblett, Rosalind. *Roman Hertfordshire.* Dorset, UK: Dovecote Press, Ltd., 1995.

Nicklaus, Jack with Ken Bowden. *My Story.* New York: Simon and Schuster, 1997.

Puttrick, Betty. *Ghosts of Hertfordshire.* Dorset, UK: Dovecote Press, Ltd., 1995.

Toms, Dr. Elsie. *The New Book of St. Albans.* Buckinghamshire, England: Barracuda Books Limited, 1976.

Ward, Peter. *Came Down to Golf.* England, 1984.

Resources

Arnell, Henry. *A History of Royal Ashdown Golf Club*, 1888-1988. England: Printed by W.E. Baxter, 1988.

Bickerton, Thomas A. *Wartime Experiences of an Ordinary Tommy*. England: Unpublished, 1964.

Campbell, John C. *Maintenance Program at the Royal and Ancient Golf Club*. Summary Report of Royal Canadian GA National Turfgrass Conference, Montreal, Quebec, Canada, 1969.

Claisen, Marjorie. *The Ryder Family and Other Recollections*. Unpublished.

Knuth, Dean. *Golf Journal*. "The Early History of Handicapping." 1992.

Kohn, Bob. *Hertfordshire Countryside Magazine*. H1233.

Murgatroyd, William B., and Booth, Alan. *Verulam Golf Club*. England, privately printed, 1997.

Smith, Julian C. *Breaking Ninety*. Ithaca, New York: printed by Thomas Shore, 1990.

Underwood, George H. *Cantelupe Centenary, 1892-1992*. Unpublished.

Underwood, George H. *Abe Mitchell, A Short Sketch*. Unpublished.